ARCHER

DR. REBECCA SHARP

Cover Design:

Sarah Hansen, Okay Creations

Editing:

Ellie McLove, My Brother's Editor

Printed in the United States of America.

Visit www.drrebeccasharp.com

ARCHER

PROLOGUE
KEIRA

Nineteen Years Old

"You know, you always wait for me to invite you inside. Are you a vampire?" I stepped back from the door to my motel room to let the Boston policeman tasked with guarding me inside.

Detective Archer Reynolds.

In my first nineteen years of life, I'd never seen a policeman who looked like him—*tall. Hot. Imposing.* And I'd seen a lot of policemen. As the daughter of an Irish Mob enforcer, being aware of police presence was practically hard-coded into my DNA.

Detective Reynolds filled my doorframe like he had countless times over the last two weeks, each time confirming that though he had to be at least a decade older than me, my body responded to him in ways I'd never felt before.

The tall, broad-shouldered detective oozed rugged authority underneath his plain clothes like a cowboy from Boston's wild West End. Maybe in uniform, he would look less breathtaking. *Or maybe more.*

1

I let my eyes rake greedily over him. His T-shirt molded to his large biceps and wide chest. His thick brown hair was combed into order underneath the Red Sox hat he always removed as he crossed the threshold, giving me ample opportunities to admire the veins snaking over his forearm muscles and the dusting of hair covering them.

His low chuckle cascaded down my spine, an incredible sound that carried heat with it every time it let loose.

I reached in my pocket when he looked at me, searching for the reminder that I was supposed to notice him, but he wasn't supposed to see me. Not really. Not the real me. My fingers found the slip of paper, and I crumpled it in my fist. I'd been in the middle of writing out my new name when he knocked, and I'd quickly shoved the evidence in my sweatpants.

Keira Murphy.

Over and over I traced the same lines until they were seamless, a trick taught to me by the US marshal that briefed my dad and me on our introduction to the Witness Protection Program. *He never expected me to have to use it so many times.*

Three years ago, Patrick 'Patty the Punisher' McKenna walked into the FBI's organized crime unit and offered up the Irish Kings, Boston's notorious Irish Mob, on a silver platter. *And it was all because of me.* In exchange for the information and evidence he provided as the Mob's most senior enforcer, the feds—Agent Lattimore—promised us a new life. So far, they hadn't quite delivered.

This time though—this trial, *this one would be different.*

Three years. Five relocations. Five *new* starts.

With each trial—each imprisonment—that Dad's information brought, James Maloney and his Mob grew even more vengeful. They found us time and again, and it was only because my dad worked for decades for the men hunting us that we managed to avoid becoming prey.

But this time, Dad promised it would be different. *Him and*

Agent Lattimore. They promised that this time their plan would work.

This time, we were brought back to Boston so my dad could testify against James Maloney himself, the leader of the Irish Kings. And in two days, the trial would be over. The verdict without a doubt 'guilty' thanks to Dad's testimony. And then we would start over one last time. New names and nothing from our past.

Including Detective Reynolds.

Pain lanced in my chest, but I ignored it. It was stupid to think I could miss something I never really had.

"I'm not sure what worries me more"—Detective Reynolds moved by me, my hungry nostrils imbibing deeply of his spiced scent—"that the idea of a gentleman is so foreign, I'm more likely to be a vampire." He stopped by the small table in the room and turned to me. "Or that the idea of inviting a vampire into your room is appealing to you."

His eyebrow curved over his smoky-green gaze, the color matching the scent of pine trees, open space, and freedom that followed him.

Maybe that was what drew me to him: freedom.

Vampires were nothing compared to the demons I'd met —only men were capable of the kind of horrors that monsters could hope to achieve.

I shut the door and quipped saucily, "How could it not be appealing to let a glittering, gorgeous man into my room when pop culture has done such a good job romanticizing them?"

Shit. My smile fell as soon as the words were out, realizing what I'd implied.

I did more than notice that Detective Reynolds was beyond gorgeous. He was the kind of gorgeous that was *arresting*—a predicament I'd grown up learning to avoid. And though his skin might not glitter, the duty to his badge, the respect of his task, and the honor of his character certainly did.

But it was the way his eyes raked over me, dark swirls of heat flickering in their depths, that were more dangerous than the weapon hidden in the small of his back. His head dipped as though to chase his gaze away from me and thoughts that betrayed the bounds of his assignment: *to protect the daughter of a witness in a federal trial.*

"I was always a Team Jacob guy myself," he said lightly, dissipating my fear that he was going to leave the take-out food he'd brought for dinner and retreat well behind the bounds of duty.

"Of course you were," I said, hesitantly approaching the table.

Jacob was made out to be the right choice—the good guy, and Edward, the bad one.

And Detective Reynolds was definitely one of the good guys.

Another reason I needed to stop being so *arrested* by him. After living in a world of vampires... or villains... it was hard to believe I'd end up with someone who didn't need to hurt others to survive.

"Me and Ranger picked Jacob. Gunner and Hunter, on the other hand..." He shook his head and chuckled, reaching in the bag and pulling out two roast beef sandwiches from Kelly's.

I loved hearing him talk about his family—his three younger brothers, younger sister, their mother—and growing up with them in Wyoming. I loved hearing about normal people with normal, loving families. It was hard not to when my childhood had been a million miles from it. Even now, nineteen was just a number—like an expiration date on a package of Peeps. *Those things could survive an apocalypse and still be ready to eat.* I knew how fragile life was, and I'd seen more death at nineteen than most in their nineties.

And I'd been responsible for it, too.

I wondered how he'd look at me if he knew that.

4

Detective Reynolds guessed early on that I was an only child. He'd picked up that my mother had died when I was young by how neat I kept the room, and I confessed that I'd been six when she passed away from cancer. My aunt Patricia, my dad's sister, came to live with us after that, but four years later, she reached her breaking point, tired of the nights my dad came home covered in blood, worried I would see— worried his work would put me in danger. She left when I was ten, and the next day, my dad told me the truth about who he worked for and what he did.

"Keira, sweetheart, I need you to know that your da is one of the bad guys. I do bad things to people because it's my job. But I promise that I might be a bad guy, but for you, I'll always be a good da and good man."

And he was. Most people would only see Patty McKenna as a criminal, but he'd done—*he did*—the best he could. And three years ago, he'd betrayed the life and family he'd adopted for decades to keep me safe, and now he risked everything to bring me justice.

"I held up my end of the bargain. Kelly's roast beef sandwiches," he said roughly when we finished. "So, what else is on your list?"

My list.

After Agent Lattimore introduced us that first day, leaving quickly to go make sure my dad was settled and prepped, the first question Detective Reynolds had asked was if he could do anything for me?

Anything. For me.

The memory stopped me. No one in his position wanted to do things for me—the police were already having to do things for me. No one wanted to do more than what was required, and I understood.

But when it felt like I'd spent a lifetime *protected—cared for out of duty*—there was something forbidden and breathtaking about someone *wanting* to do something for me—to give me a small comfort to make my situation less strained.

So, I asked him to stay and talk with me.

It seemed like a dumb request, but I hadn't really talked to anyone except my father in the last three years because no one could be trusted. And before that, when we were still in Boston, I didn't have friends for the exact same reason.

There was only my dad and me. Partners in crime.

Partners in protection. *Partners in solitude.*

Of course, I'd never confess how the seclusion gnawed at me. *I couldn't.* Not when Dad was doing the right thing for both of us. But that didn't change how lonely it felt.

And maybe that was why his compassionate question reached right inside me and unlocked the box of feelings I'd tucked away, knowing I didn't have the luxury of feeling them any longer, and I started to tell him things I never thought I'd admit to anyone.

Not the forbidden facts about me or Dad or WITSEC; I knew what things were off-limits. But I could confess what seemed even more dangerous than fact: feeling.

I was scared to start over. *Again.* Scared to cling to the lifeline of hope that *this* would be the last time when that lifeline had been cut so many times before.

"Don't leave with regrets," had been the hot detective's immediate advice. *"Regrets are rocky. It's hard to build a fresh start on them."*

And then he'd ask what I would regret leaving without, and my answer had been a list of experiences that were linked to a time in my life when everything hadn't seemed so precarious. *A Boston bucket list of sorts.*

Kelly's roast beef sandwiches. A Red Sox game. Breakfast from Bagelsaurus. Walking the Freedom Trail.

Instead of treating me like a babysitting assignment, he began trying to check off some of the items on my list. The food was the easiest. The baseball game involved him carting over his massive flat-screen TV along with some stadium food and concessions. Others, like the Freedom Trail, even Boston's hottest cop couldn't make happen.

Not while I was being protected.

A bitter smile toyed with my lips.

Protected. It was a good thing. But sometimes, protection came in the shape of a cage. It kept bad men out, but it also kept me in.

"So what else is there, Keira? You've got two more days." His voice interrupted my thoughts.

I didn't need the reminder. I'd had this day marked on my mental calendar since they'd charged Jimmy Malone five months ago. However, at some point over the last two weeks, my anticipation dwindled, weighed down with dread. By playing this bucket list game with Detective Reynolds, I'd let him in, and now I wasn't sure I was ready to let him go.

I stood and walked to the window.

"What's wrong?"

I spun, gasping to find him behind me, concern etched over his face.

"What is it?" His voice massaged all the knots of my life— knots in place to hold myself together. "Keira..."

I looked to his full lips. Curved. Firm. And quite possibly, the most criminal thing about him. My own lips parted, wondering if kissing him would taste as wrong as being attracted to him felt.

The daughter of a mobster shouldn't be thinking about kissing law enforcement.

I pulled my lips between my teeth, rubbing them together like the friction would help protect me from the words I was about to say.

"I want to be kissed."

A mistake. A crime. My small confession was the first and only criminal act I'd ever committed—admitting to wanting a man who couldn't—shouldn't—want me.

The daughter of a criminal shouldn't want to be with a cop, especially one who was ten years her senior.

But maybe McKennas were born to break the rules.

"*Fuck*," he swore roughly as his eyes locked on my lips like an arrow aimed at its target. It felt like every part of him pulsed—from his angry breaths to his taut body to his racing heartbeat.

I watched his head dip lower, every part of him—from his angry breaths to his taut body to his racing heartbeat—pulsing with the kind of life I wanted to leech.

My eyes hooded, but before they could shut completely, he shoved himself back and speared his fingers through his hair, the thick locks breaking from order into chaos.

"I'm sorry." He cleared his throat twice like the words rubbed salt in a wound. "I should go."

Words were more effective than bullets. Bullets killed quickly. Words buried deep in your consciousness and would hold you hostage forever. And these, I would carry with me wherever I went. Words from the first man I let in who then chose to walk away. *To protect me.*

"I'll be outside if you need anything."

I shouldn't have said anything, but I was my father's daughter. I was steady and controlled just as easily as I was fire and fury.

"I don't need anything," I clipped harshly, my meaning unmistakable. "Not from you."

Not from anyone.

THE NEXT DAY...

"How do you think they felt, Archer?" I savored his name

rolling over my tongue, the taste like fine liquor in my mouth. Rich. Complex. Forbidden.

My toes touched the edge of the large rimmed circle of old cobblestones outside of the old Customs House that marked the site of the Boston Massacre, and I glanced over my shoulder at him, still in disbelief that we were here.

I'd woken up this morning wrapped in a familiar weight of solitude, thinking the friendship I'd formed with the man protecting me unmendably cleaved. And then, there was a knock on my door, Archer's arresting stare waiting for me on the other side along with a Red Sox T-shirt and ball cap in his extended hand. He'd told me to change. *He'd told me we were going to walk the Freedom Trail.*

A peace offering.

And against the rules.

I wasn't supposed to step foot outside that motel room until the last day of the trial. But I'd never been a stickler for rules, especially when breaking them came with the promise of a few hours in the fresh air, warm sunshine, and vibrant energy of Boston in springtime. *And more time spent in his presence.*

"Just call me Archer," he'd instructed earlier when we reached the Granary Burying Ground. Apparently, he worried I was drawing attention to us by referring to him as Detective Reynolds while we walked through the Boston Commons.

"Angry," he replied, crossing his arms. "The colonists were being taxed. Taken advantage of. They were pissed. Although it's never smart to provoke someone who has a gun."

I stepped back and lifted my gaze. "I think they felt trapped."

"How do you mean?"

"I think the very people—the very government—who was supposed to be protecting them instead kept failing them, kept abusing their power." My throat tightened, and I had this feeling like I should stop talking—stop confessing to a feeling that hit so close to home. But I couldn't. Like there was something in him that drew out the truth from me. "I think they felt trapped by the very system that was supposed to fight for them... and anger is just one symptom of becoming a prisoner."

I tore my eyes away and blinked rapidly, surprised by the tears that had collected. I hated the anger that came over me because I knew how much risk and time and effort that my dad and the FBI had put into protecting me, and I was grateful. But a cage was still a cage even if it was for my own safety.

"And what are the other symptoms?" Archer jarred me from my thoughts.

I cleared my throat. "Imprudence. The attempt to reach out and take what you want before it's gone." I made the mistake of looking at him and wondering when he'd gotten so close. "Regret. Knowing no matter what you do, you can't unring a bell... or unfire a shot."

"Do you feel trapped, Keira?" he asked in a low voice, crowding me with his size. "Because I can help."

I shivered, knowing he couldn't but desperately wishing he could. I'd never wanted to tell anyone the truth about who I was and the life I'd lived more than in that moment. I was like a ship careening atop stormy waves yet unable to trust the safety of the shore. But Archer, he was a beacon of strength— a lighthouse promising security and warmth and something else I'd never felt before. Something just for me.

My gaze drifted down to those lips, an ache knotting in my stomach to know if they tasted like the freedom he talked about. My tongue betrayed my thoughts, traveling over my lips and moistening them.

"Archer..." I lifted my palm to his chest, wanting his heat, his steadfastness, his strength.

Taking a deep inhale, I swayed closer, wanting to follow the pull that drew me to him like a magnet to its opposing pole. My eyelids fluttered almost shut before the moment was snapped by the loud clicks of an old camera—a tourist taking a photo of the historic landmark.

But to me, loud rapid clicks had always meant danger.

I moved back so quickly I started to stumble but managed to catch myself.

"No," I finally answered him, shaking my head and hoping he didn't notice how I blinked back tears. "I'm just very protected."

"You could be in danger."

I didn't need the reminder. I'd lived in danger so long, I wasn't sure I knew what it felt like to truly be safe.

"I know." My throat constricted. I was rapidly losing the will to fight against the gravity of him. "I guess I should be grateful it's almost over then."

We continued in silence, walking until we'd followed the trail until the Bunker Hill Monument, the USS Constitution Museum closed even if we had wanted to go inside. Archer decided it was time to go back to the motel—back to the final night in my comfortable cage, promising to have pizza delivered when we got there. By the time we walked through the door, my legs felt like jelly and the thoughts about what was going to happen tomorrow after the trial started to beat loud and insistent in my mind like the thump of a war drum.

Freedom. Freedom.

"You should get some sleep. Tomorrow's a big day."

Freedom.

I'd ached for tomorrow for months—an end to a life in hiding and on the run. I'd prepared for these last few days— weeks—to drag on like a watched pot waiting to boil. Instead, they'd unraveled like a spool of twine, the time with him moving too fast for me to catch and hold on to.

And god, did I want to hold on to it more than anything.

"Why did you do this?" I looked at him and asked.

"Do what? Take you on the walk?" He tried to make it sound like it was that simple. *It wasn't, and he knew it.*

"All of it. Bring me food. The games. The movies. The walk. Why do all of this for me?"

He paused for a beat.

"Because your last memories of this place shouldn't be of a motel room. They shouldn't be of being locked away alone and safe, waiting to leave the place that's your home." He shook his head, dragging a hand roughly through his hair. "You shouldn't leave here with regrets."

Two tears streaked down my cheeks, no longer able to hide.

I didn't have any regrets until I met him, now the thought of every second spent without him, every second seemed like it would be a moment to regret.

"I'm going to leave here regretting I never got to kiss you," I said, turning myself into the revolutionary provoking the man who had the power to destroy me with a single shot.

He flinched. "I can't, Keira. We can't."

"Because I'm your job or because I'm a criminal's daughter?" If there was one thing my life had taught me, it was to know the difference between something that was bad and wrong and something that was good and wrong. And Archer... he was everything good and wrong.

"Because I'm here to protect you—"

"I don't want your protection, Archer. I don't need to be protected from you." I was so tired of being protected from life and from living it.

He swore. "And what kind of regret is a kiss going to burden you with?"

"Not as big of one as *not* kissing me will leave." My voice was small. Breathless.

"You're too young for me to kiss you the way I want."

A thrill spiraled through my body and exploded between

my legs. I notched my chin higher and hung everything I had on my next words.

"And you're too smart to believe an excuse like that."

His nostrils flared. Angry. *Hungry.* A low growl announced that something wild in him had broken free.

He reached for the ball cap I was still wearing and tossed it to the side. His hands caged my face, imprisoning me in strong shackles. I felt the low curse leave his lips, but by the time it reached my ears, his mouth was on mine.

My first kiss.

But like everything else about my life, it wasn't normal. Like everything else about my life, he kissed me as though it were a matter of life and death... *and in that moment, it felt like it was.*

I straddled two worlds in those seconds: the present and the future. *A life with Archer in it and one without.*

"*Pizza!*" The loud call was followed by three bangs on the door.

Archer pulled away instantly. I gasped for air, ready to tell him I didn't care about the food, but as soon as I saw his face, I knew it was over. I knew reality had slapped the cuffs of duty back on his desire.

And it was for the best.

So, I said nothing as he went to get our food. Instead, I memorized every fleck of gray in his green eyes, the way his cheek vibrated with every flex of his jaw, and the way the muscles in his body held him straight as though nothing could ever break him.

I cataloged every inch of him, every memory with him from the last two and a half weeks, and then pinned them all to my mind like stars to a night sky. But these weren't stars to wish or hope on, I knew better than that. These stars belonged to a constellation, untouchable—*unwishable*—but always there whenever I wanted to look.

He would be my constellation, reminding me of a place

13

and time, of talking and touches, and of a story that couldn't have ended any differently no matter how hard I wished.

Because after tomorrow, Archer Reynolds would only be the man who'd protected me, and I would become the memory of the girl he watched die.

THE NEXT MORNING...

I gasped and sat up in the ambulance, my hands tearing at my bloodied clothes like it was real blood staining the white.

My chest ached with that first inhale. The rubber bullets felt like they bruised my lungs with their impact even through my clothes and the protective padding underneath. But it was nothing compared to the pain in my heart or the stain of Archer's kiss on my lips.

I'd woken to have to say goodbye to the man I never should've given myself cause to miss. Time moved painfully slow until Agent Lattimore closed me in the SUV to take me to the courthouse and left Archer behind. Then it galloped. The courthouse. The sentencing. Seeing Sean Maloney, Jimmy's son, in the hallway, his smirk burned into my brain when he promised to find me and make me pay—something that would haunt me for a long time.

We'd walked out of the courthouse, my pulse thudding in my ears. I saw all the signals—all the signs. But nothing prepared me for the way time stopped when the staged attack happened. Another hitman for the Kings appeared, hired by Lattimore to make this look real, but for a second, I thought this might really be the end.

This morning, freedom didn't ring with a tolling bell but with the rapid-fire of bullets.

Freedom from living as two people hunted by the Irish Mob.

It felt like I blinked and we were in the ambulance, rushing to the next stage of our elaborate plan.

It wasn't enough to go into hiding. The only way to escape the Irish Kings forever was to make them believe we were dead.

Them and the rest of the world.

Archer told me I'd regret the kiss. *I would never regret it.* But as Dad drove us out of Boston, I regretted not telling Archer the truth. I regretted leaving him with the belief that I'd died on the steps of the courthouse this afternoon, a victim of mob retribution.

But there was nothing I could do. Safety came at a price, and the price of protection would always be solitude.

CHAPTER ONE

ARCHER

Four years later

"Where've you been hiding?" Jerry asked, using one finger to punch the buttons on his ancient cash register.

At almost six-foot-ten and pushing seventy, the owner of Jerry's Hardware had a permanent hunch in his back and still bent over when the drawer dinged and slid open.

I flipped open my wallet and pulled out some bills. "Was up in Yellowstone with a client."

I'd just returned home to Wisdom after a three-week stay at the National Park while the owners of a major oil corporation, Pyle Petroleum, haggled out a business deal with one of their biggest competitors. They hadn't wanted anyone —including their usual personal security—to get wind of the deal. Why? I couldn't say. People with money were paranoid about a lot of things I didn't understand, but I couldn't complain—that paranoia helped build my and my brother's company, Reynolds Protective Group, into the premier private security firm for not only the greater Jackson area and Teton County, but all of western Wyoming and even into Idaho.

"Ahh. And here I thought maybe you'd found someone and eloped."

Jerry might run the hardware store and could tell you every tool and gadget stocked inside and fifteen different ways to use them all, but he was also a closet romantic. A softie with a cheesy smile. And more than once I'd caught one of those Fabio-covered romance novels stuffed on the shelf behind the front counter.

He swore that they were his wife, Trish's, books. I swore I believed him. We both knew better.

"Just work." I shook my head with a little chuckle.

"So, you know who bought Todd's old place?" His knobby fingers slid the bills I'd handed him into their rightful spot and then started to pull out my change, adding, "Heard it's a newcomer."

"No. Mom mentioned it sold, but I didn't hear anything else," I replied absently while I bagged the new remote, motor, and chain for a garage door, waiting on Jerry to finish counting.

The sale of old Todd Sweeney's barbershop was the kind of big news that would spread quickly through Wisdom, Wyoming; it had sat empty right on Main Street for a good decade now. A new owner meant a new person. And a new person meant something new to talk about. I didn't avoid local gossip—*there was no avoiding local gossip in a small town.* But I didn't search it out. I didn't have time.

I'd also left for Yellowstone the day the rumor mills started kicking into gear.

"Heard it's going to be—"

"You can keep the rest, Jerry. I've got to run or Mom will have my head," I told him with a wry smile, waving off his attempt to count out coins; I didn't have time for that.

"Alright, well tell the mayor I said hello. Oh, and we're excited for her birthday party."

That last part was just for me—Mom's party was a surprise, if such a thing was possible in a small town.

I grabbed the bills and shoved them into my worn

18

jeans. Work was crazy, and it wasn't even our busy season, yet for the last two months, it felt like I hadn't left the office or my house until the assignment in Yellowstone. Thankfully, I managed to snag a few hours this morning to get some needed repairs done at Mom's house, so I threw on my shittiest jeans and a faded black tee. Not even five minutes from my apartment and I was tugging on the neckline, feeling like the damn thing must've shrunk in the wash.

I reached my Ford F-150 parked in the lot and climbed into the driver's seat, the keys still sitting right where I left them in the cupholder.

There wasn't much reason to lock anything around here—not when you knew everyone and everything that went on in this town.

Wisdom sat nestled in the Teton Range of the Rockies about twenty-five minutes from Jackson Hole. While it might not have the fame of the neighboring resort town, it had all the mountain views, wide-open blue skies, and quiet charm that the busy tourist town lacked.

"What's up, Hunt?" I answered my younger brother's phone call by hitting the button on my steering wheel.

"You still in town?"

I let my foot off the gas, slowing as I approached the stop sign at the end of the parking lot. "Yeah. Just finished up at the hardware store so I can fix the garage door over at Mom's."

Four weeks ago, our mother—*God bless her*—had forgotten to open the garage door prior to trying to back through it. She'd dented the whole thing to shit and then broke the motor trying to get it to go up, hoping that would *'flatten it out.'* I thought I was being a good son, offering to fix it, until work got crazy and here we were, four weeks later and she was still parking in her driveway, the crunched door still half-wedged in place.

Thankfully, our youngest brother, Ranger, still lived at home with her. Even still, I'd had that place wrapped up in more security system bells and whistles than the Rockefeller Christmas tree in New York City.

"I just got a call from Diehl over at the station. Said Zoey just called in a panic because there was a break-in at the post office," he informed me. "Asked if we could meet him there. I guess Tucker and Zane are dealing with a fence dispute up at Nelson's ranch."

I sighed. *Damn cowboys.* The Nelson Ranch was constantly leaking cows out of a broken fence that bordered the Harrow property. The Nelsons said it was the Harrow's responsibility to fix, the Harrows claimed the opposite. Cue calamity and the need for police intervention.

Not normally a problem—using resources to settle a ranch dispute—but with only a solid three-man police force, those resources quickly became scarce. And when they did, Chief Diehl reached out to us.

Myself and my three younger brothers, Hunter, Gunner, and Ranger, collectively owned Reynolds Protective Group. We dealt in personal security and self-defense, and all of us, minus Ranger, had been on one police force or another over the years; Ranger had his own special set of skills.

Our choice of profession was no surprise to anyone in town; Dad had been Wisdom's police chief for almost two decades before his heart attack. Chief Diehl was the man who replaced our father as the police chief.

I flipped my blinker in the other direction, taking a quick left-right scan before turning out onto Main Street. *Looked like that garage door was going to have to wait.*

"Someone broke into the post office?" I asked, hitting the gas a little harder. That didn't make a whole lot of sense. *Especially in Wisdom.*

Wisdom didn't boast much in the way of attractions. Two stoplights. A smattering of standard small-town businesses. *Two bars. Grocery. Movie theater. Hardware store. A family restaurant. A coffee shop. Hotel. Barbershop.*

The population of Wisdom consisted mostly of ranchers, cowboys, and overflow seasonal tourists from Jackson Hole which was about a twenty-five-minute ride from here. That was where most of RPG's clients came from—the elite who came to Jackson Hole on holiday or business and needed some extra protection.

Most people who weren't from the area were surprised at the demand for our business in the mountains of Wyoming. It was usually at that point that Ranger would chime in and rattle off, *'In 2015, it was reported that Jackson, Wyoming had the most unequal distribution of wealth in a metropolitan area where the one percent earn one-hundred-thirty-two times more than everyone else. The average annual income of that one percent is twenty-two-million five-hundred-eight-thousand and eighteen while the average income in the bottom ninety-nine percent is one-hundred-twenty-two-thousand four-hundred-forty-seven.'*

Ranger could be a little overwhelming with his eidetic encyclopedia of facts on seemingly every topic, but he got the point across: *a lot of filthy rich people lived in Teton County.* And rich people always needed protection.

After leaving Boston PD four years ago, I didn't plan on going into any kind of security again. Not after what happened. But being back here—being with my family—I couldn't ignore that this was my calling. I might've failed Keira, but it would never happen again. *And so Reynolds Protective Group was born.*

"That's what she said. I'm leaving the office now. See you in ten." He hung up just as I turned on First Street where the post office was located.

The sun bounced bright rays off the old lampposts lining the road. The air was crystal clear, and I could see each peak of the Teton Range where they sliced into the blue fabric of the Wyoming sky. This *openness* was another reason I'd left Boston. Here, guilt couldn't sneak up on me without warning, and I could spot a secret a mile away.

Sure enough, Zoey Roberts was waiting on the sidewalk, pacing and holding her arms over her chest as I pulled up alongside the curb. She waited while I shut off my truck, fear bleeding from her pale blue eyes underneath her wool cap, her black hair making her cheeks appear even more ashen than normal.

Zoey had moved to town about six months ago from Florida and had taken the mail clerk position at the post office. It was a huge improvement for Wisdom since Walter had been the only postman for the whole town for as long as I could remember.

Mail was always slow here. *Just like everything else.*

I killed the engine and got out of my truck.

"Hey, Zoey," I greeted her calmly, the young woman clearly spooked. "Are you alright?"

She nodded, taking a moment to speak. "Yeah, I'm okay."

"What happened?" I looked over her shoulder, trying to see inside the windows but the glare on the glass was too bright.

"I got here to open up for the day, and the door was already unlocked." Her throat bobbed. "At first, I didn't think too much of it because…" She trailed off, her cheeks flushing.

"Because sometimes Walt forgets to lock up at night?" I finished for her.

There were no secrets in Wisdom. And Walter Walters *(yeah, really)* was getting older and a little forgetful—*and the alcohol didn't help.* However, no matter how many times he forgot to lock up the post office every night, he knew where every local in this town lived regardless of whether their house had a number or not.

She nodded wordlessly, not wanting to get Walt in trouble.

"I went inside, and that's when I realized…" She drew quiet. "Someone was in there. It's… a mess."

"Alright, let me take a look," I said just as Hunter's Cherokee pulled up. *Good.* Zoey was obviously too shaken up to answer questions, but I didn't want to leave her standing out here alone so I could go inside.

"Hunt—"

My brother blew right by me. Only a year younger than me, Hunter and I were almost the exact same height, same build, same light brown hair and green eyes. Our mom said we'd been mistaken for twins countless times when we were younger. Even now, the most distinguishing differences between us were that I kept my face shaved and my hair neatly slicked to one side while Hunt sported a few days' shadow and disheveled waves that took the continuous brunt of his fingers sliding through them.

That, and Hunter still smiled.

"Hey, Zoey, you alright?" he asked her, completely ignoring me.

I watched my brother carefully reach for her shoulders, searching her expression for answers I hadn't been able to find. Out of all of us, Hunter and I were most alike. We followed the rules, didn't get into too much trouble, and stayed pretty level-headed. But while experience had tempered my ease of opening up to others, Hunter didn't have that problem.

My stomach twisted, the look on his face reminding me of another place and time when I'd stared at a woman with that kind of intensity.

I watched for just long enough to see some of the tension drain from Zoey's stiff form, and then I went inside. I didn't even make it through the second entry door when I saw what prompted her to call the police.

The post office boxes along the side walls had been pried open and mail was scattered all over the floor, white envelopes covering the old tile. Directly in front of the door was the counter, and as I approached it, I could see the thief or thieves had gone behind the counter and tore through the cash drawer and some of the packages in the back.

"Jesus," I heard Hunter mutter behind me. "I know Walt can be slow with delivery, but this is a little over the top." He tried to step around the papers but it was impossible not to crunch some of them; they were everywhere. "Gunner would say somebody went postal."

I shot my brother a hard stare. Our third sibling, Gunner, was the wild child of the group. Quick to laugh. Quick to joke. Quick to enjoy life's pleasures to the fullest without thinking twice. He had a good heart, but it would be a good while or take a good knock to the head to get him to settle down.

Lifting up the folding counter, I walked into the back of the post office, noting the extent of the damage.

"Did Zoey say anything else?" I asked him, pausing in front of a book that recorded the owners of each of the PO boxes.

In a town like this where so many residents lived on ranches or locations without concrete addresses, a majority of the locals had a PO box for their mail.

"Not really. She walked in. Saw the mess. Saw that no one was here. Went back outside and immediately called the police." My brother walked over to the far wall, examining the broken-into post office boxes. "Definitely a quick job. Crowbar or something similar that they used to pry them all open."

"Didn't know what they were looking for," I muttered. "Or where to find it."

His head half turned. "I asked if there was anything of value in here that she knew of or mail for any famous people, anything like that, but she couldn't think of anything." He crossed his arms and walked over to me. "You think this was a prank or something? Kids on spring break over in Jackson Hole?"

My jaw clenched.

By Boston standards, everything in Wisdom was an easy target. Businesses locked up at night, but less than half of them had any kind of security system or surveillance cameras.

Including the post office. The size of the town and the crime rate couldn't justify spending that kind of government money.

I hummed, sliding out the cash drawer under the counter. "Well, they didn't take the cash in here, so I doubt it," I said, ruling out his suggestion.

There wasn't a lot of money in the drawer. Maybe a couple hundred bucks. But still, to do all this and not take easy money… I shook my head, my gut telling me the explanation for this wasn't simple.

"Why the hell would someone rob a post office if not for money?" Hunter gripped the edge of the counter, his eyes tracking me. "And how the hell are we going to know if anything was stolen?"

I grunted, not having any good answers or explanations at the moment.

"Is Diehl here?" I could see Zoey talking, but I wasn't sure to whom.

Hunt nodded. "Got here a minute ago. I came in when he started taking Zoey's statement." Like he couldn't help himself, my brother turned and searched for the woman in question. "I also called Walt to let him know what happened and told him to head over. Maybe he'll have an idea what the hell this guy was looking for."

Nodding, my attention returned to the notebook of PO box owners. I flipped through the pages until I realized Hunter was still staring out the window.

"She alright?" I asked quietly.

His grip tightened, blanching his fingers. "I think so."

"You want to take her home?"

His head whipped around and he demanded, "What the fuck kind of question is that right now?"

My eyebrows lifted. Hunter rarely got irritated, especially with me. We usually worked on the same wavelength, but there was obviously something about Zoey that threw him off his game.

I was tempted to warn him that was dangerous. *I knew from experience.* But now wasn't the time.

"The kind I ask because I don't think the girl should be alone since she seems pretty shaken up," I replied, regarding him curiously.

"Oh." His chin dipped. He'd interpreted my question the wrong way and was just realizing it. "Sorry," he grunted. "I already asked her if there was a friend or someone she could call who could spend the rest of the day with her just so she's not alone."

Before I could respond, I came across a page that had been torn out of the notebook. The sheet containing the contact information for the owners of boxes one-fifty through two hundred was missing. I glanced around the floor, quickly scanning for the distinct lined paper filled with information.

It wasn't there.

"Can you go see if Walt can come in here?" I asked my brother, setting the notebook in the center of the counter. "There's a page missing with some of the PO box owners, and I want to know who was on it."

Hunter clipped his chin and then followed my command, disappearing outside a second later.

I stared at the notebook. Who the hell would live in Wisdom that would be important enough to justify breaking into a government building?

The bell dinged as the door opened once more. Instantly, a chill ran down my spine, the hairs on the back of my neck and arms rising to attention in a way that was both familiar and forbidden.

I brushed it off, hating that the memories of the past could still sneak up on me like that.

"Hey, Walt, can you take a look at—" I looked up, the words deadened on my tongue by the ghost standing in front of me. "*Keira?*"

My stare locked with the unmistakable—*and quite alive—*

26

emerald irises of the woman I'd watched die on the Boston courthouse steps four fucking years ago.

Keira McKenna.

Alive. Here. *In front of me.*

Four years might as well have been four seconds for how little it changed her. Sure, her hair was no longer the dark brown I remembered. Now, it was a warm russet, the color reflecting like liquid copper as it fell in long waves over her shoulders. This was her real hair color, I realized in an instant. It matched the blush of her cheeks that was burned into my memory, the freckles on her skin that connected like a constellation in my mind, always retracing the lines of her face for my fantasies, and the apricot pink of her lush lips.

My throat tightened. *This was the real her.*

Alive.

Shock blew apart my senses like a breeze through a damn dandelion, but even that wasn't enough to mask the rush of desire in my veins. Time had done nothing but strengthen the way I wanted her.

Four years.

That would make her twenty-three now—still too fucking young for my dick to jump to attention like it did, but I couldn't control it. She had a bewitching paradox about her— young but with a gaze weighted by wisdom. Innocent but with a life filled with too many hard experiences. Like a rare jewel, each facet of her personality shone differently depending on the light.

And I wanted to know them all.

"Archer."

Suddenly, I was back in that motel room, greedily savoring the husky way she moaned against my mouth, my body so on fire for her—the girl I was tasked to protect—it could've sent the whole building up in flames.

This couldn't be happening. I blinked slowly, the news broadcast from that day flashing in my mind. The gunshots.

27

The bright red on her pure white shirt. The way she was carried to the ambulance, only to be pronounced dead not long after. *Dead.*

Shot and killed.

I opened my eyes and she was still there. Breathing. *Beautiful.*

"You're alive," I charged hoarsely—dumbly—holding the edge of the counter as though if I moved, she would disappear like the fucked-up figment of my imagination she had to be.

For four years, I'd blamed myself for the death of the woman in front of me. Four years. *For her.*

My heart pounded angrily.

Dragging in deep breaths, I studied her with a piercing gaze. She wore black leggings, fur boots, and a black winter coat thrown over her plaid shirt, the green shade echoing her eyes. She'd dressed quickly, the zipper on her jacket open and the bottom button on her shirt undone. She must be the person—the friend that Zoey called; she'd rushed over here to help Zoey and ran into me instead.

For a man who prided himself on logical, rational thought, my mind bounced through facts and memories like a damn pinball machine—always returning to hit that one bumpered fact that refused to sink in: She was alive.

How the hell was she alive? Once more, flashes of the news reports skipped through my mind like a broken record. *Former mob enforcer and daughter murdered on courthouse steps.*

"I am." Her throat bobbed and she folded her arms.

At least she had the fucking decency to look as surprised to see me as I was shocked to see her. Then again, she wasn't the one who watched me get shot all those years ago.

She took a hesitant step forward and then glanced over her shoulder as though she needed to make sure what she was about to say couldn't be heard.

"How?" I rasped, too fucking shocked to think clearly.

Her full lips parted, their color deepening to match the stain in her cheeks. "Archer…"

"*How* are you alive?" The demand came out coarser the second time like my throat was parched for water, only in this case, it was dry from swallowing what had been a life-changing lie all these years. I tensed. The real question I wanted answered was, *how could you let me think you were dead?*

The pleading look in her gaze vanished, replaced by a calm resoluteness that I'd glimpsed back in Boston but had evidently grown stronger with time.

"I'm sorry, Archer, but I couldn't tell you."

Shock fractured into anger, realizing how her death had irrevocably changed the course of my life.

"Couldn't fucking tell me that you didn't fucking die—"

The door dinged again, interrupting our conversation.

"Hey, Archer, you find—" Chief Diehl broke off, the waddle of his big body stopping just inside the room. He looked between us, hardly registering the disaster of the crime scene. "Everything okay in here?"

Keira jumped into action like the curtain rose on her one-woman show. She smiled, the bright flash stealing the oxygen from my lungs. *Goddamn, she was even more beautiful than I remembered.*

"Yes, I was just about to introduce myself to…" she began, pretending not to know who I was.

"Oh, you two haven't met?" If Chief Diehl was surprised by her assertion, he didn't show it. Instead, he went about making introductions like it was his lawful duty. "Arch, this here is Keira Murphy. She moved in a few weeks ago. Bought Todd's old place."

My breath exited my lips in a low hiss.

Keira Murphy.

Keira McKenna.

One more fucking lie.

Anger cleared and the cold truth blinded me like the sun

breaking through snow-laden clouds. *Of course.* Of-fucking-course. The high-profile nature of the trial. The powerful and dangerous reach of the mob boss her father had testified against. The way she'd talked about starting over—starting new.

They hadn't been killed that day; *they'd gone into Witness Protection.* And the program had relocated her to the middle-of-nowhere Wyoming where no one would know her or find her.

Except me.

The one man who'd never forgotten her.

The one man who blamed himself for her death.

"Keira, this is Archer Reynolds. He and his brothers own Reynolds Protective Group." He cleared his throat, linking his hands in front of his protruding belly. "They do personal security but help us out from time to time."

Her tongue slid out, coating her lips with more armor for her lies. "It's nice to meet you, Archer."

It took all my strength not to flinch and give away her deceit. Yeah, I was angry. Yeah, I still wanted the truth. But the answers I did have about her past meant her lies existed to protect her just like I'd been tasked to do in Boston—a responsibility I wouldn't shirk now.

"You too," I said low and clipped my chin.

She turned back to Diehl. "I just came in to grab Zoey's bag. She said she dropped it as soon as she saw the mess." It only took a second for her to spot the black purse that had fallen on the floor next to the small packaging stand. She picked it up, meeting my unwavering stare.

Electricity cracked through the room, bright and potent like heat lightning, but without the audible thunder to give away our connection to anyone else.

"Good luck with the investigation," she offered to the both of us.

"Thank you." Diehl tipped his head. "And welcome to Wisdom, Miss Murphy."

Her smile flashed again, always bright enough to hide the secrets in her eyes.

"Nice to meet you, Keira. I'm sure I'll see you around." My low voice resonated through the room, the tense tenor carrying an unspoken meaning.

Her breath hitched, her green eyes flickering fiercely. She lifted her chin just a fraction higher to show that she felt no guilt for lying to me four years ago, and only a shadow of sorrow that I found out the truth now.

And then she walked out of the post office like I could just accept that she wasn't dead and move on with my life.

Like I could just continue living in my small-ass-town knowing the woman I'd sworn to protect—the woman my body still craved—was now living here, too.

Keira McKenna.

Heat quaked through my veins.

There was only one thing that could keep me from her. And unfortunately for her, I wasn't going to fall for the *play dead* card again.

CHAPTER TWO

KEIRA

ARCHER.

Of the two-hundred-and-three towns in the tenth largest state in the country, *of course*, I would end up in his.

Archer Reynolds. The detective whose duty was as strong as his chiseled jaw. The man with the evergreen eyes that were as endless as the open plains. The man whose lips burned something incredible onto my skin and more indelible than any tattoo I could ever give to myself.

It was Archer's descriptions of the bright skies and breathtaking mountain ranges that fueled my dreams for the last four years until I could finally settle here. Of course, I knew there was a chance—slim as it might be—that I could run into him; it was his home state, after all. But he'd always talked about Jackson—not Wisdom. I was sure I'd sooner run into Sean Maloney than Archer Reynolds in the small speck of a town orbiting Jackson, especially because the last time I saw Archer, he was quickly rising through the ranks of one of the nation's top police forces on the other side of the country. *Why would he come back here with such promise in front of him in Boston?*

No. It was supposed to be just as impossible for Archer to

come back to Wyoming as it was for me to ever think about returning to Boston.

Except, apparently, it wasn't. In fact, my life felt like a string of impossibilities decorated with danger. And now, I'd just settled into and purchased a building for my tattoo parlor in the same town as the man who protected me and thought I'd died four years ago.

"Damn," I muttered, jogging up the stairs to Zoey's apartment above the Brilliant Brews coffee shop.

The look on Archer's face when he first saw me carved new paths in my mind. I was sure I looked surprised, too, but then again, he wasn't the one coming back to life before my eyes.

I knocked on her door, clearing my thoughts of everything except my friend. "Zoey, it's Keira."

It had been two days since the break-in, and I was no closer to coming to terms with Archer's presence here than I had been the second I'd walked out of the looted post office.

I'd taken Zoey home and stayed with her that first night, and then checked up on her yesterday. She was pretty shaken up after the break-in, though she'd insisted on going into work yesterday to help Walt clean up the mess.

The door rattled when she looked through the peephole. *Neither of us could be too safe.*

She opened the door. "Hey Keira." She tucked a strand of her midnight hair behind her ear and smiled, ushering me inside.

I'd met Zoey six weeks ago when my Toyota Corolla rolled up to the post office. I'd stopped in to purchase a PO box for my new business, and when I met the raven-haired woman behind the counter, I'd recognized a familiar guarded expression in Zoey's eyes. It was one I'd worn every time Dad and I first moved, worried that the men after us were lurking around every new corner.

After Boston, that fear slowly dissipated for me. But not for

Dad. He'd looked over his shoulder for too long, it took only a couple months for me to realize he wasn't capable of fully looking forward again.

Dad had asked where I wanted to live this time, and I'd said Wyoming—clinging to the memory of the detective I hadn't wanted to leave. He promised we'd come here, but he didn't want it to be our first stop. *Just in case.* So, we drove to South Carolina and stayed there for six months. Then, we went to Louisiana. Another six months. Texas. A year. Arizona. Nine months. Every time I protested another move, he always got me with '*well, don't you want to make it to Wyoming?*' I really did, but I also saw how he could never let go of Sean Maloney's threat or the fear that the Kings would find us.

The longest we stayed in one place was Utah, our last— my last home before Wisdom. Dad had gotten sick and ended up in the hospital. Decades of a dangerous lifestyle, poor health habits, and old wounds made the chemo less effective and the cancer spread quickly. He died three months ago, begging me with his last breath to take his paintings and move on, the words '*be brave*' the last thing to pass his lips.

So, I'd packed up what few things we had, including his seven prized paintings, and drove straight to Wyoming. He never told me where the artwork came from, but he had it since before I was born. I guessed it was the closest thing we had to family heirlooms because no matter what we left behind, his paintings always came.

Even though we moved a lot, I had to give my dad credit. He tried his hardest to not bring up our former life. Every time we moved, he started out so hopeful, so determined, but eventually the fear set in. It didn't matter that there was no cause for it—no attacks or letters. No indication that the Irish Kings thought we were anywhere except six feet under. But there was no arguing with Patrick McKenna once he thought his daughter was in danger, so every couple of months, we ended up on the run again.

By the time we got to Salt Lake City, I was convinced we weren't running from angry gangsters, only ghosts.

But here was where the running stopped. Or at least, that had been my plan until seeing Archer had thrown a giant, handsome wrench in it. Who would've thought that coming to help the one person I'd befriended in town would bring me face-to-face with my single regret?

"How are you doing today?" I asked, walking with Zoey into the small kitchen off her living room.

Zoey had a one-bedroom apartment above the local coffee shop. The walls were white and sparsely decorated with photos of abstract artwork and nature. No images of her family or friends. All of her dark furniture was purchased at the local thrift shop in town which she'd recommended to me the day we'd met.

We'd gone together a week later and she helped me find a couch and a bed for the small ranch I was renting on the edge of town.

"I'm okay." She nodded, folding her arms. "Better, actually since I went in yesterday. It helped to clean up everything."

"So, you didn't find anything…"

We both guarded our secrets close at first, but our mutual respect for those secrets and our desire to have a friend brought us close enough to start sharing bits and pieces of what had driven her to Wisdom six months ago, and what had brought me here now.

"No." Her head shook, relieved. "No photos. Nothing addressed to me."

Zoey had moved from Florida because there was a stranger stalking her. She told me that the man would mail her photos of himself—of his body parts—and letters professing his love. The police hadn't done much except make a report since there was nothing threatening in the letters. So Zoey took matters into her own hands and moved across town.

Then the photos began showing up at her office. If that wasn't enough to make her leave her job, something happened with her boyfriend, who was also her boss, so she quit the marketing company she worked for with a desperate hope that would fix everything.

A few weeks later, the photos started arriving again at her new apartment, and that was the last straw.

You can only run forward while looking over your shoulder for so long before something has to give. So, she up and left her whole life—sold everything, packed her clothes in the middle of the night, bought a car with cash, and drove across the country with no destination in mind except somewhere far away.

"That's good."

"Do you want tea?" She reached for her kettle.

"I'm okay. I'm going to grab a coffee downstairs on my way out. I've got so much work to do at the shop," I told her, thinking about the towers of paint cans and laminate flooring that were about to take over my life.

It had taken two weeks of living in Wisdom for me to finally accept that this was my final stop—the place I would finally make my home. I'd been walking downtown, familiarizing myself with the local businesses and scouting job postings when I noticed the tiny barbershop across the street —Todd's—with the *For Sale* sign in the window. Before I realized what I was doing, I found myself on the phone with Todd himself, asking what it would take to buy the building.

Owning my own tattoo parlor had been part of the dream. I thought I'd at least spend a few months getting settled in Wyoming before I pursued it, but when I saw that tiny shop, the classic red and white barber poles on either side of the door, I knew it was waiting for me to get here—to take it over.

Be brave, I'd heard my dad say in the back of my mind. I hoped that meant I was justified in doing what I'd had to in

order to buy the building; I'd sold one of his paintings—
the smallest one. I'd connected online with a pawnshop in Salt
Lake City, fabricating a story that I had no information on the
artwork except that I'd found it collecting dust in the
basement of the house I'd just bought. They'd given me a
little less than a hundred thousand for it which surprised me,
but I chalked it up to Dad still looking out for me.

That was when I'd met Zoey; I'd needed a PO box for the
pawnshop to send my payment to.

"Keira, there was something missing from the post office."
She finished pouring herself a cup of coffee, setting the carafe
back into the machine and then searching for some creamer in
her fridge.

"Really? So, they figured out why the thieves broke in?" I
asked, seeing the story about the break-in on the front page of
the Wisdom Gazette, a photo of the post office blocked off
with crime scene tape taking up half the page.

"No." Her spoon clanked against the ceramic mug as she
stirred her coffee. "I realized there was something missing
yesterday, and I was afraid it might be because of you."

My eyes snapped to hers, my pulse picking up. "What?" I
pushed the newspaper away. "What do you mean?"

Zoey sank into the other chair across the kitchen
table. "One of the pages was ripped out of the book that
catalogs all the PO boxes and who they belong to," she said,
taking a hard swallow. "It was the last page that had yours
listed on it."

I exhaled deeply, the instantaneous tension draining like a
punctured balloon from my chest.

"The one that had the box registered to Twilight Ink?" I
replied and shook my head. "It's registered to the business,
Zoey. I'm sure it's just a coincidence."

I'd lived protected for almost a decade that I no longer
had to think about living carefully. Being careful was more
than just a habit, after all this time, it was instinct.

If Sean Maloney had any chance of finding me, that chance disintegrated to dust when I moved to the closed-off, mountain-surrounded corner of Wyoming. I'd left no forwarding address from Salt Lake City. I paid my rent which included utilities in cash, purchased my groceries in cash. I'd purchased my building in cash. Anything I had to register went in the name of the business.

There was nothing that linked Keira McKenna—or Murphy—to Wisdom. *Nothing except Archer Reynolds.*

"Okay, if you're sure." Zoey didn't look convinced, and I understood. She was still coming off of fresh fear while I'd had four years of relative peace to convince myself that Lattimore and my dad's plan had worked—that I wasn't in danger any longer. "I just wanted you to know."

She pulled her hands apart, rubbed them on her dark jeans, and then linked her fingers again.

"Thank you. I appreciate you looking out, but I don't think this has anything to do with me. Not now." I reached across the table and placed my palm over her clasped grip, offering her a grateful smile.

"I'm glad you're sure." She appeared slightly more relieved after my second reassurance. "I was worried I might lose you."

"Don't worry, I can tell you from experience that I'm pretty damn hard to get rid of." I grinned and she returned the gesture.

"I'm sure it was just destroyed or taken with the rest of the stuff," I mused, placing my hand back on the table and drumming my fingers. Zoey told me last night that Walt and Chief Diehl assumed there was mail and stamps missing from the post office, along with a couple packages from the back.

"Yeah. It's just so crazy that this happened here. This town seems so quiet and sleepy, even when visitors pass through from Jackson, it's just like a brief breeze of excitement before it's gone."

My gaze returned to the Gazette and I commented wryly, "Well, I'm sure Kendra will be doing her very best to get to the bottom of the crime, nosing the thief out of hiding before Chief Diehl even gets a chance."

Zoey laughed.

Kendra Moore was a reporter for the Wisdom Gazette. Her pieces were always on the front page and a little extra sensationalized in my opinion, but I couldn't blame her, Wisdom didn't give a reporter much to work with in the way of newsworthy stories.

My eyes narrowed, catching on a name in the robbery article. *Archer Reynolds.* Of course, she interviewed him. I felt a momentary flash of unwarranted jealousy that she got to ask him questions. There were questions I wanted to ask him —*why was he back here? Had something happened in Boston? Did it have to do with me?* My chest constricted. *Did he still think about our kiss like I did?*

I pushed the paper out of my sight.

I didn't have a right to ask Archer anything. Not anymore.

"It's just a matter of time before she realizes it's you who bought Todd's old shop and starts asking questions," Zoey warned, taking another sip of her coffee.

"I'm not doing an interview with her," I said resolutely. A new tattoo shop opening in town was exactly the kind of small-town news a reporter would love to do a story on, especially when the owner was a quiet newcomer. But I wasn't about to give an exposé on where I'd come from, why I'd gone into body art, and what made me choose Wisdom. "I'm keeping all my answers to myself," I added in jest.

Zoey pulled the paper over to her edge of the table and then looked at me. "Have you talked to Archer?"

Heat rose in my cheeks.

Shaken up by our meeting, I'd probed Zoey about the Reynolds brothers. She'd never mentioned any of them or their business, but I couldn't blame her. What reason would she have to bring up a security firm that mostly worked with rich clients over in Jackson? And I'd never told her about the detective protecting me during the trial because I'd never told her about the trial. Zoey knew my father had been involved with criminals, so we'd had to move around a lot, but that was all she could know. The price of safety—hers and mine—was secrets.

The first rule of WITSEC is: you do not talk about being in WITSEC.

But when I asked about Archer, I'd been forced to admit that we knew each other from when I'd lived in Boston and gave her a bare-bones story about how he'd helped me when my dad was in trouble.

"No." I pushed the sleeves of my sweater up to my elbows, already feeling my body start to warm at the mention of the man who'd haunted my fantasies for some time now. "Why?"

"Well, you said you moved before you could say goodbye." She reached for her coffee mug. "I thought you guys just might have some things to talk about especially now that you're living in the same small town."

The ball in my throat inflated with necessary regret. "It was too long ago. Plus, he knows about my father, so he will understand."

Hopefully.

I recalled the moment that understanding dawned on him about the trial—my protection. Archer was a smart guy—a stellar detective. He didn't need me to connect the dots between a fake death and the reason why I'd shown up alive in his hometown.

My eyes drifted to my own hands, remembering the way his had white-knuckled the post office counter. The shock of seeing me didn't stand a chance against the anger he felt being lied to. I didn't blame myself for lying to him, and I didn't blame him for being angry about it. It was just the unfortunate reality of the situation.

"I'm sorry."

"Don't be sorry. Our meeting was bound to happen, so it's better that we got it out of the way."

"Well, they say you are more likely to run into a Reynolds in Wisdom than you are a stoplight." She gave me a faint smile.

I laughed, feeling the strain on my chest. *Great.*

"I know Walt gave them the owners of all the boxes on that paper, so they will probably need to ask you some questions."

I exhaled slowly. "I expect he will."

Though not about the break-in.

"Have you told Hunter about what happened in Florida?" I turned the conversation on her, recalling how concerned the other Reynolds brother had been at the scene.

Her eyes bugged wide, and she shook her head furiously. "Oh, no. I can't do that."

After I'd run into Archer and then grabbed Zoey's purse, I went back outside and saw Hunter Reynolds talking to my friend, his hand gently cupping her shoulder, his head dipped down with concern. He'd been talking to Chief Diehl when I'd arrived and my only thought had been my panicked friend. When I took a good look at him the second time around, I was shocked by how similar he and Archer looked. And then I felt a little jealous at the way he looked at my friend—so warm and protective.

Archer had looked at me like that once. I knew better than to think he'd look at me like that ever again.

"But if you like him—"

"We're just friends," she protested.

"I don't think he looks at his friends the way he was looking at you," I told her, adding. "At least, I hope he doesn't because that would be awkward."

That got her to laugh, but still, she insisted, "We're just friends."

I lifted my hands and let her have this one. "If you say so, Zoey." I stood and she followed. "I've got to get going. I have a full day of remodeling to get done at the shop."

Last week had been a revolving door of professionals. The plumber. The electrician. The carpenter. Everything had been repaired and made ready for a fresh start. Meanwhile, I'd worked outside, painting over the graffiti that collected on the side of the building. Now, I just needed to get through the mountain of decor work before I was finally ready to open Twilight Ink.

"I'll stop by when I'm done at the post office and bring pizza," she offered as we walked to her door.

"You're the best." I turned and hugged her. "See you later."

CHAPTER THREE

ARCHER

KEIRA MCKENNA WAS ALIVE.

Alive.

In Wisdom.

"*Archie.*"

I flinched when something hit my forehead. A balled-up piece of paper bounced onto my desk. I looked up and saw two sets of eyes staring at me, one with concern, the other, amusement.

Hunter, Gunner, and I were sitting in my office at our Reynolds Protective headquarters, a modest lodge-style chalet that sat off a half-mile drive just outside of town. The large windows and timbered exterior made it appear welcoming though it was well protected. Bullet-proof glass, steel-frame doors, and a high-end security system advertised the kind of security we strove to provide for our clients.

The small lobby fed a hallway that contained Ranger's office, a consult room, and our file room. Upstairs, Hunter and Gunner's offices opposed each other first in the hallway that finally ended at my office in the back of the building, the windows behind my desk providing an expansive view of the Teton Range. There was a small gym in the basement, along with our server room, and a gun range in the back where we held firearms classes in the summer.

"And you guys make fun of me when I'm walking around this place in a dick daze." Gunner smirked, enjoying my preoccupation. "Not a good look for you, Archie. Not going to lie."

My expression remained hard and unmoving. Out of my three brothers and our youngest sister, Gwen, Gunner was the only one who still called me Archie. He'd been doing it since he was little, so there was no way to break the habit even if I wanted to. *Days like today made me want to.*

"Shut up, Gunner," Hunter grumbled in the seat next to him, flicking through images on his iPad that he'd taken of the crime scene at the post office.

To say that the Wisdom Police Department was ill-equipped to handle a strange crime like this was an understatement. Diehl had jumped all over my offer to have myself and my brothers stay on the case until we found the culprit and his motive for ransacking the building but not taking anything of value.

"Oh come on." Gunner lifted his hand in my direction. "What are the chances that the girl you were protecting—the one that was killed while *not* on your watch, shows up alive and well? That's shit luck, Archie."

My jaw tightened and recoiled like a loaded spring.

I'd had to tell my brothers about Keira if for no other reason than Hunter had seen me immediately afterward; in his own words, I'd been 'shell-shocked.' *He wasn't wrong.* Aside from that, this town was too small and her secret too dangerous for them to not understand the gravity of who she was—*and what seeing her did to me.* Thankfully, my brothers were the very best of men (even without my familial bias.) Sometimes, I wondered how since our dad had died when we were all young, leaving me, at sixteen, to fill his impossibly big shoes. Yet in spite of my own failings—*which I was sure were many*—they'd grown up to not only be men I was incredibly proud of, but guys I also wanted to be friends with. *Though Gunner liked to test those limits. Regularly.*

I trusted them to understand and respect the weight of the information I revealed about Keira's past and my part in it. I trusted them with my life, and I needed them to help me protect hers.

"One day, your luck is going to run out, Gun, and we're all just going to sit here and laugh." Hunter kept his attention on the photos.

"Never." Gunner rocked back in his seat and linked his hands behind his head. "What are the chances she would end up here of all places?"

Even less likely than her being alive but look how that turned out.

I grunted and turned my head to look out my office window. It was another clear, beautiful day outside—so clear, I knew if I walked up to the glass, I'd be able to see the tiny connected dots in the distance of the ski lifts at the resort.

I wondered if it was because of her—because I knew the truth and realized the life I'd led for the last four years was a lie—that now I could see everything more clearly.

A little fucking dramatic there, Arch.

Maybe. But Christ, it was still so fucking hard to believe. Keira McKenna—*Murphy*—was alive.

"Any updates on the list, Hunter?" I cleared my throat, redirecting the conversation.

"Gun and I ran through all the personal PO boxes. Diehl was following up with a third of them, and we were going to check with the rest to see if anyone was expecting anything significant in their mail," he said, closing the case on his iPad and regarding me. "Ranger took the smaller list of business boxes because we needed a little more digging in order to find out who owned them."

As though he'd heard his name mentioned, the door swung open, our youngest brother striding into the room.

Ranger looked the least like the rest of us. His hair was lighter, longer, and in a constant state of chaos around his head. His build was tall and skinny, though he did possess a surprising amount of strength when required. And his attire... Gunner joked that only Ranger was smart enough to simultaneously pull off being the youngest *and* the oldest of the group; Ranger never wore jeans, instead favoring khakis, button-down shirts, and sweater vests.

"Here are the businesses registered to the PO boxes and their owners." He walked up to my desk and handed me a list. "I organized them first based on recency of purchase and then highlighted the ones I thought most probable to have something of value being sent to them."

That was Ranger.

"I still can't wait to know who the hell thought it was a brilliant idea to rob a post office," Gunner grumbled.

"Mail theft has been a popular crime for centuries, though the various means and targets have changed." In typical fashion, Ranger answered with a slew of statistics from the vault of information locked in his head, not realizing the question was rhetorical. "More recently though, the Postal Inspection Service data showed an over six-hundred-percent increase in mail theft reports over the last three years, rising from twenty-five-thousand in 2017 to one-hundred-seventy-seven thousand in 2020."

This was Ranger's superpower: his eidetic memory. His ability to digest, process, parse, and store information was astounding. I remembered when he was a kid, I'd take all of us to the library to get our homework done. Not only would Ranger be done before the rest of us—*including helping Gunner with his*—but he'd have read at least two books by the time we left. But like every superpower, he also had his kryptonite: social situations, especially involving women in a romantic fashion, were his.

"Baby Brains to the rescue," Gunner quipped and pulled

out his phone. "Maybe someone was just looking for their lost mail."

"It's estimated that three percent of all mail sent is lost every year, but it is incredibly hard to determine in a lot of cases if mail is lost or stolen," Ranger continued blithely. "This is why the number of individual mailboxes and PO boxes is growing rapidly, to help reduce the number of thefts."

"Well, that plan backfired here."

I continued to read the report while they bantered, not overly concerned about the statistics of mail crime at the moment.

"Ranger, why is there no name listed next to this—*Twilight Ink?*" I asked, pointing to the anomaly on his list.

"Well, for that one, the post office didn't record the business owner's name, which I thought was strange. I can try to look up and see if the business is a registered LLC and work backward from there," he offered.

"I'll just go call Zoey and ask," Hunter offered a little too quickly and left the room.

"How's Mom's new garage door?" I asked Ranger while we waited.

I'd gotten a lot of things done yesterday in an effort to avoid thinking about Keira.

"Oh, she loves it." His rapid nod loosened a wayward curl onto his forehead. "She didn't seem all that worried about our safety, though I did tell her I was more than capable of shooting any intruders."

Gunner chuckled in his seat but didn't say anything.

Of course, Ranger knew how to shoot—we all did. Before opening our business, we'd all gone through a rigorous and expansive tactical and defensive training program at the elite, San Francisco-based organization, Armorous Tactical. The owner, Hazard Foster, had done a one-day training for Boston PD while I was there and his skills and experience as a former SEAL impressed me—even more so when I thought about going into private security with my brothers.

But our youngest brother who was knowledgeable beyond his years was also… innocent. With his wide eyes and warm smile, I worried what having to do harm to another human would do to him. He wasn't hardened like the rest of us, so he handled most of the research and data collection for our business, a skill he excelled at, while the rest of us worked in the field.

I was about to give some response when Hunter's return saved me the trouble, the look on his face

"What did she say?" I prompted. "Does she have the address of the business so I can talk to the owner?"

His chin dipped.

"Todd's old barbershop."

This time, Gunner didn't hide his snicker from his chair.

My jaw snapped tight. *Of course, Keira's business would be on the sheet that was taken.* We didn't even know if the missing page meant anything, but now that she was in some way connected to it, my instincts went into overdrive. If there was any chance this had to do with the criminals her father had put behind bars, I needed to know; *she needed to be protected.*

"Do you want me to go?" Hunter offered.

I shook my head, already rising from my seat. "No. I can handle it."

She'd already come back from the dead. At this point, there was nothing else left to shock me.

NESTLED along the edge of Wyoming, Wisdom was buried among the snowcapped mountains of the Teton Range. The evergreen forest covering the mountainous crags filled out

where the lines of winter began to fade. The sky was so blue here, it looked like it had been dyed and then fluffed with perfect white clouds.

Main Street was a stretch of road I knew like the back of my hand. The highlight of my childhood had been riding along in my dad's cruiser as he patrolled down the main vein of our sleepy town. We'd stop at the Main Street market and pick up a few things for dinner or at the video store where he'd let me choose a movie for movie night at home.

Every inch of Wisdom held memories.

For a time, I wasn't sure if it was a good thing, so I joined the force in Boston. Coming back, I realized that good and bad, the memories were what made this place my sanctuary. A safe retreat.

Until Keira entered it.

I pulled into the small lot next to Todd's old shop. I'd driven by the small red brick building countless times, but now that I was really looking, I could see how much work had been done in the last couple of weeks while I was out of town. The exterior brick had been power washed, the graffiti painted over, the roof cleaned, the barber poles removed and replaced with dark, wrought-iron sconces, and the door painted bright red.

I hoped Keira was here. Otherwise, I'd have to head back to the post office and ask Zoey where she lived.

I didn't mind asking. It was having that knowledge that worried me—too much temptation to know where she was staying. *To know that kissing her again was within geographical reach.*

My lips pulled tight, attempting to strangle the sensation of how her lips had felt under mine. So young and innocent. Eager and unknowing. Her taste had been tattooed on my tongue for four years, and I'd long ago given up hope of anything ever removing it.

"Shit." I stopped in front of the single step to the front door and dragged my hand through my hair. I needed to get myself under control. My temper, and the part of me that was currently thickening against my jeans.

Keira McKenna was a conflict of interest.

I knocked on the door, unable to see through its window because the blinds were drawn on the other side. There was commotion inside. A muffled female curse. And then the blinds on the door whipped up, Keira's bright green eyes catching and instantly widening when she saw me.

She unlocked the door. I noted how there were two dead bolt clicks before it was able to open.

"Archer."

I gritted my teeth, her voice doing things to me I still couldn't justify.

"Keira." My eyes raked over her from the soft pile of burnished copper on top of her head, down over her long-sleeve tee, to the leggings she had on; the whole of her from top to toe splattered and streaked with paint in various degrees. "Can I come in?"

Her eyes flashed. The question was still a habit, one she clearly remembered.

She hesitated for a moment and then stepped away from the opening with a sigh, allowing me to enter.

"I guess some things don't change."

I grunted and turned in the space, taking in the bright white walls.

The smell of fresh paint bit into my nostrils, but it wasn't enough to burn away the scent of her sweetness that wafted into my lungs as I walked by her, just close enough to amplify the buzzing in my blood.

Vaguely, I remembered the rust-colored walls and scuffed tile floor of the barbershop when it was in business. It took a second to parse the past and present and realize that the counter in front had been added as well as the partial wall in the back of the room. I assumed her table where she would tattoo clients would be behind it.

Tattoos. Another facet of this woman I'd thought about on the drive over. At nineteen, she hadn't known what she wanted to do after she left Boston. Our weeks spent together as protector and protectee had passed mostly talking about the past. But the image of Keira as a tattoo artist didn't surprise me.

She certainly hadn't needed any ink when she'd branded her image in my mind.

"Some things, but not everything."

"Yeah," she agreed, tipping her head. "You're no longer Detective Reynolds."

My gaze tracked back to her.

"And you're no longer dead," I deadpanned.

She straightened her spine. "I couldn't tell you, Archer. It was a matter of life and death."

Literally.

My fists balled under my arms. I wanted to argue with her. I wanted to protest that I'd broken the fucking rules to ease her pain. I wanted to yell that she'd begged for my kiss. And mostly I wanted to scream because I'd given it to her. I'd kissed her like a madman finally slipping into insanity.

Fuck. My jeans grew tight to the point of pain over my cock.

I'd broken the bounds of my duty to kiss someone who was not only under my protection but who was over a decade younger than me. I'd royally fucked up for one taste of her sweet lips, and she couldn't spare me a goddamn hint.

"That's not why I'm here," I responded with instead, proud of myself for sticking to my promise to Hunter to *handle* this.

There was no point in arguing about the past. It was four years too late to change anything. And I wasn't about to admit that I'd walked away from my career in Boston because I thought she'd been killed—because I blamed myself for it.

"Okay..." She dunked her paintbrush into the bucket and walked over to the nearest wall.

"Whoever broke into the post office yesterday seems to have taken a single sheet from the PO box logs—the one that contained the box number for your business."

"And?" She continued to paint, the quick strokes of her brush explaining why so much of her was lightly smattered with white.

"That doesn't worry you?" I took a few steps closer.

She paused and looked over her shoulder, halting me in place.

"That a missing single sheet of paper from a post office that was torn apart had my business name on it?" Her eyebrows popped up, making her look young. "No, it doesn't."

"So, you're saying it shouldn't worry me?" I felt my anger rising.

"Correct."

"Dammit, Keira—" I broke off and dragged a hand through my hair.

She pointed her paintbrush at me in warning, then flicked it back to herself, and then back to me. "I died four years ago, Archer. I gave up everything so I could live. If you don't think I've taken every precaution to preserve that—"

I moved toward her until her brush dropped to her side, allowing me to tower over her. *Allowing her to stand firm and unfazed by my presence.*

I stared at her upturned face, seeing a drop of white paint on her left cheek. It must've flung off when she was waving her paintbrush around.

"I need to know if there is any chance the Kings are still looking for you—any reason for them to think you're alive," I bit out in a low voice.

I needed to know if I was in danger of losing her again. My hand spurred into action without considering the consequence. I reached up and cupped her cheek, instantly blasted with the memory of the last time I'd touched her. Electricity buzzed through me like a swarm of bees, all stinging the spot where my skin connected with hers. Swallowing hard, my thumb forged a path of its own—a bridge to the past as it brushed the paint from her skin.

She trembled slightly. I still affected her. The thought fired and then instantly froze my blood. *I just didn't affect her enough to deserve the truth.*

"No. No reason. They were only after my father." Her breath faltered and her eyes dropped, signaling there was more there than she was letting on.

"And where's he?" I cleared my throat and tore my hand from her cheek, folding my arms, so I wouldn't make the mistake of touching her again.

"Gone." Her gaze snapped back. "He died three months ago."

Shit.

"I'm sorry, Keira," I rasped.

Her expression dimmed and my entire body went taut with the urge to pull her against me. Even with what little I knew about her life, I realized what a blow that would be—to lose the only person who'd ever been able to know and truly love her.

My head dipped closer like it was being pulled down in increments, straining against gravity it couldn't fight.

Get a handle on yourself, Archer. I heard Hunter in the back of my mind. *Don't think with your dick; that's Gunner's job.*

I jerked back. Falling for this woman four years ago only to watch her die had ripped the foundation of my life right out from under me. It didn't matter that she was standing in front of me, her gaze swirling with the same kind of wanting from before. She had secrets—secrets that broke me. I couldn't risk getting any kind of involved with Keira again—not until I knew every crevasse of truth in her mountain of lies.

I took a half step back, needing distance.

"And there's no reason they'd transfer their revenge onto you?" I had to ask. I had to know what the hell I was dealing with—if the fucking Irish mob was going to show up on Main Street searching for her.

She recovered just as quickly. "I'm not in danger from the mob over a missing piece of paper, Archer." She wrote off my concern. "For all you know, Walt could've ripped out that sheet to wipe up a beer spill."

My jaw locked. She wasn't wrong. Walt was forgetful because he tended to drink a little too much. Then again, she also hadn't exactly answered my question.

I scoured her face, searching for any crack in the gorgeous facade, and then let out a low hum from deep in my chest.

"You don't believe me…"

"Hard to believe someone who I thought was dead up until two days ago."

Anger burnished her bold gaze. I didn't want to be bitter, but I couldn't stop myself. I'd risked everything to do more than just protect her—to do more than just sit outside her damn motel door like a zookeeper outside a cage—and she couldn't spare me one goddamn hint so I didn't take her death to heart.

"I'm not in danger. I haven't been for years. You of all people should know that I will do—and hide—whatever I need to in order to keep myself safe." Her chin jutted up. "I haven't been found in four years, Archer. I left no trace, so I could come here and build my life. You have no idea how precious this opportunity is for me, and I'd never do anything to risk it."

My teeth grated. It was hard to argue with that. I might not know exactly how much she valued this new start, but I had a pretty good idea.

"I'm sorry that this happened, but it doesn't have anything to do with me or my past. I don't need to be protected."

I hissed, the words cutting straight into an old wound that hadn't healed much below the surface.

"I guess you never did."

She recoiled.

"Archer—"

"Don't," I warned, finding myself in front of her again, our faces just inches apart with angry air spewing from both our lips. "If you wanted to play dead for the world who knew you, you shouldn't have come here. This is my town—my home."

It held memories, but at least none of them had been tainted with her. Now, they were all at risk. *And so was I.*

"What are you trying to say?" Indignation flashed.

"These are good people here who lead quiet, simple lives. To them, the idea of organized crime is a bunch of teenagers going cow tipping as a senior prank." My voice lowered. "I won't risk the Irish fucking Kings coming to this town."

I'd seen firsthand what happened to neighborhoods in Boston that were bigger than Wisdom when the Kings came through and took over. I didn't leave all that shit behind only to have it follow me here.

"Are you trying to kick me out of town?" She folded her arms and balked, her freckle-dusted cheeks turning pink as she sassed, "Because unless I missed that you were promoted from detective to mayor, I don't think you have that authority."

Damn, this woman knew how to push all my buttons. I flexed my fist, wanting to show her fine ass the kind of authority I did have without mentioning that I might not be the mayor, but I knew her personally.

I let my head dip lower, my gaze snagging on her full lips for a second with the erotic urge to punish them. I'd always thought they were too full for someone like her—someone her age, her inexperience. She had the mouth of a fucking pin-up at nineteen, and now, that temptation turned to torture as she'd learned how to wield it.

"I'm not kicking you out. I'm telling you that you can't hide anything from me. Not here. Not anymore." My nostrils flared. "I have a responsibility to everyone in this town to keep them safe. Including you."

The pink tip of her tongue slid over her lips, tasting the promise I'd given.

"I told you, I'm not in danger."

Liar.

Our eyes locked with the kind of energy that was bound to explode into either fighting or fucking. A dangerous kind of combustion that broke so many rules—and would incur too many risks. So, I ignored the lower half of my body that angled for the latter because the upper half of me wasn't willing to risk anything else.

"Maybe. Or maybe you are the danger."

To my hometown. And to me.

CHAPTER FOUR

ARCHER

"You did *what?*"

I winced at the shrill disapproval in my sister's voice.

Gwen was the youngest in the family and the most staunchly protected by the four of us growing up. In spite of our sincere but probably suffocating concern, she'd still come out with her own Reynolds' brand of bold, working all over the country as a nurse before finally ending up in Carmel Cove, California where she met her husband, Chevy.

"I implied that she was a danger to everyone in town." Every time I repeated it, I sounded more and more like an asshole. And I'd repeated it a lot to myself over the last two days until finally, I caved and called my sister. "I know. Dick move. It just doesn't sit right with my gut that someone breaks into the post office not long after she comes to town and doesn't take a single fucking thing of value except a piece of paper that happens to have her PO box on it."

Or maybe I was still adjusting to Keira being, you know, alive, and the rift between what I thought I knew and the truth was what was really putting me off.

I pressed my lips to the beer bottle that hovered in front of them and took another good swallow, sinking deeper into the cushions of my couch.

My living room had towering ceilings, a stone fireplace, and sat directly attached to the kitchen and a small dining area. I'd built the modest ranch four years ago after attempting to live with Gunner for a single month since he had the most space in his two-bedroom apartment and asked the least amount of questions. *A bad idea.*

But after four years, I hadn't done too much else to the space except furnish it with the basics. Couch, TV, bed, and refrigerator. There were two photos on either side of the TV: one of my dad and me on Halloween, and another of my mom, my siblings, and me at Gwen's wedding last year.

My house sat about two miles down a dirt drive behind the Reynolds Protective compound. We'd ended up with almost forty acres of land in the purchase, so it made sense to build myself a place close to work.

I was sure my brothers would follow suit maybe once they decided to settle down—if ever. Until then, Hunter lived in a small condo community just outside of town though there were a good number of nights when he crashed on my couch. Ranger was still at Mom's house in town, and last, Gunner lived in a newer apartment building halfway between Wisdom and Jackson; he preferred to be a little closer to the kind of nightlife he enjoyed and the waves of visitors to the ski resort which made it easy for his hook-ups to have a natural expiration date.

There were a million reasons I hadn't personalized the space much since I moved in: I worked a lot. It was a bachelor pad. I told myself that Gunner's apartment near Jackson Hole didn't have much more to it, but that wasn't quite the truth. Gunner avoided anything permanent because he wasn't interested in a serious relationship. I felt like I didn't have a choice.

"That doesn't sound like you, Arch."

I swallowed. Like our mom, Gwen had a sharp eye, a kind heart, and a way of giving even the worst of truths in the least painful way. However, I wasn't comfortable telling Mom that I'd been seconds away from fucking the then-nineteen-year-old who I'd been protecting.

"I know." I rose and walked to the window. "I just... I thought she died, Gwen. She let me think she fucking—" I broke off and took another drink to wash down the bitterness the words left in my mouth. "I know why she did it. I don't know why I can't get over it."

"Because you never got over her."

She said the words so calmly it was like she hadn't placed a grenade in my palms and pulled the pin.

Sure, I'd been with women here and there over the last couple years. Only tourists though. This town was too small to get involved with anyone local. But every time, I wound up sated but not satisfied because I was still left wanting *her*.

Keira McKenna.

She'd been like an unfinished sentence, one that was left off at the cusp of its meaning, and I couldn't figure out how to move on—how to read past the broken thought. I thought there would come a time when there would be enough sentences after hers that the missing piece wouldn't feel so gnawing, and I could finally move on.

It hadn't happened, and now that she turned up in my hometown I wasn't sure it ever would.

How was I going to move on when it was actually possible to know the rest of her? How the hell was I going to get past the unfinished thought that was now walking around town with her autumn-soaked hair, evergreen eyes, and candy lips that taunted me with answers?

"It's not like that," I rasped, unwilling to take this conversation to the point where I confessed I was practically crippled by the attraction that still pulled between us.

"What I mean, Arch, is that sometimes, we survive

something so traumatic that it's impossible to get over—a loss so deep that hardens to stone. I know how you felt when you came home. It was exactly how I felt when I moved to Carmel. For months, I'd watched people I'd done everything to care for—risked everything to care for—die right in front of me. It's not the kind of thing you get over," Gwen said, her voice deepening with emotion. "It's the kind of thing you have to learn to make a part of you."

Gwen had worked as a nurse in New York City during the height of the pandemic. I was the one she'd called at her lowest—when she'd worked consecutive shifts because there weren't enough nurses, when she'd been wearing the same cloth masks for days on end because there wasn't enough protection, and when she couldn't watch one more patient die alone when she'd done everything she could to save them.

Even though she was my youngest sibling, she was the first I'd told about what happened to Keira because she understood.

"Except now that part of me feels like a lie—*is* a lie." It was like the knowledge of her death had been transplanted inside me, and I'd had to heal around it, only for that fact to turn out to be false and for my body to go into rejection.

"It's just a different truth to accept, Arch."

Which one? I wanted to ask. *That Keira was alive, that I still wanted her, or that somehow, it seemed even more wrong now than it had four years ago?*

"I guess." I skimmed the lip of the bottle against my mouth for a second before taking another swig.

"Well, you are the most stubborn out of the four of you."

I chuckled. "Thanks."

"You can't just try and sweep this under the rug and pretend you're okay. You need to talk to her—and not try to frighten her out of town."

"I don't know about talking to her, but I do need to apologize." I drained the last of my beer, staring out the window at the darkening sky, and then walked into my kitchen, dropping the empty bottle into the recycling bin.

"I agree," she said, adding, "You also need to let me know what to bring to Mom's surprise party."

My shoulders sagged. Mom's birthday was in two weeks, so we were throwing her a surprise party. At this point, it felt like almost the entire town was in on it, but everyone loved Mayor Reynolds, so it was impossible to contain the guest list when the whole town felt like family.

"A girlfriend for Ranger," I joked.

We all accepted that Ranger was, by far, the smartest out of all of us. Mom also declared he was the sweetest. However, while Hunt, Gun, and I had moved out—though not far—to start to create our own lives, Ranger insisted on staying at home. He worried about Mom; Mom worried about him. She wanted him to have his own life. He wanted to make sure someone was always there for her if she needed.

It was a vicious cycle that didn't seem likely to break.

But that didn't change how I'd had to listen to my mom's laundry list of worries while fixing the garage door the other week about all of my brothers. Hunter, who appeared primed and eager for a serious relationship but didn't have one. Gunner, who was quickly forming a tolerance to anything permanent that she was concerned he wouldn't realize until it was too late. And mostly Ranger, who seemed content to completely forgo anything romantic for the remainder of his life.

At least Mom knew better than to tell me she worried about me, too.

"I'll see what I can do." I heard Gwen's wide smile carry through her voice. "In the meantime, go apologize for being an ass that I know you're not."

"Thanks," I grunted.

"Love you."

"Love you, too."

61

It had taken all of three minutes to find the address for one Keira Murphy in our system.

She wasn't lying; she had taken precautions in not linking her name to the business PO box at the post office. I doubted she even registered her address with the post office, but she was renting the old Herbert property on the other side of town, and if I knew Diane, her landlord, she'd made sure that the post office knew she had a new tenant. Diane Herbert was older and had moved to Cheyenne a few years ago to be close to her son; she'd rented her one-story rancher a few times and always made sure to dot every i and cross every t when it came to alerting certain local authorities like the police and Walt that she had a new tenant.

I didn't even think about how late it was or how this was a conversation better saved for another day—*day* being the operative word—until my knuckles were rapping on the front door and Keira opened it a few seconds later wearing sweatpants and *my fucking T-shirt.*

I sucked in a breath, deja-vu hitting me hard. Flashbacks of her walking the Freedom Trail in that shirt, her ass swaying at its hem. Flashbacks of how she'd been wearing it when she begged me to kiss her—how it was one more stupid thing that justified to my desire-clogged brain why it was okay to do it. To take that kiss. *To want to take her.*

My stare snapped back to hers. Illuminated by only the dim lighting from the house, her eyes appeared the color of rich moss, and similar to the lichen, she preferred to live in the darkness of secrets and false identities, and yet, when I looked at her, her direction still pointed true.

A bewitching paradox.

"Hi," she greeted, not appearing too surprised to see me.

Her hair was down now, spilling over her shoulders like a silken sunset, the edges curling around the swells of her tits that—*fuck me*—were poking against the fabric. Lust steamed through me like a freight train, my cock swelling against my jeans.

It wasn't a good idea to come here at night. And it definitely wasn't a good idea to do it with a few beers running through my system. There was already something about her that intoxicated me—*that made me quickly lose my control around her*—I shouldn't be adding alcohol to the fire.

"I came to apologize," I told her. No sense in beating around the bush.

Her dusky gaze narrowed and made a slow journey down my front and back up again. Then she sighed and moved to the side. "Do you want to come in?"

My chin dipped. Might as well have been the fall of a gavel declaring my own fate.

I walked into the small living room, her cherry scent bursting in my nostrils with tart sweetness.

My cock now strained painfully, forcing me to quickly adjust myself while she was still shutting the door behind me. I remembered that scent, and I remembered the similarly addictive taste of her on my tongue. I ground my teeth together, at a loss for how my memories of her could be so fucking crippling.

Not memories, I finally reasoned. Scars. Improperly healed wounds that ripped themselves back open when I was around her and bled with lust. It was the only explanation.

Inhaling deep, I forced my attention to my surroundings. The room was wrapped in wood wainscoting and floral wallpaper, a gaudy gold ceiling fan had only two working bulbs. She'd lit a fire in the fireplace, bringing both light and sound to the otherwise quiet room.

"Do you want a beer?" she asked over her shoulder, heading to the other side of the room that opened into a small dining space, the table covered with unopened boxes and what looked like a stack of photographs or paintings, and the kitchen, I presumed, sat just next to it.

My jaw clenched. "No, thank you." *Definitely not.*

She shrugged and continued walking. Even in those baggy sweats, I could tell she had a nice ass—the kind that would fill my palms and give me a good hold as I drove into her.

"Fuck," I muttered under my breath and followed her.

An improperly healed wound. That was why my body reacted like a goddamn teenager.

"I wanted to apologize for Wednesday," I blurted when I reached the dining area, now able to see the small kitchen where Keira was currently opening the fridge and grabbing herself a beer from the sparsely filled interior.

"For which part?" She faced me and bumped the door shut with her hip, asking flippantly, "Saying I was untrustworthy? Telling me I wasn't welcome in your town? Or accusing me of being a danger to everyone here?"

My chest burned. *Yup, Archer the Asshole.*

She popped the cap and brought the bottle to her lips, their fullness wrapping around the glass in a mind-numbing imitation of how she'd look with her mouth sucked around my cock.

"All of it," I snapped too harshly, jerking my gaze to the hallway that led from the kitchen to the bathroom and bedroom before I really gave away how little control I had over myself. I continued, my voice softening. "I was angry and concerned, but mostly an asshole. You are welcome here in Wisdom, of course, and I don't think you're a danger. At least, not more than anything else in the Wild West. So, I'm sorry."

I folded my arms, lowering my eyes to the floor for a long, silent second before lifting them back to her.

She was doing that thing where she rolled her lower lip between her teeth while she was thinking—*that thing that did it for me, that drove me insane.*

"It's okay." She set her bottle on the counter and crossed her arms, mirroring my stance. "I'm sorry, too, Archer."

Dammit. She shouldn't be sorry. I knew only a fraction of what she'd gone through, but to have to *die* in order to live... she shouldn't need to be sorry for that. Especially to me.

"Don't apologize for doing what you were told—doing what was necessary to save your life."

"Don't tell me what to do." Her eyes glittered defiantly. "I'm still sorry I couldn't tell you."

I could only nod, staring at her all the while willing my body to remain rooted in place—a safe six feet from where she was.

"We'd been in WITSEC for three years and relocated just as many times because Maloney's men kept finding us," she revealed even though she didn't have to. "This time... putting him away... it was the biggest risk of them all, so we had to do something drastic. I couldn't... start over any more times, Archer. I'd had more last names by nineteen than some people do at ninety."

The vise around my chest tightened. She wasn't trying to make me feel more like an asshole, but she was being honest, and that honesty made me realize how cruel I'd been.

"I can't imagine how hard that was for you." I only saw how strong—and secluded—it had made her.

"It was drastic, but it worked," she assured me. "Four years and we were never in danger. Never had to run. Never were threatened. Seeing our deaths and Maloney going away... it worked. That's how I know the break-in at the post office isn't about me. Nothing has changed. Even my dad passing..." She trailed off and collected herself, the grief still fresh for her. "Their work would be cut out for them."

That didn't mean they wouldn't still be interested in her.

"I know it's not much consolation, but nobody knew," she continued before I could say anything and took a step toward me. "Nobody except my dad, me, the man who shot us, the two agents in the ambulance, and our FBI contact. And none of them knew where we were going once we left Boston."

I exhaled deep. "You don't have to explain yourself, Keira."

"Even if I could have, it was better that you didn't know— that you didn't have to carry that with you all these years. It was better that you were able to just forget about me and move on."

Fuck that. Fuck better. And fuck moving on.

"Don't tell me what was better for me," I rasped, returning her words to her without thinking.

Her eyes widened and I regretted my rash statement. She was wrong but correcting her didn't matter. She didn't deserve to have to carry the truth about what her death did to me.

"I didn't want to regret telling you," she said softly, her tongue sliding out to coat her lips. "Someone told me to not leave Boston with any regrets."

I exhaled slowly. *Regrets are rocky*, I'd told her. *It's hard to build a fresh start on them.*

"Instead, you left with my shirt and headed for my hometown." I watched her freckles disappear against the color of her blush. "Why did you pick here, Keira?"

"Because you sold it to me." She jutted her chin out, laying the blame squarely on my shoulders. "The openness. The beauty. The solitude and small community. I'd lived for so long afraid to stop and take a full breath, and when you talked about Wyoming, it just felt like if I was going to have any chance at breathing, it would be here."

I studied her while she spoke, the strength and vulnerability in her tone making it impossible to be angry at her even though in giving herself a chance to breathe, she kept taking my breath away.

"Why'd you keep my shirt?" I pressed, dropping my arms and balling my fists at my sides.

Her blush deepened, spilling along the column of her neck

and underneath the edge of her shirt. I wondered if it reached her nipples. I wondered if her skin would turn as pink as the tips of her tits or if they would redden, too.

Ironically, I took a step closer to her in order to alleviate some of the pressure on my dick.

Her throat bobbed and she looked away for a second. "Why does it matter? It's just a shirt."

"Dammit, Keira." I stalked closer, demanding her attention. "You couldn't tell me that you weren't really dying, at least tell me why you kept my damn shirt."

I couldn't let it go. I was going to tug on this damn inconsequential string until the whole fabric of civility unraveled between us.

Heated eyes dueled with mine. She moved closer to me, never one to back away from confrontation. Now, we were almost touching. Every inhale was an invasion into the other person's space, and if we chose to breathe in sync, our chests would've collided. But we wouldn't—couldn't be in sync because the nature of whatever we had was give and take from one to the other.

"Because!" she said loudly even though I was right in front of her. "Because it reminds me of warmth and safety and being truly seen—because it reminds me of you. And that's why I came here—for all those reasons I told you but because I thought that here was the closest I could ever get to seeing you again."

My breath escaped in a hiss, filling in the gaps of her ragged pants. The pressure in my chest swelled to combustible levels as my eyes roamed over the raw honesty in her face.

When her gaze fell, my hand shot up, catching her chin and forcing it up. I felt her throat bob against my palm along with the uneven gallop of her pulse. I shouldn't be this close to her. *I shouldn't be touching her.*

Her lips parted slightly, and a low groan tore from my chest. My thumb that was wedged under her chin slid over the small mound until it reached the plump skin of her lower lip. It felt like I was watching someone else even though I knew it was my thumb pulling her lip down and toying with its fullness.

"And I lived thinking I'd never see you again," I heard myself say with a deep, hoarse voice, my focus locked to my thumb as it traced her lower lip.

"Do you want me to leave?" Her breath caught.

"No." The word fired unbidden and unstoppable from my lips. My hold tightened. "But I should."

I inhaled, her sweet scent drowning me in desire.

"Why?" Her gaze dropped to my mouth. *She knew what was coming.* Hell, I knew what was coming from the moment I touched her, but that didn't change my ability to stop it.

"Because I shouldn't fucking do this." My mouth crashed down onto hers.

Fucking cherries.

I might be a gentleman who asked to be invited inside her home, but I wasn't the kind of man who asked for permission to invade her mouth. *My mouth wasn't a fucking gentleman.* My tongue speared deep inside the hot honey between her lips like I could tunnel back in time to that last night in Boston—the one that haunted me every night since.

Maybe if I'd done more than kiss her, things would've been different. Maybe if I would've been less honorable and fucked her the way I wanted, she wouldn't have destroyed me.

I turned us so her back was against the kitchen counter, my free hand gripping the edge while my other hand slid from my hold on her neck into the thicket of hair at the base of her scalp, twisting it in my grasp and tilting her head back to open her mouth wider.

God, she was so damn sweet.

She complied eagerly—frantically. Her hands curled into the fabric of my shirt, pulling me to her. Her tongue mimicked mine—long, deep strokes that both explored and claimed every inch of her mouth as my own.

She was definitely still inexperienced. My blood pounded with the thought—*and my cock throbbed to rectify it.*

She let out a soft moan when I used my mass to wedge her against the counter. I was sure it was digging into her back, the way she was half bent against it, but there was nothing I could do. She was too soft—too warm, especially the part of her that cradled against the steel beam of my erection.

I wanted to peel my shirt off of her and find the borders of her blush. I wanted to lift her onto the counter, spread her before me, and see if the rest of her tasted as delicious as her mouth. And then I wanted to bury my cock inside her heat and find out if finishing the goddamn thought of her finally fixed me.

Groaning, I slanted my mouth and angled my tongue deeper. My hand on the counter moved to her side, searching for the edge of the shirt. She trembled when my palm clamped onto the bare skin at her waist, her skin rising up in goose bumps to greet me.

I kissed her until our breaths and bodies were knotted together. I kissed her until I was convinced there was nothing more to life than the taste of her on my tongue.

I kissed her like it could change the past.

Fuck.

"*Fuck.*" I tore my mouth from hers and took two steps back.

I moved so fast she had to reach for the counter behind her to steady her, her eyes widening when she looked at me.

Way to fucking handle yourself, Archer.

"I have to go." I dragged a hand through my hair. "This…" I shook my head. "This was a mistake. I'm sorry."

I made the immediate mistake of looking at her—her ripe cheeks and red lips swollen from my kiss were enough of a sight to almost bring me to my knees. Growling low, I spun and strode toward the door, desperate to put some space between us so I could think straight.

"What? Why?" she demanded, following me like a glutton for punishment.

I gritted my teeth and wrenched the door open, inhaling the blast of cold air like it could put my dick and its desires on ice for one goddamn second. I looked over my shoulder, not trusting myself to fully face her or let go of the door.

This time, I wasn't angry with her when I spoke. This time, I wasn't trying to be harsh or cruel. This time, I answered her with the raw pain I'd managed to bury for four fucking years.

There was no changing the past.

She might be alive, she might be here, but it didn't change that I knew absolutely nothing about her except that—justified or not—she hadn't been able to trust me with the truth.

"Because you're still a ghost to me."

My chest heaved as I walked out the door without a backward glance.

CHAPTER FIVE

KEIRA

"Come... on... mother... f—"

"Keira?" I heard the side door open.

My breath escaped in a whoosh and I turned, my ass plopping onto the floor as the tension drained from my body.

"Damn. Hey, Zoey," I greeted my friend breathlessly.

"What happened to your door?" She was looking at where the handle was scratched and busted.

"I don't know." I wiped my hands on my thighs. "It was like that when I got here this morning. Probably just some local kids looking to get into trouble." I sighed. "They graffitied over my new paint earlier this week, too." Forcing me to spend three hours repainting the exterior wall.

Zoey regarded me with worry.

"Seriously, Zoey, it's fine," I assured her. "You know this place was a mess when I got it. The front door lock was completely broken. If the amount of Red Bull and Coke cans I cleaned from inside here were any indication, kids were definitely using this as a hangout spot." I relaxed a little when she finally released the loose knob and gently shut the door behind her. "I'm sure they just wanted to see what was going on."

I'd only gotten around to replacing the dead bolt on the front door since that lock had been completely broken; the side door had been fine until I got here this morning.

"Are you sure?"

Zoey walked inside, her brown coat pulled tight across her, the collar lifted up to protect her neck. Her long black hair was swept up in a high ponytail and a rise of color in her cheeks from the wind outside. It had been howling straight down Main Street all morning. Thankfully, I'd been cooped up inside my shop for the last—I groaned—five hours.

"Well, they didn't take anything. Not that there's much to take." I rested back on my palms, feeling the newly laid piece of flooring shift underneath my hands. "Although, I can't say I wouldn't have been grateful if they'd decided to steal this damn flooring while they were here."

She surveyed the sad state of my shop.

If I was being honest, seeing the side door ajar when I pulled in this morning was probably the only thing that could shake me from the memory of Archer's kiss; it replayed in my mind all week like a song on repeat, stuck on a single hot and desperate note. I'd pulled my handgun from the glove compartment and approached the building slowly, looking for any signs of life.

After the first time the Kings had found us in WITSEC, my dad started teaching me how to shoot. He taught me both the safety and the power of a gun, making sure I knew the responsibility that came with holding something so dangerous. After that, he taught me what to look for so we could both have each other's backs.

Mobsters were brutes. Not criminal masterminds. At least, not the men that were sent to track us down and kill us.

I groaned as I stretched out my legs, my knees screaming from being propped on them for so long. I hadn't invested in knee pads, but I had an inflated idea about how quickly I'd be able to get this done. When it was clear that I was losing against fake flooring, I'd resorted to stuffing my jacket underneath my knees, shimmying it along with me as I worked.

"Are you okay?" Her gaze was worried.

Resting back on my hands, I looked at how much I'd accomplished.

I'd powered through the rest of the painting—the walls matte white with a gloss white paisley design painted on top. Subtle but sophisticated. Now, I was trying to get the black laminate flooring to go down. Trying being the operative word. I had about three rows of boards together and it had taken me all afternoon.

"I would be if this flooring didn't need some sort of spell and sacrifice for it to come together," I grumbled, looking over my shoulder at my handiwork. Even the rows I'd completed were splayed apart at some of the seams. "I can't get them to go together or stay together…"

"You look… defeated."

I was—and not just by the floor.

I'd been fighting with the laminate all afternoon but mentally, I'd been fighting with Archer and the memory of that kiss. And now every inch of my body ached for one of those two reasons.

'You're still a ghost to me.'

Ass.

I hadn't seen a single brilliant inch of him all weekend, and I half-expected him at my shop's door this morning which was why I'd left for Idaho Falls bright and early. I wasn't ready to face the man who thought our second first kiss was just as much of a mistake as our first.

Archer's intentions were harder to piece together than the damn flooring, and I was done being a puzzle master for the day.

"I am. I'm about to just buy a shag carpet and call it a

day." I sighed and laid on the concrete floor, willing it to swallow me whole.

"I thought this kind of floor was easy to install," she mused, looking down at the stack of mostly unopened boxes.

"You and me both, Zoe," I told her.

I'd driven to Idaho Falls first thing this morning to pick out the floor. There was a Home Depot there with a larger selection of laminate flooring than Jerry's Hardware store in town. *And by larger, I meant it actually had a selection.* So, two hours to Idaho Falls. Forty-five minutes to decide on the black-stained faux wood. And then another two hours back. It was a day in itself, but I wasn't stopping.

I was ready for my new life here to start. *And I was ready for the annoyingly persistent thoughts of Archer to stop.*

"I thought I'd have the flooring done today," I told her. "I needed the flooring done today."

"When do you open again?"

I heard her soft footfalls move around the space but I'd already closed my eyes, about ready to fall asleep. Not the best idea, given how stiff my body already was.

"Three weeks, but I already have a few clients scheduled for a soft opening in two." I hummed.

I'd never had anything more than entry-level, seasonal jobs for the last four years. Barista. Server. Uber driver. It was hard to think about advancement when it became clear Dad had no intention of settling in one place. It hurt at first—that feeling like the vacant hole inside me searching for something stable would never be filled. But he'd risked everything for me, so I kept quiet and filled that hole with hobbies and dreams instead—anything I could take with me.

Art began to fill my time, but I learned quickly that anything more than a sketchbook was a pain in the ass to pack up and move. After the first two moves, Dad settled us in Rising Sun, Texas for a time. I hated the heat, but we went swimming one day, and I saw a man whose back had been completely tattooed with DaVinci sketches. My mind was blown.

It was like a plug in my brain was finally pushed into the correct socket, and what I wanted to do with my life went on like a light.

"How many is a few?"

"A dozen," I confessed with a proud smile.

I'd made a name for myself in Salt Lake City. *The Twilight Tattooist.* More or less anonymous, I gathered a social media following and met clients in various, always-changing locations around the city. *Or sometimes out of it.* I garnered a big fan base in Park City after one of my Olympic clients posted a photo of himself on the slopes with his intricate full sleeves on display, and it had only gone up from there.

But having my own shop—my own space, that was a game changer. *A life changer.*

"That's awesome, Keira." The happiness in her voice was genuine—the kind of genuine that worried me. It was as though she could only look forward to things in other peoples' lives because there wasn't and wouldn't be anything to look forward to in her own.

"Only if I get this damn floor done." I peeled my eyes open, staring at a ceiling that mocked me because it was still missing light fixtures. I had two massive spotlights plugged into the walls, illuminating my workspace. "My table, gun, and furniture are arriving at the end of this week. But it's going to be hard to install all of it when there is no floor."

I whimpered and closed my eyes again, wishing I had a fairy flooring godmother who could come, wave her wand, and magically make my floor installed.

"Can I help you?"

I smiled and sat up. "Thank you, but you're practically my only friend in Wisdom right now. I don't want to risk that by torturing you."

She laughed and shook her head. "Impossible, but then can I at least interest you in a drink?"

I shouldn't.

I had so much left to do.

I was exhausted.

"Yeah, let's go get a drink."

WIT IN WISDOM was my second favorite building on the block; my own being the first.

Once I'd peeled myself off the floor, dusted what I could from my dark leggings, and fixed what I could see of my hair in my reflection in the window, Zoey and I walked across the street and three doors down to the local bar.

On our first girls' night out, Zoey gave me the bar's history; it was owned by the Bolden family—local celebrities in the area since Dewitt Bolden was the owner of the Jackson Hole resort.

The bar had an old western facade just like the rest of the buildings along Main Street. I remembered the first day I drove through town and thought I'd driven back in time, half-expecting to see a gun-slinging cowboy walk onto the road with spurs on his heels. (*I'd seen plenty of gun-slinging cowboys but no spurs.*) On closer inspection, almost all of the buildings had been modernized or completely refaced, though Wit in Wisdom was certainly one of the nicest buildings.

Its classic swinging saloon doors were kept for character though they led to a more modern glass-door entry inside. The interior was a combination of old Wisdom news clippings, many about the Bolden family, and classic books that were adhered to the walls, their pages opened to a significant quote or passage.

It was almost too nice of a place for Wisdom, but the Boldens made too much money in Jackson to care about a little bar twenty-five minutes west that was probably only breaking even.

"How's everything at the post office?" I asked as we took a seat on the brown leather barstools.

"Getting back to normal," she said and looked down the bar, searching for both the bartender and any sign of Walt before adding, "Walt's been a mess, seeing the place like that. He was really… in the bottle… there for a few days. Now that I cleaned and sorted everything, he's doing a little better."

Even for someone who was new to town and kept to herself, Walt's drinking was no secret to me. I hadn't even learned about it from Zoey. The first time we came here for drinks, I picked the seat at the end of the bar, and instead of coming over to take my order, the bartender, Bruce, informed me I was in Walt's seat and then walked away, his message crystal clear: I wasn't going to get served until I moved from the other man's chair.

"What can I get you?" Bruce appeared like a phantom behind the bar.

He was an older man with white hair and a white shadow of a beard on his face. Most of the time he was reserved, all of his attention given to his craft cocktails, but every once in a while—and I'd only seen it once when he regaled some lore about a serial killer, the infamous Archangel, who'd lived undetected in Wisdom for almost a decade—he was brought into telling a story and his personality bloomed.

Bruce was a born storyteller. Emphatic, engaging, enchanting. Not words I'd ever think to use to describe a grumpy bartender, but when he was spinning a tale, those were the only descriptions that came to mind.

"Cosmo," Zoey ordered, her drink choice the only thing hinting at her former life as a high-class marketing executive.

"Make that two."

Bruce nodded and went to make our drinks.

"So, what are you going to do about the floor?"

My shoulders slumped. "I don't know. Watch some YouTube videos. Say a couple prayers. Buy a massive area rug in case of an emergency." I folded my arms on the bar and let my forehead fall on them. "Maybe I'll stop by Jerry's and see if he can help me." *Doubtful since his hardware store didn't even sell flooring.*

"You could maybe get some guys from Idaho Falls and push back the opening."

"I really don't want to do that." But it was a distinct possibility. "The clients I have coming for the soft opening have been waiting for months to see me."

"Is one the Harry Potter guy?"

Travis. I looked at her and then sat back up straight with a small smile. "Yeah." I thought about the massive back piece we'd been working on for over a year now and my smile grew. "He's coming in for a whole day so I can finish the Ravenclaw corner of the crest."

Travis had reached out to me with a gorgeous and intricate idea of having the four crests of the Hogwarts houses combined into one and inked into his back. So far, we'd done Gryffindor and Hufflepuff, with only the outlines of the other two in place.

"I've also got someone coming for me to do a full back with a replication of Monet's Water Lilies, and someone else who wants a sleeve of Van Gogh's Starry Night. Oh, and Davis. I'm doing more dripping clocks on him."

Masterpieces were my specialty. Imprinting famous works of art onto peoples' bodies.

"Ugh, no." I groaned. "I can't push back the opening. I'll figure it out. Even if it means ruining my vision with an area rug. Anyway, how are you doing?" I turned and asked my friend, worrying I hadn't checked on her enough since the break-in.

I always worried I wasn't doing enough when it came to our friendship, but I'd never really had friends before—at least not ones that I wasn't convinced I'd inevitably lose.

"I'm still struggling." She crossed her arms and sat back. "I don't know why. I thought working at the post office would make things easier, but now I think I might need another change."

"You have to do what's best for you, Zoey. Whatever makes you feel comfortable."

Her eyes slid to mine, and she nodded. "I wish I knew what that was."

Bruce delivered our drinks, and I picked mine up and took a sip.

"I have a feeling your guardian Hunter will protect you until you do," I said, brushing my martini glass against my lips. When I finished swallowing, I realized Zoey was just staring at me, her mug suspended in her grip.

"He was just doing his job," she insisted once she had my full attention.

"He looked like he was ready to do more if you'd just let him."

"I can't. My life isn't made for those kinds of things anymore." I watched her take a drink.

Zoey had been in Wisdom for almost seven months, and from what I gathered, seemed content to work at the post office and end her days with a cup of her favorite jasmine tea and a romance novel by her favorite author, Sydney Ward.

"You never know." I nudged her with my foot and grinned.

"I do know. I also know that the only thing I'm interested in pursuing right now is a second job or a different job. Maybe a receptionist or barista. Tara mentioned they were hiring the other day."

I arched an eyebrow.

"I want to start saving to buy my own house. This whole…

situation… made me uncomfortable in my apartment. Not for any particular reason…"

I reached over and took her hand with a gentle squeeze. "You don't need a reason to want to feel safe, Zoe."

I knew that once something made you start looking over your shoulder, it was hard to look forward again with as much confidence.

"Well, as soon as I need a receptionist, I'll let you know."

"Are you ready to talk about Archer?"

Instantly, my grin fizzled and I set my drink down.

"Not really," I grumbled. I'd told her that he'd come over to apologize and we'd ended up making out like it was our job to set the world on fire, but it was how many days later and my emotions were still more mixed than my cocktail. "There's obviously still unfinished attraction there." I crossed my legs, not willing to admit out loud how many times I'd tried to *finish* it with my vibrator over the weekend. "But he doesn't trust me, Zoe. And I can't… risk myself with a man who doesn't trust me."

It was the proverbial catch twenty-two. Archer didn't fully trust me because I'd lied to him four years ago. But because of that, I couldn't bring myself to trust him with the full truth about what happened.

"I think he trusts you. His pride is just wounded because you left without explanation."

I hummed. It was a little more than that, but Zoey didn't know the full situation either.

"Well, if you saw the way he bolted from my place the other night, I don't think he trusts me or himself to be around me."

Bruce chuckled, drawing my attention across the bar. I hadn't realized he was even standing there. *How the hell did he do that?*

"What's so funny?" I'd had enough of my stiff drink to feel comfortable asking.

He wiped his hand on a bar towel and then slung it over his shoulder. "It's damn hard to come face-to-face with your failure, Miss..."

"Keira."

I pursed my lips. I'd told him my name several times already on more than one occasion.

Bruce gripped the edge of the bar and bent toward me.

"I knew a boy once who moved across the country because he thought he failed his mother. Then he came back, thinking he'd failed his badge." His beady eyes met mine. "Only to have that failure follow him to his doorstep."

I set my mug down slowly.

Was he talking about Archer?

Was he talking about me?

"I think story time is over, Bruce."

My head whipped over my shoulder to the voice of a man I hadn't heard come in.

"Gunner," Bruce grunted and then faded back into his duties.

Gunner Reynolds.

Even if the name wasn't so recognizable, those eyes certainly were. That foggy green seemed to be trademarked by the Reynolds boys; it was a color that shifted so easily depending on their mood.

"I don't think we've met. Officially." A wide white smile greeted me along with an outstretched hand. "I'm Archie's younger, more handsome brother, Gunner."

This one was a player.

I chuckled, never thinking to call Archer 'Archie' but the way Gunner said it was a clear indication of the closeness of their relationship.

I took his hand, shaking it firmly. "Keira."

"Hey, Zoey." He tipped his head to the side and greeted my friend. "Hunter ask you out yet?"

Zoey choked on her drink, waving off my attempts to help and excusing herself to the bathroom in a hurry.

"I see why Archer talks about you the way he does," I said with an assessing hum, sitting back in my stool as Gunner leaned back against the bar, propping his elbows on the top.

"In a loving, supportive, and slightly jealous fashion?" he quipped with a wink. "My older brothers struggle because they like to think they know everything. My younger brother actually does know everything. But I"—he lifted his finger— "have figured out that the key to happiness is not needing all the answers."

"So, you're trying to take credit for the saying 'ignorance is bliss'?"

His head dropped and his shoulders shook with laughter.

"You caught me." He lifted his hands in defeat and faced me. "Now, before my friends get here. What can I do to convince you to give my brother the answers he's looking for?"

I balked. "What answers?"

"Whichever ones that are making him act like he got his dick stuck in a clothespin all week."

I choked on an attempt to swallow. *Jesus.* Good thing I'd finished my mule.

"I don't have any more answers for Archer, and I can't help that he didn't like the ones I already gave him."

He huffed. "I'm used to his standard degree of surliness, but this is really putting a damper on everyone's work environment. And if he shows up to Mom's surprise party like this..." His eyes widened. "Did he invite you to the party?"

Was he joking? Why would Archer invite me to his mom's party?

"It's not like that. The whole town is coming," he quickly explained. "Kind of hard to throw the mayor a surprise party in a small town without everyone joining in, isn't that right, Bruce?"

The bartender didn't look up from his task though I was sure he heard Gunner.

"Zoey, you're coming to Mom's surprise party, right?"

Zoey returned to her seat, her cheeks still slightly pink. "Yeah, I think so."

"Perfect." Gunner clapped his hands, his excitement contagious. "So, you'll come too, Keira? It's going to be great. We got the mezzanine space at the Worth Hotel. Tons of swanky food. Good music. Strong drinks. Hell, if the Nelsons bring some of their moonshine, I'll bet you'd find a good number of people willing to let you tattoo them on the spot."

My mouth opened and shut like I was a goldfish stranded out of water. "I don't know." I gulped. "I need to finish the flooring in my shop before my soft opening, and it's not going well."

Gunner scrutinized me. Unlike his brother, who cleverly and confoundingly concealed what he was thinking, it was obvious that Gunner's wheels were turning, and his expression was that of a troublemaker.

"Okay let's make a deal. If you get the flooring done, you'll come to the party." He extended his hand again, his deal sounding vaguely familiar to that of a certain stepmother and Cinderella.

"Why do you want me there so badly?" I left his hand hanging.

He leaned in. "I like seeing Archie when he doesn't have all the answers." I could hear his grin.

My head tipped. "Maybe."

Realistically, there was no way I was going to finish the flooring, so it didn't really matter. But hypothetically... I'd never had the intention to torture Archer. Hell, I'd been ready to let him have his way with me on the kitchen island. But now that this was the second time he'd managed to walk away and leave me... unfulfilled... maybe it was time he got used to the fact that we were both living in this town now.

And one way or another, it was going to be big enough for the both of us.

CHAPTER SIX

ARCHER

"I SHOULD FIRE YOU."

Gunner snorted. "For what? Offering to help a new resident to our lovely town? Seems pretty damn ingenious of you, Archie." He slapped me on the back and practically skipped across the parking lot toward Keira's building.

I flexed my grip around my toolbox.

Warning sirens should've gone off the second I saw the devious look in Gunner's eyes this morning; the last time he had that look, he'd bribed Ranger to wire up his office after hours for a massive video gaming party with his buddies. I should've known he was going to pull something like this, but I was still caught off-guard when he sauntered into my office earlier, as cool as a cucumber, and asked to borrow the flooring tools I'd purchased last year when I'd redone Mom's dining room floors.

'I told Keira I'd help her with the floors in her shop.'

I'd glared at Hunter, wordlessly demanding if he knew about this.

'You're welcome to come, too, Hunt. I think Zoey might stop by.'

But with two short sentences, he had us both by our balls, and he knew it. We were supposed to use our Saturday to get some things done around the office before Hunter and Gunner left for Jackson next week to guard a diamond heiress spending spring break on the slopes. Instead, we all left the building with one destination in mind.

Half an hour later, we'd stopped at Mom's to pick up my tools and were pulling into the lot next to the old barbershop.

Gunner stopped at the step to the front door, motioning with exaggeration that I should be the one to knock.

I shoved my tool bag against his chest hard enough to make him take it even as he swayed back. I gave him the finger and rapped on the door with my other hand.

Two locks and the door opened. Keira was no longer surprised to see me, but she was surprised to see my brothers.

"Archer…"

Damn, she was petite. Every time I saw her, I was reminded how she was small enough to fit right under all my giant warning signs.

My eyes screwed shut, recalling how easy it would've been to manhandle her small curves onto her kitchen counter. How easy it would've been to pin her beneath me with just my weight. How easy it would've been to split open her tiny pussy with my fat cock.

Fuck.

"We're here to finish your floor," Gunner chimed in from my side, striding right past me and Keira and into the building. "You said you needed it finished, right?" He looked around him. "Certainly looks like it. Unless you've opted for that industrial concrete look…"

There was a stack of flooring boxes piled on the back wall. Unopened. The two open boxes were haphazardly strewn on the floor like someone had taken out the brunt of her frustration on the cardboard.

"I… was about to," she admitted honestly, wiping her brow and then planting her hand on her waist, drawing my attention to the strip of exposed skin between her tank top and paint-splattered leggings.

My gaze raked over her hungrily. If four years did nothing to dull the way I wanted her, seven days certainly hadn't done shit to douse the blaze that kiss in her kitchen ignited.

I could see the slight sheen of sweat on her chest and the way it made her top stick just a little tighter to the perfect swells of her tits. *Dammit she should be wearing more clothes.*

Gunner cleared his throat, drawing my attention to let me know he'd caught me staring at her tits. He grinned, and I was half-tempted to punch him, but when he arched an eyebrow and let his gaze casually slide to where mine had been, I was a second from burying him underneath this damn flooring before Hunter stepped in.

"I'm Hunter." He stuck out his hand. "We met very briefly at the post office the other day."

"Yes. Nice to officially meet you." Keira shook his hand.

"And this is Ranger." Hunt stepped to the side. Ranger had been the last one to enter and was in the middle of assessing the room when the introduction jarred him.

"Pleasure." Ranger nodded quickly, a curl falling onto his forehead that he quickly reached up and tucked behind his ear. There was an awkward second when he realized Keira's outstretched hand was waiting for his.

"Ahh... Range doesn't shake hands," Hunter explained quickly, but not fast enough.

"Did you know that on average, our hands carry one-thousand-and-five-hundred bacteria for every square centimeter of skin, meaning our hands can be carrying anywhere from one-hundred-thousand to a few million germs at any given time. They are one of the most bacteria-laden parts of our bodies, so it seems counterintuitive that they should be used as such a commonplace greeting," Ranger babbled, speaking as though he were reading straight out of an encyclopedia except that encyclopedia was in his brain.

"Research has shown that a handshake can transfer one-hundred-and-twenty-four million bacteria whereas a high five cuts that bacterial transfer in half, and a fist bump transfers less than ten percent of that of a handshake."

Keira blinked at him for a second, processing the information his million-mile-an-hour mind regurgitated. And then the fingers of her outstretched hand balled into a fist.

Ranger paused and stared at her hand. The transition from fact to actual social interaction always took him an extra second, but then he lifted his own fist and awkwardly bumped it against hers.

"I had no idea. I'm glad you told me," Keira said, smiling. "It's nice to meet you, Ranger."

My youngest brother's face reddened.

"What's even more interesting," Ranger went on, fleeing cordiality for cold hard fact, "is that a Welsh study showed that a ten-second intimate kiss also transferred about half the number of bacteria as a handshake which would statistically make kissing a safer and cleaner method of introduction."

"Well, I can certainly get on board with that," Gunner chimed in. "Especially since my greeting was saved for last."

He headed for Keira with a Casanova smile on his face. *Like fucking hell.* My arm shot out like a steel beam, blocking his path.

"Your mouth is going to have to greet my fist first before it makes it to hers," I warned him under my breath.

Gunner's eyes twinkled, and I realized too late I'd fallen— *again*—for his little trap.

"So, did you start the floor or..." Hunter trailed off, returning everyone's focus to why we were really here.

"Oh, I did." Keira pointed to the wall to our right. "If you'd gotten here about twenty minutes ago, you would've seen the five rows I'd put down except they were all wrong. Every time I put one more board down, it felt like it unclipped some of the previous ones. So, I just finished pulling them all up." Her pointer finger swung to the uneven stack of laminate tiles. On top of it sat her discarded tee and sweatshirt.

"That's better, right, Archie?" Gunner asked, thoroughly earning my glare when he added, "To rip up all the half-laid mistakes and start fresh?"

Do not snarl at your brother. Do not snarl at your brother.

I blinked slowly, catching his not-so-subtle meaning, and then went over to the pulled-up tiles, running my hand along the edge to examine how they connected.

"These are just like what we laid at Mom's," I told them. "So it shouldn't take us long."

I took my bag back from Gunner and pulled out my mallet, making sure to examine it right in front of my *daring* little brother.

"Mom wanted her dining room floor redone last year, but instead of getting someone from Idaho Falls, Arch insisted we could do it for her," I heard Hunter say as I took one board and wedged it tight into the front corner of the room and then reached for a second.

Lining them up, I jiggled the connection until I heard the small clip and then gently tapped on the mallet to seat them fully.

"How did you…" Keira appeared next to me, her eyes wide in amazement. "I've been trying for days…"

"I can tell," I rumbled, now noticing how some of the plastic connections were damaged from being jammed together the wrong way. I took a deep breath, my lungs instantly flooded with the scent of cherries that drew my gaze to her like a magnet.

She was bent forward next to me, her tank dipping in the front and giving me a clear view of the swells of her tits, the valley between them, and the squiggly line tattooed just over her heart. *Fuck.* I groaned. God, I wanted to bury my face there and breathe her in. My jeans pinched my hard cock, and I stood to quickly get rid of the pain.

Thankfully, she straightened, too.

And then I saw a discarded sweatshirt and T-shirt on top of the second pile of pull-up planks. Reaching for the shirt, I shoved it against her chest.

"You should put this on," I grunted.

I left her gaping while I delivered orders to my small and slightly untrustworthy crew. With the four of us, it would only take a day to finish the room. *It better.* I needed to detox from the cherry-drug running through my veins.

"YOU DIDN'T HAVE to do this," she said softly, appearing beside me several hours later.

After trying to help for the first thirty minutes, it became clear that there wasn't enough space in the shop for the four of us plus her to work efficiently, so Keira disappeared to the small back office to get a head start on some administrative tasks that had fallen behind when she got waylaid by the flooring.

Had I known she was coming back out front, I would've put my shirt back on. Now, it would be a little obvious to walk to the middle of the room where I'd draped it over my tool bag.

I finished gulping down several swigs from my water bottle. My brothers were currently working together to measure and cut some of the boards so they adapted perfectly with the slightly uneven architecture of the front of the room.

"Gunner told you we'd help; I'm happy to do it."

Her brow furrowed and suspicion notched in my gut. "He didn't tell me you guys were going to help."

The electric saw ran for two seconds as Hunter cut one of

the boards; it was just long enough to mask the sound of my teeth grating together.

"He didn't?"

She folded her arms, and I fought to keep my attention above her tits. "No. He invited me to your mom's party and when I told him I couldn't go because I needed to get the floor finished, he made me a deal: if the floor gets done, I'd come."

Dammit, Gunner. "He invited you to her party?"

That came out wrong, and I realized it instantly.

"I don't have to go—don't think I can go," she covered quickly.

"That's not what I meant." I sighed. I was making a mess out of this—of myself. She was a part of this town now, I couldn't be surprised every time she was invited to be a part of the community. "Of course, you're welcome to come. The mayor's birthday is always a big deal in Wisdom."

She didn't look convinced. Instead her attention drifted to where my brothers were working and laughing—they made the time pass quickly with their rowdy banter.

"You must be happy to be back home with them."

My skin prickled. "I am."

I thought leaving would fix things—fix how I fell short. It hadn't. But coming back, even under the conditions I had—or maybe especially because of them—had been some kind of balm.

"When did you move back?"

I inhaled sharply. I should've expected that question, but in the middle of dealing with unexpected crimes, unexpected desires, and unexpected kisses, I'd forgotten to remain prepared for it.

Their conversation grew louder, so I quickly chose escape over explanation. "One second," I muttered and stalked over to my brothers, grabbing my tee along the way and tugging it back on. "You guys good?"

"Doing good. Shouldn't need more than another hour to finish up here," Hunter replied.

"You want to trade places, and I'll go do the back room?" Gunner offered cheekily.

The back room.

I'd been avoiding it because Keira was working back there and there was enough of the front to tackle, but since we were here and blowing through the work, we really should just do that, too.

"No. I've got it."

I went back to Keira without waiting around for Gunner's next jab.

"I'll put the flooring down in the back while they finish up out here," I told her, leading the way to the small office. It was cluttered with a few stacks of boxes of tattooing supplies, papers, and folders stacked on top like she'd used the boxes as a makeshift desk.

"You really don't have to do this, Archer, but thank you," she repeated, tucking a strand of strawberry red back behind her ear.

"Not going to half-ass helping you." I caught the way she shivered and my hands slid from where they were clamped on my hips. "Is it okay to move everything?"

She nodded.

We moved the first couple boxes in silence, but finally I caved, needing a distraction from the way our bodies bumped and brushed along the way.

"So how did you end up picking tattooing? Last I remember, you had no idea what you wanted to do when you grew up." That last bit made her sound like she'd been a child when we met.

"My dad told me he was a mob enforcer just before my eleventh birthday, Archer. I'd been grown up for a long time by the time we met," she replied easily, reminding me that though the trial had pieced together more facts about her past, I still didn't know the details.

"At eleven?" I forced out while moving one of the boxes, wondering what kind of man tells his kid at eleven that he kills people for a living.

"My aunt lived with us until then, but she couldn't stomach my dad's work any longer; she worried what kind of danger that lifestyle would bring into my life as I got older. So, she left, and he told me the truth; I was bound to find out sooner or later." She didn't sound angered by it even though his line of work had upended her whole life.

"And he wouldn't leave it?"

Her head tipped like the thought hadn't occurred to her. "He'd been part of the Kings for so long… close with Maloney for almost his entire life. That world *was* his family."

"That must've been hard."

She toyed with the hem of her shirt. "He was my dad, and except for a couple of times, that was the only side of him I saw. He promised me even though he was a bad guy, he was a good man—a good father."

"And was he?"

"He risked everything for me," she replied with a small voice, and then her head snapped to mine like she hadn't realized what she said. It was like she'd let go of the tiniest end of the string that held her together just waiting for me to reach out and unravel it. "Anyway, he loved art and drawing was an easy hobby to have when we moved around a lot," she forged on before I could interrupt. "Especially after we left Boston the last time, I kind of lost myself in art for a while, trying to capture everything around me before it changed again."

"Why did it keep changing?" I looked up from where I kneeled on the floor. It didn't make sense. She said they hadn't been found—hadn't been in danger. *So why did they keep running?*

Her eyes flared.

"Everything changes, Archer. All the time. That's life," she said without really answering. "But art... my dad and I bonded over art. Art that has stayed the same over centuries. DaVinci. Monet. Van Gogh."

"And tattoos?" I knew her answer before she spoke. I saw it written on her face just as clearly as it had been all those years ago—the want of something stable and immovable to keep her grounded.

"Tattoos are the most permanent and personal kind of art." She leaned back against the wall, watching me intently as she spoke. "Once they're a part of you, they don't leave—can't leave." She paused and recanted, "Well, they can. But it's a process to remove them. So, they're basically there to stay."

Unlike everything else about her life.

"Where did you learn?" I asked, hoping it wasn't so damn obvious that I wanted to know everything about the life she'd lived after I watched her die. Every place she stayed. Everything she did. Every person she met.

Anyone lucky enough to be let in.

"Different places. New Orleans. Austin. Salt Lake City." I heard her move closer to me but I felt my attention focused on the boards I was snapping together.

I went to reach for another slat when Keira held it in front of me.

I met her gaze. "Thank you."

"When I was apprenticing with a tattoo artist in Austin, I remember this girl came in and picked out some Chinese symbol design. She'd just turned eighteen. A few minutes later, her mom barges through the door, yelling and pleading for the girl to think about what she was doing to her body—that she was marking it with something that would stay with her forever." She chuckled.

"And what did you think?"

"I thought... how comforting it was to know that something that meant so much could never be left or taken from you." Her gaze fell to the floor, but I swore I saw it glisten, and a sad smile tipped her full lips. "Permanence isn't something that should be feared... or taken for granted."

I sucked in a breath. Her words felt like the snap of a hot rubber band on my heart. I simultaneously hated the life that had shaped her and admired the strong, wise woman she'd become because of it.

"So that's what you do." I took another board from her outstretched hand. "Give people permanence."

Her exquisite mouth curved. "Something like that."

"With Chinese symbols?" I teased gently, her velvet laugh caressing me.

"Not quite." She pursed her lips. "I ended up with a large following for my... well... let me just show you."

She grabbed her phone from the top of the pile of papers I'd moved to the corner, tapped a few times on the screen, and then turned it so I could see a collage on her Twilight Ink social media of the pieces she'd done.

"Holy shit." I stopped what I was doing so I could tap and scroll through the photos.

Her tattoos were incredible, massive replicas of famous works of art. Some on peoples' backs. Some on their arms. Some on their front. And some on their— "What the hell is this?"

I tapped on a particular photo of a man whose tattoo of a melting clock dripped down from his abdomen onto his upper thigh; for her to have done the tattoo in that location, the guy had to have been naked.

He certainly looked fucking naked in the picture even though certain parts were expertly cropped out.

Keira chuckled.

"That's Davis. He has a particular obsession with Dali," she said, taking her phone back before my grip shattered it.

"Was he naked for this?" I demanded, not caring that I sounded like an overprotective ass.

Her head cocked, and she scrutinized me, a coy smile lifting one side of her mouth. "It would've been pretty hard for me to ink this on him with his clothes on."

Motherfucker. I had the urge to bite her lip until she rethought her response.

I'd felt a lot of things for Keira. Protective. Worry. Sympathy. Lust. Ache. But jealousy was a fucking new one. In fact, I couldn't remember ever experiencing the sensation before—*and Gunner's annoying flirtation didn't count.*

"You don't think it's good?" she asked innocently.

She was toying with me.

"I think I'm glad that it's done." My jaw pulsed.

"That one is," she revealed nonchalantly. "He's actually one of the clients coming for my soft opening. I'm replicating The Ship by Dali on his back."

The hell he was.

"Soft opening?" I forced my breaths to steady.

She walked back over to her pile of folders, oblivious to the surge of jealousy pumping through my veins as she set her phone down.

"I have a dozen previous clients who want more work done that are making the trip here for me to tattoo them, so I can adjust to working in my new space." She lifted a sheet of paper from her pile, presumably the list of people coming to see her; all I saw was red. "That's next weekend. After that, this place will officially be open."

All I heard was that she was going to have naked men in here as soon as next weekend, and the damn caveman in me couldn't think straight.

"And do you have any?" The only thing worse than her tattooing a naked man was the thought that she'd stripped down so someone could do the same for her.

Our eyes clashed like sparks and kindling.

"One," she said, holding my eyes as she reached up for the edge of her shirt.

Air snagged like barbed wire in my throat, watching the fabric dip lower and lower on her chest until the top swell of her breast was bare almost to her nipple.

The staggered line I saw earlier was now clearer.

"Be brave," she murmured. "The last advice my dad gave me before he died. I recorded it, so I could tattoo his voice wave." She released her shirt, the expanse of skin covered in an instant. "Ironic that I got into tattooing because I valued permanence... but then this was the only tattoo I could picture giving myself."

"Not ironic," I told her, stepping close. "You know it's more than just about permanence. You want something meaningful—something or someone that you care about to be with you no matter what."

"Maybe." She shuddered, looking away and swallowing hard. "Or maybe I'm more indecisive than I realized."

Liar. I let my eyes roam her face even as my hands lifted to either side of her head. She craved something to fill the well of solitude inside her, and damn if I didn't want to be that something.

"Anyway." She shook off the conversation and ducked out of my reach. "I'm just glad the flooring will be done so that I don't have to move my clients for my soft opening."

My gaze traveled from her around the room and then ventured toward the front, my protector instincts speaking louder.

"Do you have security cameras in here?" What I wanted to demand was that I would be in the room for every fucker who was naked around her, but I settled for asking about security cameras.

Her brow furrowed. "Worried about me, Detective Reynolds?"

I tipped forward with a low hiss at her taunt.

"It's my job to keep you safe."

Her tongue swiped across her lips. "Not anymore," she

97

countered, but her eyes betrayed her, drifting down to my mouth for a second before she caught herself. "I'm not in danger anymore except maybe from laminate flooring."

"I'm going to install security cameras anyway," I declared.

"Archer, I'm not—"

"It doesn't hurt to be extra cautious," I reminded her firmly, watching her lips purse instead of argue. "Plus, if you're not in danger, why did you keep moving around after Boston?"

If they had been safe, why hadn't they stayed put?

Her expression flickered but she didn't budge—like she didn't want me to know she was still hiding something. "My dad couldn't stop worrying."

"Is that the whole truth?"

Her eyes widened a fraction. "Yes. Some habits are hard to break."

Like wanting her. My cock throbbed, knowing she was just a few easy inches in front of me.

"Archie! You finished back there?"

I shoved off the wall forcefully, putting solid distance between Keira and me when I heard Gunner's voice. *Shit.* I forgot we weren't alone. *I forgot I wasn't supposed to get close to her.*

"For now," I called back, my eyes never breaking from hers.

Keira folded her arms, her chin tilting higher in the way that exposed the smooth column of her throat. She'd always teased me about being a vampire, but the things I wanted to do to that throat might actually make me a solid candidate.

"I'm installing a security system for you." My tone wasn't debatable. "Safe or not, you shouldn't be alone in here with strange men."

She walked up to me and flattened her palm on my chest, sending air cracking through the hard seam of my lips. "Your eyes look greener than usual right now," she mused dryly. "I wonder why."

I growled low, watching her like a feral beast as she rolled her lower lip slowly between her teeth.

"Arch, you ready to go?" Hunter's voice approached.

Keira dropped her hand, my chest burning like a hot stove in the shadow of her touch.

"Thank you for helping me today," she said solemnly. "And for always protecting me."

Hunter entered the back room before I could reply, immediately insisting that Keira come see the front of her shop now that the floor was finished. I hung back until they were gone and then walked over to the sheaf of paper she'd pointed to earlier.

I would always do whatever it took to protect her. Job or not.

Taking out my phone, I snapped a quick photo of the list of clients coming up here to see her. I didn't care if they were former clients or not. I wasn't letting anyone alone with Keira until I'd vetted them first.

It remained to be seen if she'd still thank me once she knew what I'd done.

CHAPTER SEVEN

KEIRA

I WASN'T QUITE SURE I'D MADE THE RIGHT TURN AS THE DRIVE wound farther away from the road with no building in sight, but as soon as I rounded the bend and the thicket of pine trees opened into a clearing and I saw a sleek wooden lodge looking building and a familiar Ford F-150 parked out front.

Archer's truck had been a staple at my shop all week.

Every day once he finished up with his work for RPG, he'd head over to Twilight Ink to work on installing a security system that seemed so over the top for a small tattoo shop that I was surprised the building didn't collapse under the weight of the tech.

There were cameras, motion detectors, and a keypad lock. My favorite thing? The five silent alarm buttons installed as tiny touch pads throughout the inside: one by the front door, one underneath the lip of the counter, one back by the back window, one on the wall next to my tattoo gun, and one in the back room next to my desk.

One tap was all it took to call not just Wisdom PD, but Reynolds Protective. *Honestly, I wouldn't be surprised if it alerted the FBI and National Guard, too.*

My foot pressed on the brake as I reached the small

parking lot out front, and I slowly pulled in next to Archer's truck.

Even though he'd gone over the basics with me yesterday about how the system worked, he wanted to review it again somewhere where I wasn't quite so 'distracted.'

He would be distracted too if he had a business opening tomorrow.

He'd only been there for a week, and already I was craving his presence for longer. It was a dangerous feeling to have for a man who couldn't be mine, and it was because he hadn't just shown up to install the security system.

Archer brought dinner with him every night from some of the local restaurants in the area. A few I'd already had, most I hadn't. He'd claimed that since I'd introduced him to some of Boston's most famous eats, it was his turn to do the same.

So, he showed up with paper bags and cartons of food, and we fell into conversation like we were back in that motel in Boston, talking about living in Wisdom, what Wyoming winters were like, and the plans I had for my business. And when we were done eating, the conversation continued while he worked, though nothing was said about the past or our kiss, but we circled around it like vultures just waiting for the first scent of weakness to delve deeper.

I walked up the three steps to the front door. Before I could ring the bell, there was a beep and the door opened, revealing Gunner's playful smile.

"Hey, Keira. Welcome to Reynolds Protective." He ushered me in.

"Thanks." I scanned the entryway.

The large windows and small seating area had a modern, comforting feel. The paint and abstract art on the wall were all blue tones, adding to the calming atmosphere. I guessed that was chosen thoughtfully since most people who walked through these doors were in fear for their life.

"How's the floor holding up?"

I tipped my head. "Holding up?"

"Figured Archie might've paced a worn path through it by now. You know, frustration and all."

I stared at him blankly, refusing to be goaded. It didn't matter if my and Archer's chemistry was so explosive it was a good thing it couldn't be bottled; I wasn't going to talk about what was or wasn't happening with his younger brother.

"It's holding up perfectly." I smiled. "Thank you again for your help."

"Of course." He chuckled, taking my hint. "So, I guess we'll see you at Mom's party then on Sunday?"

"I don't know…" I folded my arms and turned to face him, giving the rest of the building my back. "Your brother didn't seem too happy about your little deal."

"I think he's getting over himself."

My chin jutted in his direction. "Is he? Because it looks like you've been demoted to playing receptionist this morning."

Gunner threw back his head and laughed. "While I do enjoy playing receptionist, especially to beautiful women, sadly, Hunter is already looking to hire someone for the job." Approaching me, he added, "I just happened to see you pull in, so I thought I'd say hello."

He stood in front of me, and I realized how easy it was for him to be a ladies' man. That devious quirk of his mouth promised sinful delights, the rebellious lock of hair draping down on his forehead gave him boyish charm, and the muscles stacked on his torso were as well-honed as his brother's—Gunner Reynolds was a burning hunk of a man, but I might as well have been a bucket of water for all he was able to set me on fire.

"Gunner." The low growl permeated through the open space.

My gaze slid up from Gunner's bobbing eyebrows to the small balcony overlooking the firm's foyer. The eldest Reynolds stood there like a god peering down from Olympus, gripping the railing with white knuckles and lightning bolts shooting from his murky eyes.

Instantly my body sizzled to life. It wasn't fire that awoke each and every one of my cells, it was Archer's electricity. His imposing masculine energy and the way it was always centered on me ran a steady current through my veins that was just waiting for a massive surge to bring me to my knees.

"Think that's my cue," Gunner said low, looking at me and then winking at his brother before taking off down the hallway on the main floor.

I looked up. "Hi."

He finally released the banister. "You can come up."

The thudding of my heart deepened as I climbed the stairs—getting nearer to him always did that to me.

"I finished getting everything online with your system this morning," he said when I reached the landing, his eyes scanning me before he snapped them away. My skin tingled from the sting.

"I really think this was a little overkill for a tattoo parlor," I repeated the thought I'd had multiple times.

He paused in front of his office door, towering over me and dousing me in his protective shadow. "Your father testified against the Irish mob—a criminal organization that was able to track you down numerous times in WITSEC and threaten your life." His words weren't spoken as much as growled. "I don't think any amount of security is *overkill* for that."

I managed to hold off rolling my eyes until he gave me his back, opening the door and allowing me to enter.

The office was everything I would've expected for Archer Reynolds. Big wooden desk with a large leather desk chair. Big windows wrapping around the back corner of the building. Big view of the breathtaking Teton Range. All reminders of how Archer was in control of everything about his life. *Everything except how he felt about me.*

He strode over to his desk, and I had to admire the way his powerful legs moved with such sleek grace. *And that ass.*

"Why are you so worried about me, Archer?" I asked, hating that inextinguishable bud of hope that held on to him, wanting to hear him admit he cared.

"Because it was my duty to protect you, and I failed."

Wait, what?

"What are you talking about?" I demanded, walking closer. "I didn't actually die, Archer." I motioned down the length of my body. "It was all fake."

He jerked like my words whipped against an open wound, and when he looked at me, I'd never seen such raw pain in a man's eyes before.

"Not to me."

"Arch—"

"Here are the instructions on how to arm and disarm the system, as well as instructions on how to change the codes if you want," he interrupted me, holding up one folder with a wave and then picked up another. "This is an outline of what happens when you hit the panic button. I also had Ranger provide estimates of how long it would take law enforcement to reach you once the button is pushed."

When I got close enough, he handed me both folders. "Is this really necessary?"

"Someone broke into your building—"

"Oh my god—Kids!" I interrupted him with a huff. "Kids broke into my building," I insisted, regretting that I hadn't replaced the busted back doorknob before he managed to see it. "Do you think anyone from the Kings would just break in and not take anything? Not leave a note? Not wait for me?" I folded my arms, hating that I was even talking about this after so many years. "If the Kings had found me, Archer, I would be dead, not dealing with a broken lock."

He visibly flinched at that last mention of me being dead but quickly recovered.

"You know he's trying to get parole, right?" His voice was low and coarse.

"What?" My eyes whipped to his. My arms unfolded slowly like they lost their strength and structure until they hung limply at my sides.

His jaw was like granite. "James Maloney petitioned for parole six weeks ago."

My insides curdled. *That was when I'd moved to Wyoming.*

It had to be a coincidence, otherwise someone would've come for me by now. The Kings didn't leave idle threats, and Sean promised to find me and make me pay, and that impatient bastard would make good on that threat as soon as he had the chance; he wouldn't wait six weeks. He wouldn't wait a day.

"I didn't know that," I said, hating how my voice grew tense.

"Their organization fractured after your dad put him away," Archer went on to tell me. "His son didn't quite garner the same respect as Jimmy, and with so many arrested because of your father's information, the Kings stronghold in Boston was crippled."

"Well, his son was a piece of shit," I charged too quickly, unable to stop myself.

The darkness welled up inside me, spreading like a dark fog. Pervasive and cold, but without substance, so it was hard to rein in.

I didn't know about Dad, but I certainly hadn't kept tabs on what happened in Boston after we left. When we decided that the only way for us to live was for them to think we died, I took the death of Keira McKenna to heart. Like I was outside my own body, I watched myself die on those courthouse steps, and I buried her under each mile we drove away. I buried all thoughts about that city and the memories of the vile men who lived in it and what they'd done to me. To us.

"Keira..."

I snapped out of it and saw how Archer was looking at me. *Shit.* Sometimes, it felt like he was the only one who could see me. Maybe it was because he knew who I really was. Not everything. *Definitely not everything.* But more than almost everyone else.

"Did something else happen in Boston between the Kings and your dad?" he probed, his natural instinct for fishing out truths going into overdrive when he sensed I had something to hide.

"You know what happened, Archer. My dad didn't want me around that life, but he knew they'd never let him go quietly," I replied, quickly brushing him off. "And to Jimmy Maloney, in prison or on parole, I'm still dead."

His jaw tightened.

"Well, I think that the daughter of the man who put him away should be guarded twenty-four-seven," he returned, catching my eyes. "But I'll settle for the security system."

I hummed and pulled the folders against my chest, holding them there and asking, "Is that all?"

Why did I need to come here just for that?

"No." He cleared his throat and I knew I wasn't going to like what he said next. "When did you put out to your clients that you were opening your own place, Keira?"

"I don't know." I gulped. "Maybe five weeks ago to some of them. Why?"

He picked up the last folder, staring at it for an extra long second before he said, "What if it was one of them who broke into the post office and tried to get your address?"

I gaped. "What?" My head shook incredulously. "That makes no sense. First, the post office had nothing to do with me. Second, why would they need to do that when they knew I would have to give them the address eventually?"

I didn't understand what he was getting at, and I didn't like the way his gaze was practically burning a hole in the folder.

He finally looked at me. "Did you know that the client you showed me a photo of—Davis James—grew up in Boston?" he asked, shocking me into silence. "Or that he flew into Jackson Hole the day before the post office incident?"

I couldn't believe what I was hearing—*what I was realizing.*

My mind flipped through memories like a Rolodex of information, searching for the right card with the right moment. And then it came to me.

"Did you... did you *investigate* my clients?"

Archer's lips tightened and he stood taller with self-righteousness. "I'm trying to protect you."

I grabbed the file from his hands and opened it. Sure enough, there were pages upon pages stapled together of all of Davis's information from previous addresses to high school transcripts to his credit history.

"I can't *believe* you," I muttered, feeling the sudden invasion of my independence as sharply as a hot knife through butter. I went to look at him but my eyes snagged on where his hand rested on the neatly stacked pile of folders on his desk. *No.* "You looked into them all?" I wasn't sure if it was a question or an accusation, but the hot flash of dignified guilt over his too-handsome face was the only answer I needed. "I can't believe you did this."

My mind scrambled, trying to figure out *how* he had done this. But then I recalled that my soft opening schedule had been on top of the pile of papers in the back room, left on display because I'd been too distracted by Archer.

"Do what? Try to protect you when I think you're still in danger?"

"That you would invade my *privacy* and take pictures of my clients' information in order to spy on them!" I swatted his arm with the folder, but it was about as effective as beating a rock with a piece of tissue paper. "You don't get to do this, Archer. Not now. Not anymore."

I couldn't tell what I felt more—grateful and warmed by

the extent he'd gone for my safety or afraid that once again, my life wasn't my own—*petrified that it would never be.*

With an angry cry, I dropped all the folders on Archer's desk and headed for the door. I needed to get out of here. All of a sudden, the fresh freedom of the Wyoming air began to dissipate into the suffocating musk of confinement.

"Keira..." His growl came after me, catching up with the goose bumps on my neck just before his hand locked on my arm.

I spun but kept moving toward the door, my back meeting the hard wood and my front faced with Archer's hard body and equally stony expression.

Pieces of my anger ignited in his presence, catching into little balls of fire with every harsh breath that clashed with his. Each inhale bumped my chest against his.

"Don't do this," he pleaded, inching closer. "Don't make me out to be the bad guy."

I shivered. Archer Reynolds was as far from being a bad guy as one could get. I knew that with certainty since I'd grown up around enough real bad guys. But what he could be was too good for his own good.

"Then don't make me feel like I'm in danger over random little things you string together."

The hard tension on his face deepened as his mind fought with his emotions. He wanted to believe me, but it went against what he felt. And I understood. At least part of me did. When he'd seen me last, I was in danger. While my life after death had sequentially peeled away my bondage of fear, he hadn't seen any of that. To him, I would always be the girl in danger—the girl it was his duty to protect.

"They aren't little to me."

His lips twitched as his head dropped lower. I felt the heat of his breath against my lips and they parted, wanting to taste whatever part of him I could.

"I won't be put in a cage again." I tipped my chin higher, breathing unsteadily.

His body radiated against mine, and I reached up and flattened my palm to his chest, breaking the touchless barrier between us.

"I will put you wherever is necessary to keep you safe."

Everywhere except in his arms.

Safety was one thing, but the way his eyes dropped to my mouth, jealous of every breath I drew into it, betrayed the real danger brewing between us.

"I'm not in danger from my clients." I sounded like a broken record. My voice fell slightly, desperate to reassure him —to make him understand. *Desperate to believe that wasn't where this was headed.* "This ended in Boston, Archer. I've been free for four years."

"Well that makes one of us."

What was he talking about? I drew a sharp breath, shocked more by the tortured look in his eyes than the sound of his anger.

He growled and pushed himself away from me, taking the blanket of heat away from my skin as he stalked to the other side of his office like a lion that was both angry and wounded. *Perhaps angrier because he was wounded.*

"What—"

"Just because you want to believe you're safe here doesn't mean you are," he interrupted me, gathering the folders I'd strewn across his desk and hitting them on the dark wood to even them out. "And until the strange, *random* things stop happening to *you,* I won't stop protecting you."

He was in front of me again, handing me the pile of folders like I was just supposed to accept his overbearing intrusion into my new life.

"Ghosts don't need to be protected," I lashed back.

Air evacuated my lungs when the heat of his fingers notched under my chin, lifting it until I was looking at him.

His nostrils flared, and I watched his mouth come for mine, my eyes fluttering shut just when his head veered to the side, landing his lips next to my ear.

"They do when they keep haunting me."

I swore I felt his mouth at the tender junction between my ear, jaw, and neck. I swore I felt the brush of his lips there, waking my goose bumps to life like he was their Pied Piper.

And then he was gone—back to standing in front of me like he had so many times before. A bastion of restraint. A frustrating masterpiece of a man who both cared too much and not enough.

"I'll walk you out."

CHAPTER EIGHT

ARCHER

"ARCHER?"

The hand on my shoulder startled me, and I realized I'd been washing the same damn plate for far too long.

I blinked and the lamp-lit street and auburn sunset came back into focus through the window above the kitchen sink. I remembered where I was: at Mom's house. I'd just finished having dinner with her and my brothers, and I'd come in here to wash the dishes and have a moment alone.

As soon as I started, my mind went somewhere else—it went back to my office, watching Keira scold me and then plead with me yesterday afternoon.

I won't go back in that cage.

Her protest broke my heart. I wasn't trying to put her back in a fucking cage. I just wanted to make sure she was safe. Maybe she was. Maybe I didn't know what the hell I was doing. Maybe I was so fucking traumatized by watching her die that now I was willing to shove her back in a cage just so I'd never have to go through that again.

Don't be a selfish ass, Archer.

But if that wasn't enough of a stressor, the way she talked about Sean Maloney was left like a stone in my shoe—small but pressing on a bad button every time I retraced the memory.

"Are you alright?" Mom probed.

Lydia Reynolds rested the side of her hip on the counter next to me and gave me that classic scrutinizing eye.

She was a force of nature. A benevolent one, but still powerful.

After Dad died, Wisdom had pulled together to help her raise us. A single mom supporting five kids was a tall task—but not too tall for this small town. Once we were all old enough and out of the nest so to speak—all of us except Ranger—she decided it was time to give back to that same community by running for mayor. She was elected not long after I left for Boston and had held the position ever since.

"I'm fine, Mom." I grabbed the towel slung over my shoulder and began drying the dish.

Even as mayor, she still lived in the same house we'd grown up in—the two-story log cabin sat a block off Main Street on a slight hill. From the kitchen window, I could see a good strip of the western facades, including the small former barber shop that now had a *Twilight Tattoos* sign proudly illuminating the window.

We'd all had dinner at her house tonight—more or less a weekly tradition unless we were out of town with a client or Gunner was spending the weekend 'living life' in Jackson Hole.

"You're always fine, and that's what worries me." She took the plate and towel from me to help me dry.

I gave her a look. She wasn't supposed to help with clean up after making her famous eggplant Parmesan for us, but I knew she wasn't standing here to help—*at least not with the dishes.*

"And you're always asking questions."

She wanted answers. Answers to why I was grumpier than usual, to why I'd only participated in less than a quarter of the conversation at dinner, and to why I was the first to volunteer to do the dishes though, according to Ranger, it was technically his turn.

"That's because I'm a mother. It's part of the job."

I sighed, my hands moving in the monotonous circular motion on the next plate as I listened to my brothers talk and laugh from the other room.

I couldn't give her an answer. But I could give her a name. *Keira.*

"Just dealing with a difficult case," I finally muttered and handed her the plate to dry.

And a debilitating distraction.

Maybe I was overreacting about everything. But she was dead and then she was alive and then I kissed her and—*fuck.* Every minute I was around her, I was torn with wanting to protect and punish and pleasure her. But she hadn't come here for me, I reminded myself.

"The one with the girl from Boston who's opening up the new tattoo parlor?" she asked with a benevolent omniscience.

My teeth clenched. Three brothers and one small town… I shouldn't be surprised that she knew all about it.

"Who told you? Gunner?"

"No."

As soon as she denied it, I knew the answer. "Ranger."

Gunner enjoyed giving me shit for Keira far too much to let someone else in on the fun. Ranger, on the other hand, didn't pick up on certain nuances—like it wasn't the case that had me in knots, it was the woman. He didn't know what it was like to be fucking strangled by feelings on the inside for someone else; he didn't understand that was the kind of thing —the very last kind of thing I'd want to talk to Mom about.

"I'll be fine," I repeated gruffly. "Guess it's just hard to see someone you thought was dead come back to life."

She hummed softly. "I think it's hard to see someone you have unfinished feelings with die right in front of you. I think it's even harder to accept that those feelings don't go away with death, and now she's alive, you have to deal with them again."

My breath came out in a low hiss. *What feelings? Desire?* Yeah, I'd been two layers of clothing away from fucking her in that motel.

When she was nineteen.

And under my protection.

"It was just unfinished business." I cleared my throat. "And now she's just being reckless."

A slight exaggeration.

"Does she know why you're back here?"

I tensed, turning my head away from her for a second before passing her the next wet plate. "That doesn't matter."

"It certainly looks like it matters. You hardly said two words at dinner, and this whole time, you've been watching Todd's old place like it'll vanish if you look away too long."

"With her there, it might," I grumbled.

She sighed heavily. "I wish you'd stop running, Archer. It breaks my heart."

I inhaled and exhaled slowly. I wasn't going to have this conversation with her—no, this wasn't a conversation.

"I'm not running, Mom. I'm right here, handling my responsibilities and protecting people who I think might be in danger." I handed her the last plate and turned off the sink.

"Are you?" she asked quietly in the way I knew meant what she was going to say next would be the real blow. "Or are you just trying to punish yourself for things that were out of your control?"

Every time she said that, I made it a point to stare at the scars around her neck—to remind myself that I'd failed her. That if it hadn't been for the FBI—if it hadn't been for Special Agent Roman Knight and the Behavioral Analysis Unit—she would be dead because I'd failed to stop a serial killer. Today, she wore a turtleneck underneath a thick flannel shirt, but I could still see the marks from where the Archangel tried to kill her.

"None of it was out of my control," I said through locked teeth. "Not you. Not her."

"You know better than to believe that," she tutted, grabbing the dish from me and drying.

I huffed and muttered, "I don't know what to believe."

"Well, what I believe is that if you offered up a little bit of your truth, maybe Keira would feel more comfortable doing the same." She shouldered her way in front of the sink.

"What are you doing?"

"Cleaning up from dinner," she said and then nudged her chin in the direction of the tattoo parlor. "I think you have a bigger mess that needs your attention."

"Oh my God, K, if you saw the muscles on him, the way his ass moved down the mountain... Mm mm mm."

I stopped partway through the door, my attention homed in on the conversation going on in the back of the shop.

I'd stayed to finish the dishes, but I knew before I left that my next destination wasn't home.

It was late—well past when she should be working on a client, yet the lights were still on in the shop and her Corolla was still parked by the side door, a large Range Rover next to it.

Every muscle in my body was tight, but not with fear. *At least not with the fear that she was in danger.*

I walked fully into the space, seeing how all the little details had come together since I'd finished installing the security system two days ago.

The front desk was neatly organized, a datebook closed on

top with a stash of pens resting in an apple mug. Along the wall to my right hung several of the photos of her clients that I'd glimpsed on her phone the other day, showcasing the skill and artistry of her work. The small, black beaded chandelier cast a dim glow and ornate shadows in the room. The space had a speakeasy vibe of secrecy and subtle independence.

"Now, I told him he had to be gentle with me after today——"

"Hold on, Davis."

I straightened, hearing Keira's voice, and closed the door firmly behind me. I didn't want her thinking I was trying to sneak in here unheard. It was bad enough I couldn't stop myself from showing up just before the end of her session with this Davis character to make sure she was okay.

And partially to make sure the fucker wasn't naked.

She came around the partial wall, the loud clunks of her black combat boots stopping short when she saw me. Irritation furrowed her brow. Meanwhile, the sight of her knocked the breath from my lungs.

She was wearing the tiniest shorts known to man and a cropped black tee that had *Twilight Ink* written across the chest. My body went hard. If I were a betting man, I'd place all my money on the guess that she wasn't wearing a bra underneath the damn thing, though the dark color made it hard to tell. Her hair was up in a high ponytail but hung down over her shoulder, and my fingers curled, wanting to fist around the length and use it as a red rudder.

Fuck.

Instantly, my cock was wedged along my leg, throbbing like I hadn't jacked off in the shower every morning since I saw Keira that morning at the post office.

"Archer." She folded her arms and I caught the shadow of her tattoo on her chest as her shirt slid down her shoulder for a second before she fixed it. "I'm with a client right now."

"K, who is—Oh my god." The man from her photos—Davis—appeared next, pressing the tape on the side of his abdomen to make sure the bandage over the newest part of his tattoo was stable. *Luckily for him, he was wearing fucking pants.* His hand rose and covered his mouth, looking me up and down.

Davis had to be about Ranger's age and of a similar build —skinny but toned. He had dark hair that I'd called purposely disheveled and a beard that looked a few days old but highlighted his bright white smile and matching dark eyes. And from the neck down, he was covered in ink. A massive collage of some of Dali's greatest works. *All done by Keira.*

In the photo, it was impressive. In person, it was breathtaking.

Not something I ever thought to think about a guy's chest, but damn, she'd made it her canvas and created a work of art.

"Introduce me," Davis whispered loudly and swatted Keira's arm.

Her lips pursed and they glared at each other for a second before she turned back to me and said tightly, "Davis, this is Archer Reynolds." She paused. "He... installed the floors for me."

Installed the floors? Seriously? That was the connection she was going to go with.

A low noise rumbled out from the fire in my chest. My gaze clashed with hers, and I wondered if her friend saw the sparks, too.

"Archer, this is Davis James, but I think you already know that," she taunted me.

Before I could say anything to her, Davis sauntered up to me with his hand extended.

I took it firmly. He immediately pressed his other hand over mine as we shook and said, "It's a pleasure with a capital P to meet you."

There was no doubt in my mind that the only person Davis was attracted to in this room was me. I didn't know whether to be relieved at the knowledge or irritated that she

117

couldn't have just told me. Instead, she let me think that she'd been locked in this building all day working on a naked guy who wanted to fuck her.

Because it was none of your damn business, Archer. None of her is your damn business.

I clenched my teeth.

I'd made my bed. I only had myself to blame that I'd chosen to make it without her in it.

Then he half turned to Keira and said in a whisper loud enough for me to hear, "What are they putting in the water up here, K, because I need to bottle some of that shit and take it with me." He fanned himself.

"Can we talk?" I asked her.

"I told you, I'm bus—"

"Oh, no." Davis wagged his finger and backed up. "I won't be your excuse. Not for this, honey."

"Davis." She turned and hissed.

"Nope. No can do." He lifted both hands and continued to back away. "Plus, I've got to get back to the resort. And Ben." He pouted. "Although, trust me, if I could trade places with you right now, I totally would."

I could only imagine the face she was giving him as he bolted back behind the partial wall, presumably to grab his things.

Not even thirty seconds later, he was back, bare-chested underneath his massive puffer coat and a coy grin on his lips.

"Thank you. You're incredible," he told Keira, grabbing her shoulders and kissing her forehead. "Have a good night."

I was pretty sure that even Ranger would've picked up on his intonation of the word *good* to know what he was implying.

Yeah, not happening.

Unfortunately for my throbbing dick.

"Traitor." I heard her mumble, remaining with her back— *and perfect ass*—facing me as Davis headed for the door I was semi-guarding.

"Take good care of my girl," he drawled as he walked by me.

My tight smile unfurled into a scowl. I wanted to snap back that I would only ever take the best care of her—even if she didn't realize it. But that wasn't what bothered me.

She wasn't his fucking girl.

She was mine.

The thought hit me just as the door banged shut, leaving the two of us alone.

"Well, here I am. Safe and sound. Are you satisfied?" She turned slowly. "Or do you still think Davis is a threat?"

Once more, my eyes snaked over her lack of clothing.

"No, I don't think he's a threat," I admitted because it was the truth. Clearing my throat, I put my eyes in time-out. I stared blankly at the apple pen holder on the desk and pretended like there wasn't a living, breathing, redheaded forbidden fruit standing a few feet in front of me. "And I'm here because I want to… apologize… if I overstepped."

"If?"

My head snapped back to her. "I want to apologize *for* overstepping."

She took a few steps in my direction. "Except you keep doing it, Archer."

"Apparently, protecting you is a hard habit to break," I rasped, my throat tightening as she stopped within arm's reach. "Is this what you wear with all your clients?" The question dumped out before I could stop it. "I think Davis had more tattoos covering him than you have clothes."

Her eyebrows rose and she cocked her head. "This is some apology."

Dammit.

There was something about her that drove me insane. *Wanting her. Not being able to have her. Not knowing the truth about her.*

Okay, fine. There were several things about her that drove me insane.

I filled my lungs and tried to stay calm. I tried to ignore how damn bad I wanted to kiss her and soften the tight line I'd forced her lips into.

"You're right. I guess I'm not good at those either." I dragged my hand through my hair, meeting her unwavering gaze. "What can I do to make it up to you?"

Her mouth formed a little 'o' and I died a little inside from the pain it sent rocketing through my damn dick.

She hummed, the sound dangerously close to a moan. Her eyes wandered over me while she thought for a moment.

"Do you have any tattoos, Archer?"

Fuck.

"No."

Twin emerald irises sparkled when they pierced mine. The wet tip of her tongue slid over her lips like she was preparing to taste satisfaction in her request.

Her chin lifted. "Let me give you a tattoo."

Something primal jolted in my chest, hearing her say she wanted to mark me.

I had nothing against tattoos. Gunner had a couple of them, and even Hunter had one for our dad. But I'd never felt something so deeply or thought something so important that I needed it inked into my skin.

But this. Here. Now. *With her.* It suddenly struck me with such significance, that not only was I willing to agree because I wanted her forgiveness. I wanted the damn tattoo because I wanted her to give me something that she couldn't take back.

I wanted one fucking piece of her that I couldn't lose again.

And if I was being honest—if I was being responsible and respectful—this was the only thing I should take from her.

"Okay."

CHAPTER NINE

KEIRA

I DIDN'T KNOW WHAT SURPRISED ME MORE: THAT HE AGREED to let me tattoo him or that I had asked.

It was the champagne, I decided. When in doubt, blame it on the champagne. *And Davis.*

Davis was a plastic surgeon at the hospital my dad was treated at in Salt Lake City; that was where we'd met. Well, technically, we'd met at the Starbucks around the corner. I'd been replicating a DaVinci sketch in my notebook and he'd snooped over my shoulder.

Similarly to me, he'd lived much of his life growing up along the East Coast and felt like an outsider almost everywhere he went, not trusting those around him to respect and support the brilliant and bold man he was. There was obviously a difference in our lives, but the painful loneliness was something that we'd bonded over and eliminated with our friendship.

Davis loved Jackson Hole. Not because he skied. Or particularly liked the snow. But because he liked the *après-ski* crowd who flooded the bars when the slopes closed looking for a good drink and an even better time.

Davis was at my door bright and early this morning with a

giant pink bottle of champagne and a matching celebratory smile. He was here for his tattoo, of course, but he was also here to celebrate with me.

I'd finally found my spot—the place where I belonged. *Assuming whatever happened with Archer didn't drive me away.*

Setting the champagne to the side, we'd caught up on life. How his work was going. How my move had gone. What Wisdom was like. If I met any hot, gay cowboys for him. *You know... the important things.* I'd finished tattooing his dripping clocks over an hour ago, and that was when we popped the cork.

One plastic champagne glass after another until the bottle was gone and I'd spilled about my blast from the past. At least Davis kept to himself that he already knew who Archer was when Archer showed up unannounced.

"This way." I led Archer back to my table, feeling the heat of his brazen stare along my back and then lower.

I grabbed the glasses and empty champagne bottle that sat on it and threw them in the trash.

"Are you drunk?" he demanded.

I straightened and quickly turned to face him.

"No." *But I should definitely refrain from spinning so fast in the near future.* "We were just celebrating." His gaze traveled over me, making my nipples pebble painfully against my shirt. He didn't look convinced, so I quipped, "I'm not nineteen anymore, Archer, so that makes this legal."

His eyes whipped to mine, something fierce coming alive in their depths that made me feel like he could devour me with just a single look.

Shit.

Double shit.

"That makes the champagne legal," I mumbled for clarification, but the damage was already done. Thankfully, I managed to refrain from also clarifying that fucking me would have been legal previously. "So." I cleared my throat, wondering if my cheeks looked as warm as they felt. "Where do you want it?"

That didn't sound so great either.

"I get a choice?" One eyebrow peaked.

"No, you're right," I broke in quickly. If it was his choice, I'd probably end up having to work on his foot. Or forearm. I had this one shot—this one moment where Archer Reynolds was in my debt, and that champagne was going to push the limits as far as he'd let me. "Take off your shirt."

The hard corners of his jaw pulsed. He stood there for a second, and I thought he might refuse, but then he lifted one hand over his head and fisted the neck of his T-shirt, bunching the fabric, and then pulled it off in a visual symphony of moving muscles.

I didn't know where it went. On the floor. On the side table in the corner. He could've eaten it for all I knew because my focus was stolen completely by the muscled perfection in front of me.

My lips parted, air crawling between them.

It had taken everything in me not to stare earlier in the week when his shirt had come off while his brothers were here. For four years, I'd wondered how his bare chest looked without anything covering it. I had ideas. I imagined things. I even told myself that what I imagined couldn't be too far off given how well all his clothes seemed to fit.

But it was like how I thought I knew what the wild mountains of Wyoming looked like because he'd shown me photos or that I thought I was prepared for the crisp evergreen-scented atmosphere because I'd bought a Wyoming candle from a farmers' market.

Then I'd actually arrived here. I hadn't even made it into town before I pulled my car over on the side of the road, got out and walked in a daze several feet into a field, and then dropped to my knees in awe.

Nothing prepared me for the wild majesty of this place. No thought. No picture. No dream.

And nothing prepared me for the sculpted masculinity of him.

A bronzed, broad canvas of muscled hills and valleys.

And tonight, I had an excuse to touch him.

I bit into my lower lip, using the pain to pull me back to reality. Tearing my gaze away, I patted the table, not trusting myself to speak.

I went to wash my hands at the small sink, cranking the water to ice cold in hopes it would dull the fire running through my blood. The table creaked a little as he sat on it.

"Do you have something in mind?" I asked as I dried my hands. "Or something you definitely don't want."

"No Chinese symbols."

I laughed instantly, his joke the brief reminder my body needed to keep breathing. When I faced him, the laughter fizzled.

He sat on the edge of the bed, legs wide, and his hands gripping his knees. He'd gone from a work of art to a specimen of sculpture, all hard curves and sharp lines. And the intensity of his expression—his smoldering eyes locked on me like those of a hunter. *An archer whose gaze spiraled through me like flame-tipped arrows.*

"Anything else?" I asked, breathless.

He shook his head. "I'm all yours."

I sucked in a breath. *If only that were true.*

"Alright, let me think for a minute while I get everything set up." I quickly turned away, needing to regroup as I grabbed my tools and began to set up.

"Thought you might've mentioned that Davis had no interest in you," Archer said a few seconds later, his voice roughened.

In retrospect, I should have told him Davis was as gay as the sky was blue. *Especially had I known he was going to go full-*

blown background check on my friend. But the way jealousy emulsified the desire and restraint in his gaze was something I couldn't bring myself to make go away.

"I didn't think whether or not he's interested in me had any effect on my safety," I said, daring him to admit it just had an effect on him.

The table creaked again as I grabbed my cleansing wipes and a disposable razor. I thought I heard something mumbled that sounded an awful lot like, *"You'd be surprised,"* as I faced him.

"And do you wear… this… for all your clients?"

My face flushed hotter as his stare lingered on my chest where my nipples were beaded so tight they ached. For his hard touch. His firm mouth.

"No," I blurted out. *Definitely not.* "But it gets hot with my spotlight on for several hours, and then we had champagne."

He grunted, only marginally satisfied by my answer.

"I have to clean the area," I explained for the both of us, rounding in front of him.

He sat tall, watching me on edge as I stepped between his legs. I felt the warm moisture collect between my thighs as I inched closer, the seam of my shorts rubbing against my core.

I pulled out an alcohol wipe and then realized I hadn't put gloves on. Maybe I'd forgotten. Maybe it was an unconscious choice. This wasn't just a small display of permanence I was giving him, it was something personal. And I wanted to feel his flesh tremble under my fingertips as I inked it.

My eyes bored into the flat plane of his left pec. I hadn't chosen that spot for the tattoo until I was in front of him, my hand already reaching for the upper crest of the muscled plate over his beating heart.

"Going straight for the chest then," he rasped as soon as the cloth touched down on his skin.

I was surprised the isopropyl alcohol didn't catch on fire from the heat of him. Working in slow circles, I cleaned the area that, at this close range, I could see didn't need to be shaved.

"Don't worry, Archer," I murmured. "It will be something discreet."

"So no Van Gogh's Starry Night?" His chest rumbled underneath my fingers, and I pulled back suddenly, heat pooling between my legs.

"Not quite." I spun and walked back to my side table. I'd had no idea what I was going to tattoo on him until that moment, his joke triggering an idea so simple and strong, it bowled over me like an avalanche. "But you just gave me a good idea."

Archer. Starry Night.

I bit the corner of my cheek to hold back a smile.

"Did you do those paintings?" His chin jerked in the direction of the back room. I looked and saw the stack of wrapped boards resting against the door.

Crap. I forgot I brought those over earlier. Damn champagne.

"Those are some paintings of my dad's that he's had since before I was born." *One less since I'd sold it to buy this building.* "They're really all I have left of him, so I figured they'd be safer here… now." *After he'd turned this place into Fort Knox.* "Maybe one day I'll have walls to support paintings of my own, but for now bodies will do."

"I'm sorry, Keira."

I didn't say anything after that. I couldn't. I wanted to let him in, but I was afraid. I was strong for so many things, but for this—the opportunity to put myself in a position to lose Archer again—I was afraid. After everything that had either been taken or given up in my life, the only things—the only people I could afford to allow in were the ones that inked themselves as permanently as a tattoo on my heart.

And Archer made it clear that wasn't going to happen for us.

"You're not going to give me a Twilight tattoo are you?"

he probed a few seconds later, and I clung to the small comedic breeze that lightened the mood.

Smiling, I grabbed my black ink; it had a little bit of indigo mixed in so it would heal close to a true black on his bronzed skin.

"Tempting, but no," I returned. "Unless you want Team Jacob forever marked on your chest?"

"I think I'd prefer to keep that between us." His low chuckle stoked the fire that burned low in my stomach.

I turned away once more, grabbing a new, fully charged battery for my wireless SpectraFlux tattoo machine and attaching it to the unit. I should've asked him to lie on his back. It was easier for me to work and made it almost impossible for him to flinch back, though I doubted he would.

But I didn't ask.

I didn't want to hunch over him for the next few minutes, I wanted to stand in front of him. I wanted to stand between his legs, my chest inches from his, my hands on his hard body, while I gave him a piece of me that he couldn't turn down or give back.

The air thickened as I got closer like I was wading deeper and deeper into a pool of pure tension. By the time I was back between his thighs, my gaze level with his, I felt almost lightheaded from the proximity.

"Ready?" The question rode out on a breathless exhale.

When he didn't respond, I found him staring down at me with an animalistic gleam of lust in his eyes. Then I noticed his white-knuckled grip on the edges of the table. And finally, the distended ridge jutting against his jeans, his erection bending the sturdy fabric against its hardness.

He grunted low, and I quickly snapped my attention back to his collarbone. Rolling my lower lip between my teeth, I focused on the chest in front of me. Bare and wide and blank.

I placed my left hand on his sternum, hearing the low hiss that burst from his lips.

"Lean back a little," I instructed, not trusting myself to meet his gaze as he rested back on his hands.

The position gave me a better angle to work at, but it also meant I had to tip toward him to work. My hips rubbed against the insides of his thighs, and heat churned in my core, aching for relief.

Splaying my fingers, I brought my other hand that held my tattoo gun up to his pec.

God, he was so strong. He wasn't even doing anything— not like the other day when he was working on the floors— and still his skin was taut over the swell of strength underneath it.

"I'm going to tattoo your outer collarbone," I told him, hoping the explanation would help me focus. "The area is usually less exposed to sunlight, so less prone to fading over time." I slid the tips of my fingers to the area in question, the surface like hot velvet under their tips. "The skin here also tends to stay relatively firm over time, so it shouldn't stretch out or distort too much."

When he didn't say anything, I glanced up, instantly pinned by his hot, piercing gaze. *Big mistake.* Suddenly I felt all the peripheral feelings I tried to ignore. The pressure of his legs against mine, practically holding my core to his groin, the heat pulsing off his skin, the steady thump of his heart against my palm, and the inches that separated my mouth from his.

This was dangerous—the most dangerous situation I'd been in for years.

"Good to know," he said roughly.

I bit into my cheek and snapped my eyes back to my canvas.

"Also, this might hurt," I added quickly, even though I didn't think any pain would faze him at this point.

I turned the handheld pen on, the low vibration and noise of the unit magnified by the already buzzing current of electricity in the air.

I felt his chest rise with an inhale under my palm as I brought the needle to his skin. *This was it.* There was no going back.

"Good," he said low, just as I pressed the tip to his chest, making my first mark.

Heat flooded me when the first trace of black buried itself under his skin. He didn't move—didn't flinch—as I embedded the first star in his flesh. Instead, his breath released in a steady stream, as though the pain was a relief for the pressure built up inside him.

The first star only took me a few seconds before I moved onto the second placed just next to it. I kept them small and rounded, with the pointed peaks only visible up close, this way from a distance, this would look like nothing more than a cluster of freckles near his shoulder.

"You okay?"

"Fine." The word came through clenched teeth.

Three stars were done. Fifteen more to go.

"Will you tell me what you're doing? Or do I have to wait until it's all done to find out?" His voice was like a rough, warm breeze against the top of my head.

My breath caught, and I pulled the machine back and looked to him. For a second, I imagined he was asking those questions four years ago. Four years ago, he'd had to wait until I'd been killed to learn who I really was.

I licked my lips. "I thought I'd give you a tattoo of something that would never change."

He glanced down. "Morse code?"

I grinned. "Something that hasn't changed for thousands of years." His eyebrows perked up. "Stars."

His low hum made the ache in my core intensify, an insistent pulse that begged for friction. *Begged for relief.*

"A constellation."

My chin dipped. "Orion with his belt and bow."

The archer of the stars.

"Significance?" he asked and then cleared his throat. "I'm not up on my Greek mythology."

My needle paused at the star of one of Orion's shoulders.

"Orion was the son of Poseidon and Euryale, daughter of King Minos. He was able to walk on water and was known as a giant and handsome huntsman." I wiped my cloth over the first six stars of his belt, head, and shoulders, and began the five stars of his shield. "He was known for his strength and courage."

Archer's chest rumbled just as I finished the final star on the shield. I wiped the area and then moved onto the six stars of Orion's raised arm and sword.

"So how did he end up in the stars?"

I gulped. "Well, there are several different versions of how he died."

"Tell me yours."

I shivered. Mine. *My story.* That was all he ever wanted and yet, I refused to give all my precious wounded pieces to a man who wouldn't give me any of himself in return.

The needle dipped into his skin as I spoke once more. "After several mishaps, Orion finally ended up on Crete where he became the companion to Artemis, the Greek goddess of the hunt." My throat bobbed. "Artemis had taken a vow of chastity but found herself falling for her companion. As time passed, she was tempted to break her vow to be with Orion."

I paused and took a breath, feeling like I'd forgotten about breathing over the last couple of minutes.

At this point, my hand was on autopilot. Compared to the kinds of tattoos I normally did, this one was the kind of design I could do blindfolded—a good thing because it felt like our story was woven into the threads of the myth I was telling.

"The god Apollo saw that his sister, Artemis, was on the verge of sacrificing something that couldn't be undone, so he tricked her into killing Orion. He bet that she couldn't hit a point so far out at sea, but Artemis was the goddess of the hunt, so of course she could."

"And that point was Orion," he surmised.

My chin dipped, and I tried to swallow but couldn't.

"Realizing she killed the man she loved, Artemis went to Zeus and begged him to immortalize Orion as a constellation, one that could be seen from any place on earth." I was on the last two stars as my story came to a close. "So, Orion sits on the celestial equator which makes it one of the most globally visible constellations."

I pulled the tattoo machine away from his chest, picking up the cloth I'd draped over his thigh and wiped the skin two more times.

"She turned him into a celestial tattoo."

I snapped my gaze up to his. "Talk about permanence," I tried to joke, but there was only a deep huskiness to my voice. My arm lowered, but instead of coming to my side it latched to his thigh, feeling the muscles ripple and harden instantly. "So now you're forever marked with a symbol of strength and courage."

His eyes swirled, the burnt edges of his irises tainting the familiar foggy green.

"I'm forever marked as a man who died so the woman he cared for wouldn't have to break her vow," he corrected me, but he wasn't talking about Artemis or Orion.

He was talking about himself and me. *He was talking about my vow.*

I shuddered.

My vow of secrecy. My vow of safety. I'd sacrificed him and what we had because I'd sworn not to reveal that my death would be fake.

Maybe he was right. Maybe that was why I'd given him this tattoo—why I'd chosen Orion; I'd been a guarded prize who'd fallen in love with the skilled protector sent to keep me company, and in the end, killed how he felt about me in order to save myself.

Without breaking his gaze, I set my tattoo machine on the rolling stand next to me and brought my fingers back to his chest—to my masterpiece. I traced over the skin. It was so hot and firm to the touch, the cells creating a hum of their own.

My breaths faltered as I traced along the hard set of his collarbone until it dipped in the center of his neck.

"Keira…" he warned me.

But I didn't listen.

He was my constellation. The thing I'd looked to no matter where I was because it was the memories of him that guided me—that brought me here. *That brought me back to him.*

The flat of my palm traveled up the side of his neck, following the hammering beat of his pulse until I reached the hard curve of his jaw.

I drew a trembling breath, swaying closer to him. My eyes found his, fell into their depths, and willingly drowned.

"I'm sorry, Archer."

For the past. And for the present. But mostly, because I couldn't stop myself from kissing him.

CHAPTER TEN

KEIRA

FOR A SECOND, HIS MOUTH REMAINED UNMOVING UNDER MINE like I was Medusa whose kiss had turned him to stone.

I whimpered, curling my hand around the back of his neck and pulling him tighter, my tongue sliding out along the hard seam of his lips.

And then he came to life.

He came down from where I'd pinned him to the heavens of my mind, the stars of his memory coalescing into the man in front of me. *My own concrete constellation.*

I might've made the first move, but it only took a moment for him to take control. One arm slung around my lower back, his grip settling on my ass and yanking me firmly against him. His other hand snaked up the back of my neck and into my hair, finding the tie that held it up and tugging it free.

Our tongues sparred in the heat of our mouths, two hunters vying for the same prize. *Artemis and Orion.* Every stroke and lick like a hot arrow sinking deep into the beast of desire.

"I shouldn't have come here," he growled hoarsely into my mouth even as he held me firm to his waist, the heat of his cock wedged against my hips. "I shouldn't have done any of this."

His regrets were no match for the desire that exploded between us. I pinched his tongue between my teeth and sucked until he punished me with a hard kiss. Seconds later, he drew back, both of us panting, filling the air with seductive smoke from the fire that caught inside us.

I moved my hand to his tattoo. "Shouldn't have let me tattoo you?" I curled my fingers into his skin.

"That too." His lips scattered rough kisses along my jaw and then down the column of my neck, biting and kissing a possessive path.

"You can use my machine and tattoo me," I offered huskily, turned on by the thought of him inking me.

His lips curled against my skin, the nip of his teeth chasing my flurried pulse. I shuddered under the magic of his mouth.

"I don't need a machine to mark you, Keira," he swore into my trembling skin.

I inhaled sharply. *Oh God.*

I just processed the meaning of his words when his mouth suctioned violently onto my neck, drawing blood to the surface of my skin.

"*Jesus, Archer,*" I panted as he sucked, each pull of his lips stoking the knot of fire in my core tighter and tighter. *Hotter and hotter.*

He gorged for several minutes and then finally let my skin pop free, drawing back to examine the masterpiece of his mouth. I stared at his eyes, imagining that I could see in them the raised purple hickey he'd given me. I bit my lip to keep from moaning when another rush of wet soaked my shorts.

Reverently, his hand slid from my hair to my neck, his lips curving into a pleased smile.

"My new tattoo?" I rasped, feeling the delicious heat of the hickey burrow into my skin.

Smoky green eyes flicked to mine. "One of them."

"One?" I gulped.

His fingers meandered to the curve of my shoulder and then along the edge of my collarbone, pausing in the same spot of his tattoo.

"Fifteen stars." He traced lower, reaching the top curve of my breast before his hand turned so it was the backs of his knuckles that dragged along my thin T-shirt. "Fifteen bruises."

I couldn't look away. It was as though there was an invisible string that tied my gaze to those long fingers. My breaths turned stunted, each inhale waiting on edge for the moment his next touch would send a bolt of pleasure through my veins.

"All over this perfect body that I've dreamed of for four fucking years," he went on hoarsely, torturing himself as much as he was torturing me.

He'd dreamed of me. All this time.

I wanted to cry. *I wanted to scream.* I wanted to climb on top of him and beg him to never let me go.

"Archer—" I broke off with a sharp cry as his knuckles slowly bumped over the peak of my nipple, sparks plummeting down between my thighs. Without thinking, my hips bowed forward, searching for pressure... for him... for friction to help ease the ache.

His mouth latched on another patch of skin at the base of my neck, repeating the hard pulling until I rocked against him in time with his firm sucks. It made me lose my mind, the way both my skin under his mouth and my sex tingled with the swell of blood and angry nerves.

I moaned when his hands made it to my waist, clamping possessively in the dip.

"I'm going to end on that sweet clit of yours," he swore, and my mouth dropped open, instantly going as dry as the Sahara. "I'm going to suck her so fucking hard your orgasm will brand you from the inside out. It will ink into your nerves a kind of pleasure that will never be erased—the kind of pleasure that will turn you to fucking stars."

My legs trembled, my muscles turning to jelly with want.

No one had ever touched me there. *Aside from myself and a vibrator.* I was still a virgin, and Archer knew that. The way he looked at me, I knew he did. *The way he knew me...* He knew it would be impossible for me to give myself to someone who didn't know me—the real me. The irony was, for my own safety, no one could know the real me.

No one except for him.

As soon as I reached for his shoulders to steady myself, Archer lifted me up, expertly adjusting himself as he manhandled me until I was the one sitting on the table and he stood between my legs, my feet curved around the back of his thighs.

His palms framed my waist, his long fingers almost touching where they splayed across my back and stomach. His eyes took mine, holding them with ferocious intensity as his hands slid higher.

Like a wildfire, his grip burned along my rib cage, his fingers sliding underneath my shirt until he filled his palms with my breasts.

"*Fuck,*" he swore and I arched into him.

His hands were massive—easily large enough to completely cover my whole breast with his grip. Long, strong fingers teased me until I was mush. A choked cry broke through my lips when he pulled his hands back, returning them to my waist and forcing me back.

Pinning my shirt up just below my breasts, he bent over me and pressed his mouth to the base of my ribs.

More hard sucks.

More blatant hickeys.

In this position, my sex was pressed directly along the rod of his cock, giving me a steel pole to grind against, but it wasn't enough. I moaned loudly, hoping he could read the sound that begged his mouth to go where I needed it most.

Minutes went by as he decorated my abdomen with tantric tattoos, the bruises of desire a bright purple against my pale skin. At some point, my head tipped back and my eyes grew hooded, my body clinging to the pleasure that built each time he sucked hard, only to be released in fragments as his mouth moved on.

"Archer, please," I begged shamelessly.

He paused, and I caught my breath. When I looked at him, his broad shoulders were wedged between my spread legs, his gaze locked on my core. I held the air deep in my lungs, milking every ounce of oxygen from it as he gently rubbed the backs of his knuckles along the seam of my shorts, pressing a little harder on the ball of my clit.

"Archer!" I bucked against him.

His eyes snapped to mine, murky with drunken desire.

I stared, enrapt, as he moved with skilled precision, hooking his fingers into my shorts and thong and removing them both from me in one swift motion, leaving me bare from the waist down. He embedded his shoulders back between my thighs. The skin around his collarbone turning red from where I'd marked him. *My own skin turning red and flushed, waiting for him to mark me.*

He turned his head against my inner thigh, inhaling like he wanted to drown in my scent. And then his mouth returned to its mission. He bit into the tender skin before suctioning his lips and drawing blood to the surface.

One more hickey on the most sensitive skin right next to my pussy.

I grew wetter knowing that was where he was heading— knowing that I'd soon feel that delicious suction where I wanted it most.

"I'm going to tattoo your little hungry clit with my teeth," he growled, taking another bite into my skin. "I'm going to suck you so hard my lips will be branded inside your pussy."

Oh god.

I couldn't even catch my breath before white spots burst in my vision as his fingers slid along my seam from entrance to clit and then pulled away coated in my wet like I was a tipped over jar of honey that he'd tried to catch the spill.

"Do it," I pleaded wantonly. *Shamelessly.*

My swollen pussy throbbed. My legs trembled where they framed the sides of his dark head. I'd never been this turned on. *I'd never let myself get this turned on.* Nothing was permanent in my life. Not safety. Not pain. Not pleasure. Both good and bad were luxuries that a nameless nomad couldn't afford.

Until now.

Until here.

Until him.

"This is so damn dangerous." His hot breath wafted over my slick sex, his mouth drawing closer.

"That's what we are," I told him. "What we've always been."

A dangerous attraction in a perilous world.

"Keira…" he groaned and I saw the turmoil in his eyes even as he lowered his head to my spread folds, fighting himself until the very last moment.

Because he couldn't fight this.

His eyes closed and those firm lips sealed over my throbbing clit.

I cried out, pleasure knifing so hotly through my body I bucked against his mouth.

Big hands clamped on my hips, pinning me to the table.

"You know the rules, Keira," he ground out. "No moving during a tattoo."

Fuck.

He punctuated his command with a hard suck on my clit, and it took everything I had to not move—not flinch against the hard sting of pleasure. And then his mouth was back, shackled to my sex while his tongue swirled and lashed over my most sensitive area until I was nothing but a sea of melted nerves.

My hands worked into his hair while my legs curved around his shoulders. Anything to bring me closer to the devastating lash of his tongue.

"You're so fucking wet," he rasped between deep, hard sucks.

Two fingers pushed inside me, stretching my clenching muscles. I languished back on the table, lacking any kind of defense against the pleasure raging over my body. He stroked me from the inside, pressing along the sensitive front wall of my pussy while his tongue licked over me on the outside. It felt like fire and ice spiraling together to create an impossible kind of pleasure.

"Fuck, Archer, I think I'm going to come," I admitted in broken gasps.

I was too torn apart by lust to care about embarrassment, and I wanted Archer too badly to pretend like I could hold off my orgasm after only a handful of minutes under the assault of his tongue.

"Oh, you definitely are," he promised roughly against my quivering sex, the gleam of his lips telling me how drenched I was.

Ever promising.

My eyes squeezed shut, my body tangling into a million knots all held together by the tip of his magical tongue as it twisted me higher and higher. The ends of his fingers notched into that sweet spot inside me and pinned me to the precipice of pleasure, but the firm tug of his lips I expected to send me over the edge never came. Instead, his tongue did something I couldn't describe. All I knew was it felt like a silken snake moving through my pussy—it slid and pushed, curved and pinned, and finally squeezed until I felt a sharp pinch of pain.

And then that pain exploded into bright, searing, *consuming* pleasure.

I screamed.

I screamed so loudly I expected Officer Diehl and the whole of Wisdom to be at my door in minutes to investigate the sound.

But I didn't care. I couldn't.

Pleasure ripped me apart at every seam of my cells, spiraling them up like shooting stars and pinning them to the night sky. I bucked and writhed, unable to stay still any longer as I orgasmed. But no matter how I moved, Archer's mouth never left me. His lips devoured me slowly through my climax, savoring every clench and shudder, lapping up every rush of release.

I wasn't sure how long it took until I was limp and panting on the table, entirely broken apart and sated, that I stared up, still seeing stars floating in my vision.

Oh my god.

Archer Reynolds had turned me into a constellation with the tip of his tongue.

I gulped.

"Fuck, Keira," he hummed low when he was done licking me clean.

My legs slid from his back as he rose up, towering over me like a god who'd finished with his feast. He drove one hand through his hair that I'd sufficiently tousled, the other moved to the front of his jeans, palming and adjusting his cock where it bulged.

I didn't know where the strength came from, but I sat up and hooked my ankles behind his knees so he couldn't move away.

"Archer..." I licked my lips, lifting my hand and placing it flat on his chest, my fingertips resting just at the edge of his tattoo. I wanted more. *I wanted everything.* "I want you."

I started to drag my hand down—down over the firm

muscles of his chest toward the ridges of his abs when his grip claimed my wrist and held it prisoner.

"No," he said raggedly.

The word pierced my chest like a flaming knife, and I couldn't breathe.

"What do you mean, no?" I didn't understand.

"I mean I can't fuck you."

My desire ignited into anger. "But you could tongue me to death?"

"Dammit, Keira." He brought my hand to his mouth, his teeth sinking into the fleshy part of my palm.

Apparently, I wasn't the only one who liked to create marks on people.

"I can't... I won't take it from you," he said, his voice pained. He pressed his lips to the skin his teeth had marked, the tenderness bleeding the anger from my chest.

"What? My... virginity?" My eyebrows lifted higher. "It's not a big—"

I didn't get a chance to finish.

"It's everything, Keira. If I fuck you, I want more than just the trust it takes for you to give me your body. I want you to trust me with it all," he explained through clenched teeth. "Your past. Your secrets. Your fears. Every fucking thing because that's the kind of man I am—the kind of man I've always been. I won't settle for parts of you, and that *is* a big fucking deal."

It was my choice whether I wanted to bare myself completely to him. To be entirely... vulnerable... in a way I'd protected myself against for so long. It was my choice to tie myself to the single piece of my past when the only dream I'd come here with was to finally make my own future.

"Archer..."

"If this is your shot at permanence, I won't be the exception," he rasped.

My mouth dried, fear taking hold of me like a hand around my throat.

"No, you just want to be the rule."

The rule of law. The rule of duty and responsibility. The rule of protection. *The rule that couldn't be broken.*

I wanted Archer, there was no question. But to give him everything... to let him in and risk losing him... I was more afraid of that than anything else in the world. So, I backed down and told myself it was the right move. Maybe what happened tonight was just leftover kindling from our past lives that needed to burn, and now that it had, we could both move on.

"So, what happens now?" I asked thickly, dragging my eyes from his tattoo to his face. "We forget about tonight?"

Those lips that destroyed me with pleasure now only brought pain when they firmed into a hard line, refusing to emit a response.

"If that's what you want."

Bitterness collected like a ball in my throat, hurt burning into my rib cage with every breath. It wasn't fair that he could pleasure me so expertly, demand everything, and then not even reach for me as I pulled away. Before I could stop myself, old hurts—loss, betrayal, and self-isolation for the sake of survival—reared their angry heads.

"I guess I can pretend like this never happened," I said with forced casualness and a shrug, disentangling myself from him and sliding off the table.

I collected my shorts and thong, quickly tugging them on under the icy burn of his stare.

"Well, you are good at that," he fired back with a growl, but I refused to shiver.

I spun and faced him. My gaze snagged on his tattoo, watching it rise and fall under the ragged movements of his chest.

"Except I marked you," I returned flippantly, folding my arms and noting the moment of satisfaction I felt when his eyes dropped to my breasts. "We can't pretend that doesn't exist, but I guess it's not that noticeable."

His eyes glittered as he stepped closer, holding my gaze as he collected his shirt and jacket into his white-knuckled grasp. When he spoke again, his voice was low and strained like a thread about to snap.

"This isn't the first indelible mark you've left on me, Keira," he swore roughly. "It's just the first one you've seen."

And with that parting shot, he released me and walked out of my tattoo parlor.

I cleaned up, made it home, and immediately crashed into bed without changing. My body felt like a barely held together blob of Jell-O just before exhaustion claimed me. And there, I found Archer again behind my tired eyes and in the longing depths of my dreams.

But it was better this way—better for him to remain a constellation in my life, made of stars that would never dim or disappear or be put in danger.

Maybe that was why Artemis begged to have Orion knitted into the fabric of the night—because she couldn't have him but neither could she lose him.

CHAPTER ELEVEN

ARCHER

I ALWAYS THOUGHT OF MYSELF AS A RESILIENT PERSON. ABLE to stay strong when my dad died. Able to stay strong when my family needed me. Even able to stay strong when I'd moved back here in the wake of Keira's presumed death. But I was wholly unprepared for the strength required to stay away from Keira once I'd had a taste of her.

For two days, I'd thrown myself into every possible thing that could've consumed my time. Client work. Preparing contracts and proposals. Reviewing applications for the personal assistant position I'd put up an ad for. Phone consults. For the business, I was sure it looked good that the head of the company was willing to get on the phone with a client on a weekend, but it was nothing more than a self-preservation tactic.

A desperate attempt to breathe when my body drowned with wanting her.

Wanting those full lips under mine. Wanting her velvet skin filling my grasp. Wanting her sweetness back on my tongue. *And the feel of her around my cock.*

Fuck.

I adjusted myself, hard as stone in a second recalling how

close I'd been to burying myself inside her pussy—something I'd dreamed about more times than I was ready to admit.

I didn't know what it was. It certainly was more than physical attraction. More than the chemical response of my brain to her perfect tits and the curve of her ass. If it was just that, I wouldn't have stopped myself Friday night.

But I didn't just want her body, even if it was something she hadn't given to anyone else before... *especially because it was something she hadn't given to anyone else before.*

I wanted her truths. I wanted to know every dark corner of her past. Every bad thing she'd seen. Every hurt she'd experienced starting over. I wanted to know each and every way I could make her smile because that was a feat in itself—bringing lightness to a woman who'd endured more darkness in the first twenty-three years of her life than anyone should have to. I wanted to learn the exact point of her blush that made the freckles sprinkled across her cheeks disappear.

I wanted everything. But obviously, she still didn't trust me enough to give me that. It was understandable. That didn't change how it ripped me apart inside.

Again.

My phone buzzed in my pocket. A text from Gunner to let me know he was on his way back with Gwen and her husband, Chevy, from the airport. Mom didn't know Gwen was flying home; it was our birthday surprise for her.

I tapped back my reply and then set my phone on the desk, pinching the bridge of my nose like it could refocus me to the only thing I should be thinking about right now.

Mom's birthday party.

It started in just over an hour at the Worth Hotel downtown—the only really nice spot in Wisdom. Owned by the Worth family for generations, it attracted both the overflow elite from Jackson Hole and those looking for a quieter place to stay rather than at the busy ski town.

I wondered if Keira was going to still come.

"Fuck."

My head snapped up, a knock on the door surprising me. A quick glance out the window showed Hunter's dark blue Cherokee in the parking lot.

"Yeah?" I called.

Hunter appeared in my office, sporting a blazer over his button-down shirt and jeans.

"You clean up nice," I remarked.

Sometimes, it was hard to remember that Hunt was only a year younger than me. I guessed that time and circumstance changes people differently. Dad died, and I'd become the head of the family, and that small gap of only a year felt like it widened by bounds.

"Well, we don't get to dress up too much around here." He shrugged and then approached my desk. "You alright?"

"Yeah. Perfect," I replied, even as I winced from the painful pressure in my dick.

He didn't believe me. I read his expression as easily as I read my own. In fact, when we were growing up, there were plenty of people who thought that Hunt and I were twins.

"You planning on changing for the party?"

I looked down at my jeans and dark tee and then back to him. "There something wrong with what I'm wearing?"

"Well, the perpetual scowl you've had on for two days is really starting to stink," he deadpanned, slowly strolling up to my desk.

"I haven't had a scowl on for two days," I grumbled, knowing it was a lie.

"We can either call it a scowl or we can call it the blue-ball glower which is what Gunner suggested."

I rolled my eyes. Scowl it was.

"So, what's going on with you and Keira?" he asked, reading right through my *scowl* to the reason for it.

Hunt and I were similar in that way, too. Perceptive

enough to read between the lines of the slightest and vaguest tells. But who was I kidding? My scowl was nowhere near slight or vague.

"Nothing."

"Don't give me that shit, Arch. It's me. You can tell me." He set the folders he was holding down on my desk and grabbed the back of the chair in front of him.

His demand surprised me. Everyone joked that Hunter was my shadow. If I took two steps forward, so did he. I enrolled in the police academy, and so did he. Between the two of us, we formed the solid and responsible foundation for RPG. But when it came down to it, there was a point where my emotions could take hold—usually anger—and that was when Hunt would break his second-in-command mold and step in.

And now was that time.

"It's complicated."

Understatement of the decade.

"No shit. You thought she died. Then she was alive. Then you tried to take over her life like it was still under your protection. And, shocker, that didn't go over well."

That was only the start of it.

It wasn't until Keira walked back into my life that I realized my obsession over what happened in Boston hadn't been because I'd failed to keep her safe, it was because I'd failed to act on what I wanted. Now that she was here, I could act—would act. *If only she trusted me.*

"There's nothing between us, Hunt, because she doesn't trust me—she doesn't want me enough to trust me," I told him, sinking back in my chair with a rough laugh. "Me. The man who swore to protect her."

Christ, at the end, I'd even risked her hating me in order to do my duty and keep her safe.

And still she pushed me away.

"So?"

"What do you mean 'so?'" I folded my arms.

"I mean that you don't just protect people. You step in and take responsibility and unilaterally make decisions for someone's safety without regard for their input—"

"But—"

"And in most cases, it's fine—more than fine. It's your job. You've made it your job from the moment Dad died."

I tensed. I wasn't prepared for him to bring up Dad. I wasn't prepared to see him as my responsible and understanding thirty-three-year-old brother instead of the younger brother I was hell-bent on protecting.

"And yeah, it was your job... duty... in Boston. But not here." He sighed deep. "She didn't come here expecting you or your protection, but you keep shoving it down her throat."

Wasn't the only thing I wanted to shove down her throat.

"I'm not... doing that."

He reached for the folders he set on my desk and slid out the bottom one, letting it fall on top. "Detailed information about the rest of her names on her client list for this coming week."

Dammit.

My teeth locked together.

"She could still be in danger."

"And she could not be," he returned. "The post office thing was random, I'll admit, but based on everything you've told us, wouldn't the mob just kill her if they'd found her?"

I hated this recurring point. *Facts could be fucking annoying.*

"All I'm saying, Arch, is that you're dealing with someone who's had very little say in her own safety for her entire life. I know you want to swoop in and be a knight in scowling armor, but if she's here to make a life, don't you think she gets a say in that?"

Trapped.

Her interpretation of the Boston Massacre came back to

me from four years ago when she'd asked how the colonists felt going up against the British soldiers.

'*They felt trapped... the very people who were supposed to be protecting them kept failing them. They were trapped by the very system that was supposed to fight for them.*'

And here I was. The one man who knew more than most about what she'd gone through to get this second chance—hell, to get a first chance at living her own life—and instead of helping her fight for that, I kept trying to put her back into the same cage.

"I'm starting to wonder whose side you're on." I grabbed that top folder and pulled it in front of me.

I overstepped with Keira. I knew I overstepped which was why Friday night had happened. It was just pretty damn hard to sever the instinct I'd been left with that day in Boston—that she was mine to protect.

Maybe I was going about this all wrong.

Maybe I'd thought that protecting her was what made me deserving of her trust. It was the case for most people. But Keira wasn't most people. Keira had been threatened while she was supposed to be safe and protected. Life had taught her that protection spelled imminent danger; it was why she and her dad had gone the route that they had.

I thought protection was the easiest way to get what I wanted—to get her.

It wasn't.

"Your side," he said firmly. "Which is why I'm telling you that Mom's party is another opportunity to build that trust since she will be there."

I kept my eyes trained on the bland manila paper.

"Zoey told me earlier that they'd both be there," he revealed with a small smile.

My gut tensed.

It was these moments when all the responsibilities I'd taken on since Dad died were worth it—to see my younger siblings be able to smile with ease and without worry. I'd gladly sacrifice that luxury for myself in order for them to have it.

However, this specific one, I needed to talk to him about.

"Speaking of…" I reached over and palmed a different stack of papers that I'd set aside for the day, dragging them back in front of me. "Are you going to ask her out?"

Hunter's head cocked. "Don't you have enough of your own relationship troubles to worry about?"

I shook my head. "I wish that were the case." I thumbed Zoey's resume off the top of the stack and held it in front of me, scanning down the list of credentials that brought her to the top of the group. "She applied for the assistant position," I told him.

Before I could even extend my hand, he reached over and took the sheet from me like he needed to read it to believe it for himself.

"She didn't mention…"

I heard the low rumble of hurt in his voice.

"I'm sure that's because she didn't want any special treatment from the guy who keeps flirting with her." Zoey Richards struck me as the kind of woman that didn't want any kind of preferential treatment, not just in a job application but in life.

"Good point."

"I don't need the details, but I'm not sure hiring someone that you're seeing is a good idea. Or hiring someone that you want to date is a good idea."

His mirrored green gaze met mine. "I would never hold her employment over her just for a date."

"I know that, Hunt." I took the paper back from him. "I just don't want to make this complicated for anyone."

His throat bobbed. "Is she a good candidate?"

"The only one." I sighed heavily. "Unless Gunner really pisses me off and then I'll hire Lily White."

"Jesus, she applied?"

I nodded.

Gunner made sure to keep his romantic flings to either jobs that took him out of town or with tourists that were passing through, this way there were no mistaken expectations. Hunter was like that, too, but he was much more discreet in his romantic pursuits (before Zoey moved here, at least.) Gunner, on the other hand, had learned that lesson the hard way with Lily White.

According to Gunner, they'd spent a weekend together over a year ago, but she still kept hounding him, believing that deep down, he really wanted to be with her.

It wasn't the truth. She was pretty but vapid and a little conniving. She was also a local; her family-owned White's Department Store over in Jackson, but they lived in town. So, not only was Gunner constantly running into clothing mishaps from online ordering because he refused to go to the only decent clothing store within a seventy-mile radius, but he still had to try to avoid her at the local spots in town on a weekly basis.

"Alright, well, if Zoey's the best candidate then she's the right choice," he went on matter-of-factly. "I don't think you should use my feelings for her as prejudice either way."

I watched my brother as he put aside his personal wants for the sake of duty and responsibility to our business. He shouldn't have to, but I didn't have much ground to stand on to argue when it's all I'd ever done. I was just as familiar with sacrifice as Keira was familiar with solitude.

"What else did you bring me?" I asked, changing the subject.

He nodded to the other folders that had been on top of Keira's. "Top two are background information and risk analysis from Ranger on Gunner's next job."

"Job?" I arched an eyebrow and chuckled.

The great-great-great-grandsons of Jeremiah Worth were

coming up to Jackson next month and they always hired us for personal security—specifically Gunner. They were all around the same age and had similar interests. Sometimes, it felt like Gunner was getting paid to have a weekend with the guys, but what could I say? They were paying for it.

"Just following protocol." He grinned.

"Yeah." I gave a cursory flip through the paperwork and then set them on the other stack of case folders on my desk.

We were booked solid for months. Hunter and Gunner primarily taking any cases that were outside of the Jackson area while I tried to handle the local ones, although there were always exceptions.

"Alright, I'll take a look." Without thinking, I reached up and itched just under my collarbone, yanking my hand away instantly when I scratched my tattoo. "Shit," I muttered, knowing that scratching could ruin the tattoo.

"You okay?" Hunter looked at me curiously.

"Yeah, fine," I brushed him off.

It didn't hurt. Not really. They were only a handful of tiny fucking dots. But it was just enough to give my chest a constant annoying itch for the last two days.

A literal itch I couldn't scratch—just like the woman who'd given them to me.

"You want to ride over together?" he offered, checking his watch which prompted me to check my own.

I paused for a second. It would probably be a good idea. At least, I could talk to Hunt about work and not be left alone to think about Keira.

"Yeah, that might be—" I broke off, my cell buzzing violently on the desk. *Why was Diehl calling me?* "Hold on," I told Hunt and answered the call, "Hey, Diehl. What's up?"

My brother waited, as curious as I was to know why the chief of police was calling.

"Hey, Archer, sorry to call you today. I know Lydia's party is starting soon."

In thirty minutes, to be exact.

"Not a problem. What's going on?"

There was a long exhale on the other end of the line—an exhale I recognized from my time spent in Boston. We didn't deal with a whole lot of unnatural death here in Wisdom, but in a city like Boston, that exhale read like a kind of Morse Code.

"I need you to come out to Walt's place."

"Shit." I stood and reached for my thick flannel jacket draped over the back of my chair. "Alcohol?" I asked though I knew in my gut the answer.

"No." The police chief paused. *"It's bad Archer. I don't know if he'll make it. Not something I've seen the likes of before."* His voice ended with a tremor.

"Shit, I'll be right there," I told him and hung up. "You're going to have to go to Mom's party without me. I'll get there when I can."

He didn't move. "What happened?"

"Walt's been attacked. Diehl didn't elaborate." I didn't want to say any more until I was looking at the crime scene.

Hunter's eyes bugged wide. "I'll come with—"

"No," I interrupted him with a commanding tone—one I knew Hunt was hard-wired to obey. "I can handle this. I need you to go to the party."

His chin clipped down. "Alright. Anything else I can do?"

I shoved my phone in my pocket and felt my jaw tightened down. I didn't want to say it, but my gut told me I had to. "Make sure Keira is there. And stays there."

"Fuck." My brother exhaled.

I couldn't agree with him more.

CHAPTER TWELVE

KEIRA

I SHOULDN'T HAVE COME.

But how could I resist?

Laughter floated through the historic hotel, the lobby filled with the unfettered joy of a town of people who banded together, forming a kind of family whose bond was as strong and in some ways, stronger than blood.

The plaque next to the double front doors of the Worth Hotel indicated it was chosen as one of the top Small Historic Hotels in the US, and once inside, I could believe it.

The subdued exterior opened up into a luxurious lobby that oozed old-world class with its wood-paneled walls and patterned velour furniture. But it was the fragrance that got me. Evergreen and cinnamon. As though this was the cozy corner of the world where old Saint Nick chose to relax for the other three-hundred-and-sixty-four days of the year.

Up the center stairs led to the mezzanine where the party was held. Balloons and streamers wound color through the space, and the 'happy birthday' banner hung hilariously from a large moose-head bust above the large stone hearth. On one side of the room stretched a table filled with food, cookies, and most importantly, birthday cake.

I might've been drawn to the beauty of Archer's descriptions of Wyoming, but after Dad died, it was something deeper that drew me here. The idea he'd left me with of his family and community seemed like the only thing strong enough—safe enough for my roots to grow. And seeing the Reynolds family together—Lydia Reynolds' ageless grace, the three boys, and the youngest daughter, Gwen, whose movie star smile matched her mom's—it made my chest ache in a way it hadn't before. Partially for Dad, for the missing half of our dynamic duo. But also for something more.

For Archer. The man who was mysteriously absent from his own mother's birthday party.

I couldn't believe he'd skip out on the party just because I was coming; that didn't sound like him. But I couldn't bring myself to ask where he was.

'If this is your shot at permanence, I won't be the exception.'

My mind still reeled from what happened at the tattoo shop, my body still trying to frantically piece back together all the fragments he'd fractured me into, but it was my heart that suffered the brunt of it.

I moved to Wisdom to start over. To settle down. To build roots that had been ripped up and replanted so many times, I wasn't sure they even knew how to grow deep any longer. But around Archer... they didn't simply want to grow, they wanted to unravel and entwine and tether myself to him in ways that nothing could separate.

"Birthday punch?"

I looked up as Zoey handed me a glass of deep red liquid. I took it with a smile of thanks and drank a sip. *Fruity and sweet.*

"I feel like all of Wisdom is crammed into this hotel right now," I mused, looking around the room.

"All of Wisdom *is* crammed into this hotel right now," she agreed.

All except a single man with an Orion tattoo.

"Hello there, Miss Keira."

"Hey, Jerry." I smiled at the owner of the hardware store. It was hard not to know the man I'd seen almost every day for the last month, always needing something or other for the shop to come together.

"You must be all settled in and ready for business. I haven't seen you in a couple days."

"My soft opening was on Friday, but I'll be open officially at the start of next week." A thrill ran through me. *Open for business. Open for life.*

"Oh, wonderful. Congratulations." He then turned to Zoey with a twinkle in his eye. "I've got another one of Sydney's books for you to borrow, if you want to stop by this coming week."

"Of course." She nodded, her cheeks coloring slightly as he patted her shoulder and moved on to catch up with his wife.

"You and Jerry should start a club," I told her. "Romance in Wisdom… or something like that."

Zoey had come with me to the hardware store to pick out paint for my shop, and when I went to pay, I was surprised to find my new friend and the older, rough-around-the-edges store owner exchanging romance novels like they were illegal drugs.

"Maybe." She flushed and her eyes slipped back across the room.

I didn't have to check and see what—*who* she was looking at.

"You know, instead of curling up with a romance novel, you could spend the night with a real-life hunk," I moved close to her ear and murmured, laughing at her subsequent horrified expression.

"No." She shook her head. "We're just friends."

I rolled my eyes. "That's like putting a car in park and then saying it doesn't drive." I nudged her and slid my eyes back to Hunter. "Tell me your reservations again."

"Well, I just applied for a job at Reynolds Protective, so that's at the top of the list."

I spun to her. "Really? You didn't tell me." Zoey shifted her weight. "I'm sorry, I didn't mean that as an accusation."

"I know. It was a spur of the moment kind of thing. I still haven't decided if I regret it or not." She took a drink of her punch. "My plan was never to stay long-term at the post office, but after what happened..."

"It's still worrying you."

"I know it has nothing to do with me or what I went through, but I just don't feel safe there anymore." Her eyes turned glassy. "And what safer place could there be to work than RPG?"

I couldn't argue with her there. Technically speaking.

"So, you'll be okay seeing Hunter on a daily basis?"

She took another drink. Several gulps this time. "Of course. I'll be working at the office; they'll be out... bodyguarding. It'll be fine."

I wasn't convinced, and from the sounds of it, neither was she.

I understood why my friend kept the charming, second-oldest Reynolds son at arm's length, but I wasn't sure she realized how much harder that would be when a constant, close proximity was involved.

I'd learned that the hard way.

Our conversation ended when Tara and Jamie came over, insisting we try some cookies they'd made for the party because they were going to start selling them in the bakery case at Brilliant Brews. A few minutes later, Hunter appeared and asked to speak to Zoey, and the other girls quickly took the opportunity to excuse themselves and bustle over to the mayor to see if she was enjoying her birthday treats.

I exhaled slowly and took a step back against the wall. Laughter and conversation enveloped the space. The warm lights and bright party decorations brought a vibrancy to the already lively event. I hadn't met Mayor Lydia Reynolds yet, and I wasn't sure I was going to. But judging by the crowd of smiling faces always surrounding her, she was as well-loved in this town as her sons were.

My gaze dipped around the room once more. Archer still wasn't here.

"Keira."

I turned. Gunner appeared by my side with a tipped smile on his face. I was sure it had an effect on some women, but not on me. Sadly, that smile did nothing compared to his oldest brother's heated scowl.

"Gunner." I arched an eyebrow.

"Glad to see I won our deal," he said confidently.

"Did you just come over here to gloat?" I arched an eyebrow and ran my gaze over him; it caught on his shoes. "Um... do you know you are wearing one black and one brown shoe?"

"Dammit, don't keep looking," he hissed and turned, leveling his shoulders with mine so we both stood with our backs to the wall, observing the crowd.

"Am I missing something?"

"No. I'm the one missing a pair of matching shoes, but I was hoping no one would notice. I mean black... brown... they're both dark colors. Can you really tell?" he grumbled.

It wasn't that noticeable, especially given the setting of the party, but I enjoyed giving him a little bit of a hard time.

"Do you really want me to answer that?" I bit back a smile. "How do you not have matching shoes? Socks, I can understand. But—"

"Because," he bit out. "Because I ordered these from a discount shoe website and when they got here today, I realized they fucking sent me two different colors."

My mouth formed a small 'o' while I tried not to laugh. "There isn't a place to get shoes around here?"

"In Jackson." He flashed a big, fake smile as though we

were talking about something not as serious as mismatched shoes. "But I can't go there."

I lifted my chin, pushing my lips out in a silent request for more information.

"I have a rule. Don't mix pleasure with clients or local community."

I was starting to get the picture. "And you have that rule…"

"Only because I made the mistake once."

"Of course." I hummed but couldn't stop my shoulders from jostling with a restrained laugh. "And now you have to wear mismatched shoes."

"Just until I can return them," he said, holding a straight face for a second before laughing. "So, what are you doing hiding over here?"

"I'm not hiding," I bristled. "Hunter came over and stole Zoey away. Tara and Jamie went to see your mom. I was just taking a minute to… observe the crowd."

"The crowd."

"Yes." My chin bobbed.

"Minus Archer."

My shoulders slumped. "Minus Archer."

He waited a second before saying, "Hunt told me Chief Diehl called Arch right when they were about to leave. I guess something happened—" Before he could finish telling me, he was interrupted.

"Gunner, you said you'd wait for me," the tall brunette in the silver sequin dress scolded, walking up to her brother and giving him a playful smack on his arm before turning her attention to me.

"Hi, I'm Gwen," she introduced herself warmly and then hugged me like this wasn't our first meeting. "It's so nice to meet you."

"Nice to meet you, too." I awkwardly hugged her back.

I observed up close the youngest Reynolds sibling. She had

the kind of thick, dark hair that reminded me of the dyed hairstyle I'd had in Boston. Her hazel eyes had flecks of green like her brothers, a trait I guessed they got from their father since Mayor Reynolds had brown eyes. Her smile twinned with her mother and Gunner's, and she had a similar kind of oozing warmth as though someone spilled sunshine all over her that couldn't help but draw you in.

And it certainly didn't let her husband wander far.

"And this is my husband, Chevy, and our dog, Oscar." She pointed to the small furry head of the Pomeranian peeking out from the doggy backpack Chevy was wearing. "He's an old guy and will get way too excited with this many people around," she explained, adding with a wince, "And probably trampled."

Together, they were one of the most beautiful couples I'd ever seen. Gwen's husband was broad and handsome, his shoulder muscles straining against the straps of the backpack. It was strange to see such a big man wearing a doggy backpack, but the way he looked at Gwen explained it all; he'd do anything for her, and she loved her dog.

"You know, Chevy, seeing you with the backpack in person is a gift for everyone here tonight," Gunner joked, and Chevy flipped him the bird.

We all laughed, and an unfamiliar lightness spread through my chest.

Gwen leaned closer to me like we were the oldest of friends and explained, "I sent my family a photo of Chevy wearing the backpack when he first bought it for Oscar. So, this is a real treat." She placed her hand on her husband's large arm while she spoke, glancing at him lovingly.

Chevy took it in stride. "And have you reached the point where you have no matching shoes left, Gun, because all the mates have been thrown at your head?"

"Shit. Does everyone know?" Gunner folded his arms.

"Well, we only noticed because Ranger noticed, but then

Mom told Ranger not to say anything, so I guess she really was the first to see," Gwen paused and pretended to think for a second. "Yeah, I'd say everyone knows."

We all laughed, including Gunner, so it was obvious he didn't take the fact too seriously. Truthfully, I wondered if there was anything—besides family and his job—that Gunner took seriously.

"Anyway, Keira, I absolutely love your hair. That red is just gorgeous, isn't it Chevy?" Gwen gushed and looked to her husband.

I flushed and thanked her softly, remembering how good it felt when the dark dye from Boston had finally begun to fade. After years of having every hair color under the sun, I swore that once I got my natural color back, I'd never dye it again.

Chevy agreed with only a nod. Gorgeous hair or not, the man couldn't take his eyes off his wife for longer than a few seconds. "I'm going to take Oscar outside for a few minutes to stretch his legs," he murmured and excused himself.

I smiled to myself, seeing a tough guy who was clearly smitten with the small ball of fluff.

"Hey, Gunner, I think Mom is waving for you to help her cut the cake." Gwen looked at her brother.

He frowned. "I don't see—" He broke off with a stifled *oomph* and I caught the retreat of Gwen's elbow. "Yup, I see it now. Ranger looks like he's giving everyone a lesson on pi and radius and diameters. So, I'm going to go handle that before the lesson in advanced geometry kills the party and the cake." He grinned at me. "We'll talk later."

I bit my lip watching him walk toward the cake table where the mayor stood with a few friends and her youngest son who pointed and made hand motions that confirmed he was explaining the best way to cut it. Still, I didn't want Gunner to go just yet. I wanted to know more about why Archer wasn't here and what crime had been committed.

"So, what do you think?" Gwen asked, taking her brother's place by my side.

I shoved my hands into my pockets. "About the party? It's great. The food is great. It's great to see so many people come out to celebrate with her."

And it would be great if you would stop saying great.

"Well, yeah. I mean, that's Mom. When Dad died, the whole town kind of jumped in to support her and us, so they always like to have a big birthday party for her," Gwen explained, sliding her glance from her mom to me. "But I was talking about Archer."

I went to swallow and choked. *Subtle.*

"Oh." I licked my lips and went to take another sip of my punch but realized the glass was empty. "He's very… respected and determined and cautious."

Archer and I were a murky topic, and I wasn't about to dip my toes into the deep end to try and explain it to his sister whom I'd just met.

"So… overbearing, protective, and stubborn?"

I looked over and met her gaze and saw her cheeky grin. "Maybe those things, too."

We both chuckled, and she then proceeded to tell me how he'd originally approached Chevy when he found out they were seeing each other. By the time she was finished, I had tears rolling down my face and my cheeks hurt from laughing.

"I don't want you to think I know a lot about what's going on because I don't, but"—she held up a finger—"I do know that my oldest brother who called me a few weeks ago asking for my help."

"Oh?" I ducked my head.

"Spoiler alert: Archer decided to shoulder the weight of too much responsibility when Dad died, so for him to ask one of us for help… well, let's just say I walked over to the window to make sure that pigs weren't flying."

I laughed softly.

"It's obvious that my brother cares about you in a way I haven't seen from him before," she confessed, tipping her body to face me and resting her shoulder on the wall. "It was the first time I've ever heard him uncertain about something."

I felt a little woozy. Like my universe tilted a little further toward the man it wanted at its center.

"I don't think Archer is uncertain about anything," I murmured. "Especially involving me."

He was certain that I was in danger. He was certain that the mob and my clients were after me. And he was *definitely* certain that he needed to build me up the other night and then walk away when I didn't bend.

All or nothing had been his demand.

"I know he can be… trying," she admitted. "But he has a good heart."

"I think so, too," I said with a voice that wasn't much above a whisper.

"If there's one thing that he and I share, it's that we both run from failure. Especially when someone else gets hurt. It's like we don't know how to not blame ourselves." She sighed. "As a nurse, it took me a long time to accept that there would be times where I could give everything—do everything right—and it still wouldn't be enough to save someone."

The sudden depth of the conversation turned my breathing shallow.

"I've made my peace with that. Archer still struggles," she said with a low voice. "It's why he's back here."

My eyes snapped to her.

What I wanted to say next was drowned out by the Happy Birthday song booming through the room. Instantly, I was wrapped back into the lights and joy of the party, watching the candles on cake flicker expectantly.

The song ended and Archer's mom blew out her candles to loud cheers. I clapped along with everyone else as the cake was sliced, my eyes searching for Hunter.

I excused myself from Gwen to go in search of Hunter. I needed to know the reason why Archer wasn't here.

"Keira?"

I looked over my shoulder. Lydia Reynolds stood there with that wide smile and her hand extended with a plate.

"Hi, I'm Lydia." She beamed. "I've been looking forward to meeting you all night."

Meeting me? I gulped.

"I... umm... it's a pleasure to meet you too, Mrs. Reynolds—Mayor Reynold—"

"Lydia," she corrected me with a laugh.

"Lydia," I murmured and dipped my chin.

Lydia Reynolds was a woman who'd aged gracefully. She had to be approaching sixty, but the fullness in her cheeks and the light in her eyes when she smiled gave her a youthful appearance that no amount of years could dim.

"Would you like some cake?"

The fruit-filled vanilla cake looked absolutely delicious and my mouth watered. I wanted to talk to Archer's mom, but I also wanted to talk to Hunter and find out what had detained his older brother; Gunner's brief admission gnawed at my stomach.

"Sure." I took the plate and smiled. Maybe she could tell me where Archer was.

"I know you've already been in town several weeks, but I wanted to officially welcome you to Wisdom," she said graciously. "And congratulate you on your new business."

"Thank you." I shoved a bite of cake in my mouth.

"When do you open? I'd love to stop by."

"Next week." I covered my mouth so I didn't look like a slob.

"Wonderful." Her smile widened. "I can pop in and schedule an appointment for a tattoo."

I choked on the remains of my bite of cake. "For... yourself?"

It wasn't that I hadn't done tattoos on older people, but I was just surprised that the mayor of Wisdom was asking for one.

"Of course." She chuckled. "Just don't tell my sons. Especially Gunner." She shook her head, eyeing her middle child lovingly. "He wanted to get matching tattoos a few years ago, and I had to turn him down because the design he suggested was just so ridiculous. More than mismatched shoes."

I covered my mouth to stifle my laugh.

"He's my wild one, but so easily takes everything in stride." She sighed. "My oldest son on the other hand takes things hard."

I hummed, afraid to agree out loud.

She stepped closer to shield us from the rest of the group. "Do you know why he moved to Boston?"

"For the accent?" I joked, and she laughed.

"Do you have a minute? I'd love to show you the downstairs lobby and give you a little history of Wisdom," she said, her expression hinting that it wasn't the hotel's history she was going to share.

As soon as I nodded, she linked her arm through mine.

It took us a couple of minutes to make it to the stairwell since she was stopped by locals along the way, making sure to introduce me and tell everyone about my imminent business opening. The way she talked about me made my chest burn— the air of pride and warmth of compassion. It reminded me of when Dad went on to his nurses about my work.

Finally, we reached the stairs and the music and conversation faded behind us.

"My husband was the chief of police for Wisdom," she began, taking each step slow. "He passed away from a heart attack when Archer was only fifteen."

"I'm sorry," I murmured.

"Archer took on too much. I tried to stop it from

165

happening, but my oldest has always been stubborn like his father. As soon as he knows what needs to be done, he does it." She squeezed my arm, and we reached the base of the stairs. "I suspect you already know that."

"A little," I murmured, savoring the feeling like I was being shown behind the armor of my very own knight.

Lydia led us down a hallway of old framed photographs of the town and its generational residents.

"He always knew he wanted to be a policeman like his dad. So, when Archer finished the police academy, he came back to Wisdom and joined the local police force." She paused in front of one frame, and I recognized the six of them immediately. "The day he was sworn in."

I bit my lip, unable to stop myself from focusing on Archer. His face so stoic compared to the excitement on his siblings' faces.

"As I'm sure you've seen, our local policemen mostly deal with bar brawls, ranch disputes, and the occasional runaway cow," she said, making me laugh. "However, about four months after he joined the three-man force, a serial killer who'd been living in the area stopped in our small town and chose his next victim."

I shuddered, a chill blazing down my spine with the ferocity of an arctic wind.

I watched her reach up and fold down the front of her collar for a second, allowing me to see the thick scarring around her neck. I couldn't help the way my mouth dropped a little. I'd learned a little bit about torture and wounds and wound healing over time. My dad had a ton of scars earned from carrying out the mob's business, so with just one look, I knew instantly that Lydia Reynolds almost lost her life because of that wound.

"You," I breathed out the word.

It was rare to come across a serial killer in person, although I had a feeling Ranger would be able to give me an exact statistic. Technically, I guessed that maybe even Dad might fall under the classification, but not because he had a need to kill; it was just his job. But to come across a surviving victim of a serial killer... I had a feeling that statistic was even rarer.

"I don't remember much about what happened, only the aftermath." She pressed her collar back in place. "The FBI— Archer's friend, Roman—got there in time to save me, but Archer could never let go that he hadn't. It wasn't his fault, but he couldn't see it that way. In his eyes, his failure was almost fatal for me. So, he took a job in Boston. He said he wanted more experience dealing with harsher crimes, but I could see in his eyes that it was punishment for not being good enough."

I didn't know what to say. I guess I always just assumed Archer ended up in Boston because what kid doesn't want to leave his middle-of-nowhere hometown? But now that I thought about it, the way he spoke of this place never indicated that he was glad to leave.

After talking to Gwen, and now this, my heart ached for the boy who thought he had to protect the world and then punished himself simply because he'd never be able to stop every evil.

"I... didn't know," I said thickly. It was all I had.

Lydia faced me and took both my hands in hers, squeezing them gently. My gaze dropped to our linked hands and then snapped back up where it was pinned by hers.

"That was why he moved to Boston," she repeated in a soft, sad voice. "Because he thought he failed."

I was missing something—I knew I was. Air slipped like spilled milk from my lungs, and my heart lingered between beats like it didn't want to move forward until my brain found the piece it was missing.

And then with emotional and hopeful eyes, she handed it to me.

"And that's why, four years ago, he moved back home."

Oh god.

My stomach plummeted to the floor, the final plaque of Archer's armor falling.

It was me.

It was all because of me.

"KEIRA!"

I jumped, the thunderous boom breaking my trance. Spinning on my heel, I faced the man we'd been talking about, his handsome face having a different kind of definition in this new light.

"Archer." Lydia stepped forward, concern clouding her face. "What is it? What happened?"

Every hard line of this man was under strain as he came over to us.

"Hunter said something happened with Walt…"

Walt? From the post office?

"He's in the hospital."

I froze.

"What?" Lydia gasped, and Archer immediately grabbed her shoulder when she swayed. "How? Was it the alcohol?"

The muscle in his jaw vibrated. "No, he was attacked."

"Oh, my lord." She pressed her hands to her cheeks, her eyes welling with tears. "I've known Walt since… before you were born."

"I'm sorry, Mom—"

"No, no. Don't be sorry." She nodded. "Just tell me, do you have any idea who did this?"

The shake of his head was quick, but the way he looked at me when he did it lingered much longer.

It couldn't have to do with me. *How could it?*

"Not yet," he added gruffly. "Diehl went with him over to the hospital in Jackson."

"Alright, well I should go, too—"

"Mom—"

"Don't mom me." Her tone hardened and she wiped her tears. Suddenly, I saw the woman who'd risen up and raised five children in the wake of her husband's death and then became mayor of this town. "That man changed his mail route in order to walk you boys home from school each day, so I wouldn't have to leave work or worry. I need to be there. I'm the only family he has."

We both knew she wasn't really his blood. Based on what I knew of Walt, he didn't have any living relatives, and that meant that Lydia was his family in the only way that mattered.

"Take Hunter with you," Archer said in a way that left no room for question. *Not surprising.*

She acquiesced with a nod and then walked quickly back toward the stairwell.

"Keira…"

I shivered, all of that intense, adrenaline-filled focus was now on me.

"Is this because of me?" I asked with a small voice, feeling myself tumble back to the girl I'd been when I first met him. Vulnerable and alone.

"I don't know, but I need…" He exhaled. "I need to talk to you."

CHAPTER THIRTEEN

KEIRA

I DIDN'T ASK QUESTIONS BEFORE CLIMBING INTO ARCHER'S truck. Silence blanketed us like a sheet of dense snow, and even with the heat blasting in the cab, it took several minutes to thaw.

Archer kept his eyes on the road, but I couldn't help myself from taking him in.

Two days and I ached to touch him.

I looked at his hand on the steering wheel, the thick fingers wrapped around it with a firm grip and remember those hands on my waist. *Pushed inside me.* I remembered the width of those shoulders pinned between my thighs, all bronze muscle and sinew. I hesitantly dragged my gaze higher to his face that was full of anger and concern, his mouth drawn tight.

I shivered, recalling how tight those lips had closed on my skin. Two days, and his hickeys were still on my skin. Every day I checked them and tried to ignore the small hole forming when I thought about how soon they'd be gone.

But the thing he'd done with his tongue. I still couldn't figure it out.

"Chief Diehl went to pick Walt up on his way to the party.

We try not to let Walt need to drive anywhere," Archer finally began, his voice hoarse. "He lives in a double just behind the post office, so he doesn't go far to work. Diehl found him on his dining room floor beaten to a bloody pulp." He exhaled loudly, expelling some of the pent-up frustration. "Called the ambulance, but it has to come from Jackson, so it took fucking forever."

"What happened?"

"When Diehl called, he thought Walt was dead, that's how bad they beat him. Honestly, I have to wonder if whoever did this thought he was dead, too, that's how weak his pulse was," he said.

I didn't respond. We both knew—from opposite sides of the law—how violent crimes worked. If whoever attacked Walt wanted him dead, he would be dead.

"I couldn't even recognize him, Keira," he rasped and the truck picked up speed, the weight of what happened dragging his foot closer to the floor. "That's why I didn't want Mom…" He trailed off with a muffled curse.

My stomach knotted over itself seeing him like this—*watching him fray.* Archer wiped a hand over his mouth, his arm coming down heavily on the console where his fingers instantly balled into a frustrated fist.

"I'm sorry, Archer. She'll be okay. She's a strong woman," I told him and without thinking, I reached over and set my hand on his, shocking us both.

I should've pulled back, but I didn't. Instead, I just stared at my small hand over his big one.

"I know. I just…" He shook his head.

"Want to protect her from pain," I murmured, everything I'd learned only a little earlier about this man hitting me with full force.

He grunted.

"Who do you think did it?" I curled farther into the seat.
Please don't say the Irish Kings.

171

"I don't know. Hopefully, if Walt—when Walt pulls through this, he can give us some answers. Diehl is going to have someone at the hospital until he wakes up," he said. "But whoever it was knew what they were doing."

"What do you mean?" I asked, and then recognized we were driving toward the edge of town—toward my house.

"I didn't see defensive wounds and there was a piece of a zip tie on the ground next to him. He wasn't bound when we found him, but I think whoever did this had him tied up when they beat him."

My heart thudded slower, the scenery outside the window turning into a gray blur. Dad never spoke in specifics about his work, but every once in a while, he'd make comments that revealed the nature of how these kinds of crimes went.

"Violence is a message. It's either to send information or take information. Sometimes both."

Archer spun the wheel with one hand and pulled into my driveway, surprising me with our destination.

"So, you came to... bring me home?" I asked, blinking twice in surprise.

Of all the things I expected from the man who'd installed a security system without my request and did background checks on my closest clients without my knowledge in order to make sure I was safe, I was expecting a lot more than for him to just drive me back to my house.

I looked at him, practically able to hear the stone of his chest cracking with the deep inhale he took to keep calm.

"What are you doing, Archer?"

He put the truck in park and sat silent for a few seconds.

"I don't know."

I should've probably got out of the truck and thanked him for the ride. Instead, I faced him fully and left my back to the door.

"Do you think this has to do with me?" I asked again.

It was possible. Anything was possible. It just wasn't like anything that had happened before.

"I don't know," he said more roughly this time. "Let me rephrase. There's no evidence that this has anything to do with you."

"But you came for me anyway."

A deep growl rumbled through the truck's cab. "I did," he rasped. "I don't know how not to, Keira. I don't fucking know anything right now except that I need to keep you safe."

Heat suffused through my body, tingling right down to my toes. The way this man needed to care for me was unlike anything I'd ever experienced. Then again, no one had even been given the opportunity to care for me before. *How could someone care for a person they really didn't know?*

"And how are you going to do that?" I watched his jaw clench slowly and realized the answer. "You're going to sit outside my house all night in your truck, aren't you?"

"It was either that or take you back to my house."

"That sounds more like you," I admitted, managing to hold back that I wouldn't have complained.

"Yeah." He finally looked at me, and the depth of emotion in his gaze punctured the breath from my lungs. "But I want you to trust me, Keira."

He took down my barriers without even knowing it. And who was I kidding? I'd always trusted Archer Reynolds. It was everything else I didn't trust, including myself.

"Then tell me one thing," I murmured thickly, my heart beat raggedly against my chest like it was trying to go to him.

"Anything." His heated gaze locked with mine.

"Why did you come back to Wisdom?" I forced down a swallow. "Why did you leave Boston?"

The questions spilled out and then I held my breath. It had nothing to do with Walt and what happened. It had everything to do with why we were here.

His stare turned tumultuous—a green storm over murky seas.

"Because you died," he finally rasped with a deep, rugged voice. "I thought they'd killed you, and I knew it was my fault. I was the one who took you out of that room. Paraded you around the city..." His throat bobbed. "I blamed myself, and I couldn't... I couldn't stay there. Everywhere I looked, I only saw you. Your eyes. Your freckles. Your smile."

"Archer..."

"How you looked when you told me you felt trapped. How you looked when you told me you wanted a kiss." His voice grew harder. "How you looked when I walked away from you that last night—*fuck.*" He hissed low. Meanwhile, I couldn't breathe at all. "I told you not to leave Boston with any regrets. Well, it turns out I did. And I had to figure out a way to live knowing I'd never get the chance to make them right. So, I came back to the mountains thinking it would be easier to forget about you, forget about my failure, here."

The whole of me burned like his words were fired directly into my center with the force of a bullet, but instead of passing through, they exploded into a cloud of ache. A gnawing want that felt like when you held your breath for too long and your lungs burned for air. Well, I'd held myself—all of me—back from Archer for too long, and now I gasped to let go.

"I see," I choked out.

"No, you don't, Keira. I came back here because of you. And now you're here."

"Well, I came here because of you, and now you're here," I countered.

We'd both ended up in a place that we'd thought would be a haven from the chance we lost to be together. Instead, we'd found each other, and neither of us seemed ready to believe that this could be real after everything we'd been through.

His eyes shimmered. Gone was the fog from their color, leaving only deep saturated truth.

"So, what do we do now?" he asked, the rich rumble of his voice sending a wave of goose bumps over my body.

I inhaled slowly and then exhaled.

I remembered the countless times—countless hours I'd spent over the course of years tracing out each and every one of my new names over and over and over again until it was second nature to write a lie.

And in this moment, I realized I spent the last four years tracing over the lie that I didn't regret him—that I didn't regret leaving Boston or lying to Archer the way that I had.

But being in Wyoming with him over these last couple of weeks erased all of that. It stripped back the lies I'd put in place to protect myself and left only the worn, faded truth.

"What we do now is not wake up tomorrow morning with one more regret," I murmured, reaching for the doorknob and fleeing the truck with Archer's stare pinned to my back.

The next few minutes required no thought. I went inside my house, threw a bunch of clothes and my toothbrush into a backpack, and walked back to his truck.

Through the window I saw him sitting there, his elbows propped on the steering wheel, his thumb trapping the bridge of his nose as he gently shook his head.

I opened the door to the cab, and Archer sat back with a start. His hot gaze made my breath catch.

"What are you doing?" he rasped.

The night breeze blew a strand of hair across my face and it tangled on my dry lips.

"I told you. I don't want to leave this night with another regret." I notched my chin higher and held his gaze, electricity sparking in the dry heat between us.

"Keira…"

I climbed back into the passenger seat, carefully placing my bag of things between my feet. Sitting upright, I faced him, all my senses spilling like marbles when he reached over and caught my chin between his thumb and forefinger, pulling me toward him and imprisoning my attention with a single look.

"What do you want?"

"For you to take me back to your house."

His nostrils flared. "You're sure?"

I gulped, reading every single question embedded within those two words.

If I was sure I trusted him. If I was sure I wanted to spend the night with him. If I was sure I wanted to give him my virginity. If I was sure that I wanted to start my life by getting into a relationship with the only link to my past.

And if I was sure I was willing to let him claim all of me.

My pulse went haywire—like a lit fuse burning toward something brilliant and fragile and explosive.

"I've lived enough lies, Archer, to know what is the truth," I told him breathlessly. "And the truth is, past, present, or future, I will always regret every chance I give up to be with you."

CHAPTER FOURTEEN

ARCHER

I RELEASED MY BREATH WHEN I TURNED DOWN THE PRIVATE drive behind our building that led to my house. The night was clear like black obsidian, speckled with the glitter of stars. Thousands of them, including Orion, like they'd been burning for millennia for this night, too.

"This is your house?" Keira asked as the drive curved in front of my ranch.

The front windows were framed by massive wood beams and reflected the headlights of my truck. Rustic elegance is what the architect had called it; a sanctuary was what it was. Away from work. Away from town. Able to escape everything except the memory of her.

"Built it when I moved back." I pulled into the two-car garage, shut off the truck, and took her bag off her lap to carry it inside for her.

I held the door open for her, allowing her to step inside the laundry room where she promptly stopped and looked over her shoulder at me.

"This is gorgeous."

The house had an open layout, so from where we stood,

she could see clear through the spacious living room to the kitchen and dining room.

"Jerry's two oldest sons own a construction company."

"Makes sense," she murmured, and I could hear her smile.

I'd been good friends with Jack and Mateo in high school —our friendship one of the reasons they'd walked away from a variety of brushes with the law with only warnings. They were hell-raisers when we were younger but had since straightened out. Their last act of defiance was to go into custom homes rather than take over the family's hardware store; they left that to their youngest sibling, Tom.

"They're good friends, so they built this for me. They do high-end work for the wealthy residents of Jackson and the surrounding areas," I offered as explanation for the sprawling home with its dark beam accents and panels of windows. For any other person, the generous single-story ranch would've run well into the millions. Instead, I paid cost for materials and got their time at a discount.

I flipped a switch on the wall and the gas fireplace in the living room burst to life. The towering stone hearth rose all the way to the twenty-four-foot ceilings with two recessed lights shining dimly above it.

She walked into the living room, her head turning in every direction, absorbing details as she went. Meanwhile, I absorbed her. The sway of her hips. The shimmer of her hair like an inextinguishable flame.

"Do you want a drink?" I offered.

"What have you got?"

"Coffee. Water—"

"Wine?" Her gaze locked on the bottles sitting on the island. "I am legal now."

A bolt of lust rocketed through me. *Legal hadn't stopped me from wanting her when she was nineteen.*

"Forgot I had those," I muttered.

I didn't normally keep much wine in the house except a

bottle for Mom because that was all she'd drink. However, I'd bought several bottles to bring to her party that I'd ended up leaving behind for obvious reasons.

I went into the kitchen, set Keira's bag on one of the counter stools at the island, and got out two glasses, pouring some red wine into each while she continued to meander around the living room, running the tips of her fingers along the arm of the couch and then the edge of the mantle. *Never thought I'd be jealous of inanimate objects before.*

I walked over to her and handed her a glass.

"Your walls are empty," she said and took a sip, her tongue sliding out to lick away any lingering liquid.

My already hard cock throbbed, wanting to feel that pink velvet tip run along its length.

I quickly turned away and took a huge gulp of the wine, willing myself under control before my dick decided to punch through my jeans.

"Not really the decorating type," I said gruffly. "Nothing really to decorate for."

Nothing and no one.

"So, all this just for you?"

She sounded farther away, so I glanced back and realized she was standing in front of the fire again.

I hummed low, feeling myself drawn to her. "For now."

Her head snapped to me and I quickly clarified, "I have a big family. At some point I'm sure my mom's going to move in here when her house gets to be too much, and Ranger will probably come with her."

"You think?" Her head tipped and she took another sip. "He seems to have a pretty independent mind. He was talking to Zoey and me about real estate investments at your mom's party."

I stared at her.

My first instinct was to say yes and tell her that I knew Ranger, but her question made me pause and really consider the way I saw my brother. With him being the youngest after Gwen, when Dad died, it was hard to see the two of them as siblings; they didn't really know Dad, so the only person who'd ever filled that role was me.

But over the last few months, I realized there were changes in Ranger. He'd asked to start handling some of his own cases for RPG. He'd finished up the basement at Mom's that had its own entrance to give him more independence while still living there; and he'd bought his own car.

"Maybe," I said, finding it hard to agree that one more of my siblings might not need me any longer. A selfish thing to think but protecting and taking care of them was what defined my entire life.

"You're a good man, Archer Reynolds, to think about your family the way that you do," she stated, pulling me from my thoughts.

I knew why I *needed* the space and that was enough to mask why I *wanted* the space. Dreams of a family, of finally settling down, were always in the back of my mind, but when I inflated them with hope, they swelled like a balloon with a small hole, growing larger until I realized that everything I breathed into them was slowly leaking out through a missing piece. *A missing piece that happened to be standing in my living room right now.*

"When was this?" She pointed to the picture of the five of us with my mom on the mantle.

"After Gwen's wedding last year." I moved closer to her, feeling the heat in my blood intensify.

"So serious," she murmured, talking about me. "Is this you and your dad?" She moved to the second photo—arguably the second decoration in the entire house.

I nodded. "Halloween when I was eight. Every year, I wanted to be a police officer, but that was the first time he let me wear his hat and badge to go trick or treating. The hat kept falling over my eyes when I tried to pick out candy." We both laughed. "It was the best Halloween ever though."

Her fingers moved like she was about to press them onto the glass, but then quickly pulled them away and took another sip of wine.

"What is it?" Something had bothered her.

Her smile was sad. "I wish I had more photos with my dad." She licked her lips again. It was hard for her to talk about him—because he was gone and probably because she'd lived for so long knowing that talking about him risked both their lives. "I wish he was here now to see this place." She faced me. "To see you." She smiled. "He'd like you."

I arched an eyebrow. "You think?"

Her forehead furrowed. "Why wouldn't he?"

"Because—"

"Because you're a cop and he was a criminal?" She broke in defensively, her temper rising. "That life was over for him a long time ago, Archer. From the second he went to the FBI, he lived on the right side of the law—"

"Because I almost fucked his daughter when she was only nineteen," I growled low, eliminating the space between us and towering over her. "Because I haven't stopped thinking about her since." My head dipped lower, our hot breaths mingling like an unspoken conversation between our lips. "Because the things I want to do to her now border on criminal."

"Oh." Her cheeks flamed, but she didn't back down. It took a second, but then her chin rose, her eyes glittering in the firelight with a dark lust that called to my own. "And what things would those be?"

Air released in an audible stream from my tight lips like a pressure pot about to burst.

"Making her come stay with me because I need to keep her safe."

Her breath trembled. "You gave me a choice."

"I'd like to think I was going to," I ground out.

What she didn't know was that I'd been seconds away from following her into her house, hauling her over my shoulder, and taking her home with me. *Thankfully, she'd come back to the truck when she had.*

"Make her strip in front of the fire." My head dropped closer, my pulse pounding in my skull. I cupped her cheek, pressing my thumb to her lower lip, moistened from her tongue and stained from the red wine.

She turned out of my hold and set her glass on top of the mantle. For a second, I thought I'd said something wrong—stepped too far over the boundaries I'd already crossed. But then she'd pulled her top over her head and dropped it on the floor, leaving her upper body bare except for her black lace bra.

Fuck.

The scrap of material had no padding, rather it looked like one more tattoo on her perfect pale skin—painted lace over the small swells of her tits, caught up only by the beaded furls of her nipples.

"Keira." A raw and ragged sound escaped my chest, but it didn't stop her.

Her jeans were next—down to her ankles and then kicked off to the side. Her panties rode up high on her hips, the matching black making my cock twitch, but it was the faint bruising left by my mouth that turned my blood molten.

God, did I want to mark her.

Mark her and mark her and mark her until there was no inch of her skin that didn't read 'mine.'

"Well, so far, you haven't forced me to do anything," she murmured coyly and faced me, allowing me to see her from the front.

My breath caught like a bullet lodged in my chest.

She was exquisite. A masterpiece of silken skin, flushed color, and heady desire. And I was undone.

"Keep talking like that and the things I do to your mouth won't just be criminal, they'll be lawless," I warned.

She shivered, my eyes instantly drawn to her nipples, the dusky red color boldly peeking out from the lace. "I want…"

"What?" I prompted with a growl. "What do you want? A kiss?"

I tensed, my blood like gasoline ignited by her touch. I'd asked her the same question four years ago and she'd replied with a kiss. Now, I wanted so much more.

Her eyebrow rose. "I wanted a kiss four years ago. There's been tax and inflation piling on that request," she replied, her small husky laugh driving me insane. She flattened her palm over my chest. "Now, I want to see you. To touch you."

She balled my shirt in her small fists and pulled it up over my head.

"I want your touch. I want more hickeys." Her hand slid down my arm to take my wrist and bring my hand to her breast.

Christ. Red rimmed my vision, and my dick felt like it was about to explode.

"I want that thing you did with your tongue." She tipped forward and flattened her tongue over my nipple, flicking it before giving it a little bite.

"*Fuck.*" I flinched.

"I want everything, Archer." Her hand slid down over my abdomen, its destination clear. "Your hands. Your mouth. Your cock—"

I crushed my mouth to hers with a savage growl, yanking my palm from her chest and imprisoning her wandering hand in my grip, tugging it above her head. I moved my other hand at her throat, using it as a rudder to tip and tilt her head to give me the best access to the haven between her lips, now a heady mix of sweet and tart from the wine.

She moaned, and I grew drunk on the sound.

I kissed her hard, driving my tongue into every corner of

her lush mouth and claiming it all for myself. I couldn't regret the lack of gentleness when she kissed me back with equal fervor, her tongue tangling in a hot battle with mine.

My hand slid around and cupped the back of her head. Instantly, she pressed herself flush to my front, the soft center of her stomach cradling the hard beast between my legs.

I hadn't been with a woman in so fucking long. I couldn't remember. I didn't *want* to remember. That thing she wanted with my tongue? It was something I'd learned quickly when I realized I had no interest in actually fucking a woman who wasn't Keira—a shitty situation for me since I'd still believed Keira to be dead.

She moaned and bit my tongue, shooting a hot arrow of lust straight down to my cock.

I returned the favor. To her tongue. To her lips. I sucked them until they were so full and swollen, I knew they'd be sore tomorrow.

Good.

"I want you to think of me anytime something comes close to this mouth of yours," I swore and then claimed her lips once more.

This time, the kiss was deeper. I kissed her like the goddamn world was ending, like there was nothing left except her and me in this moment, and I was going to take everything I could from it knowing just how easily it could all be gone in the morning.

Several long minutes later, I pulled back with a groan, both of us panting

"Keira," I rasped, my fingers untangling from her nape to brush the strands of hair back from her face.

"I want you, Archer," she repeated like I didn't know—like I couldn't feel how tight her tits were against my chest. Like I couldn't feel the pulse of heat between her thighs begging for my attention.

I shifted, about to cart her off to my bed, but one look at her red swollen lips, and I couldn't resist the beast inside me.

I rubbed my thumb over the ruddy flesh and then ordered, "On your knees."

Her gaze swirled with wanton hunger, never leaving mine as she obeyed.

I kept her one hand held high in my grasp, using my other to flick open the waist of my jeans. She licked her lips purposely slow as I pulled the denim over my hips, allowing my thick cock to hang free.

Her sharp inhale was like its own goddamn caress. I watched her eyes slide along my length, from the weight of my balls to the thick root of my cock, she followed the pulsing veins all the way to the purple tip that beaded with a drop of precum.

"I want to taste you," she declared.

"You're going to do more than taste me." I slid my fingers around the back of her head to grab hold of her ponytail. Bending forward, I whispered huskily in her ear, "I told you I don't need a tattoo gun to mark you, baby." Her unabashed response to the endearment made me swell even thicker. "I'm going to tattoo the back of your throat with the tip of my cock."

Her little whimper killed me as I straightened, and I'd barely grabbed hold of my heavy length when she leaned forward and captured the meaty tip between her lips, swiping her tongue over the end to taste the salty drop.

"*Fuck!*" I threw my head back with a long groan, knowing this was the end for me. Four fucking years of pent-up frustration only to finally have her perfect mouth around me.

Using her ponytail, I tipped her head back until it forced her jaw open wider.

Air evaporated from my lungs as I pushed in deep until I bumped against the back of her throat. I felt her gag reflex activate, and I almost lost it right then.

"Suck on me," I instructed, instantly feeling her mouth clamp down around me. "Good job, baby," I encouraged and slid back, giving her a chance to breathe.

But she didn't want it. Her small hands positioned on my hips and pulled herself forward, her mouth following my retreat.

"You want it to hurt a little…"

Her eyes flew up to mine and she moaned along my length.

"Fuck," I hissed and stuffed my cock back into her mouth.

I stared in a daze as the firelight flickered over her pink skin. Her lips were slick and spread, her cheeks puffed out to make room for all of me. Gritting my teeth, I drove into her heat, tapping the back of her throat before giving only a slight relief.

Her tongue stroked my shaft, begging me to go deeper. I gripped her hair tight and rocked deep into her mouth once. Twice. And hard. She'd be bruised in the morning. *Marked.*

I growled low, the suction of her mouth so intense, my balls tightened on the second thrust as pleasure knifed through me. With a hoarse shout, I roughly yanked my dick free before I lost it against the back of her throat.

Her lips popped and she sputtered.

"Fuck, Keira." I brushed her hand away when she went to wipe the sides of her mouth, using my fingers to do it for her.

"Did I do something wrong?" Her voice was raspy from my assault. "Was I not doing it right?"

I groaned. "God no, baby. You had me losing my mind," I confessed. *More than my mind.* "But I don't want my cum down your throat. Not tonight."

Her gaze widened in understanding and like she weighed no more than a rag doll, I picked her up into my arms, my hands filling with the swell of her ass. I tensed as my cock bumped up against the heat of her core. It would take nothing to move her panties to the side and bury myself inside her—lose myself in fucking ecstasy.

"Where are we going?" Her question tightened my restraint.

I walked us through the kitchen, heading down the hall that led to the master bedroom. I kneaded her ass as I carried her, knowing one day I'd spread those cheeks and take that tight little hole, too.

"I'm not fucking you in front of the fire," I told her. "For four years, I've fantasized about this moment. You better believe the first time you take my cock is going to be in my bed."

She moaned and dropped her lips onto mine, a wild hunger living inside her that was finally free. My eyes shut as we kissed, hardly needing any of my senses to find my way to the bedroom or the massive sleigh bed in the center of it.

I stopped just at the edge of the bed, setting her legs down so I could take off her bra and thong. Next went the rest of my clothing. I splayed my hands around her waist, sat on the edge of the bed and pulled her onto my lap.

"Fuck," I hissed, her slick pussy pressing right on my dick.

I pulled the tie from her hair, tilting her head back so my lips could search out unmarked spots on her neck. Her skin was hot against my tongue, eager to be sucked. Her hips began to rock against me. She was soaked, sliding so easily along my length it was a miracle I didn't just fucking slip inside her cunt.

My mouth moved to her tits, hungry for her cherry nipples. I pulled one between my teeth, applying pressure until she squirmed and gushed wet against me. When I finally sucked her, she let out a delicious little whimper that went straight to my dick.

God, she was so sweet. Forbidden sweet. Like a star I'd wished on so many times that the weight of my desperate wishes finally pulled her down to earth. And I didn't care what punishment the heavens might invoke, I was keeping the brilliant heat of her celestial body all for myself.

"Archer," she moaned, her head dropping back.

Smiling, I tortured her breasts one after another until she was panting and moaning, her body contorting and trembling like it was made to melt under my touch.

"I need…" she broke off, grinding her slick folds along my length. "Please, Archer… I need… more."

"Me, baby," I growled, biting the underside of her breast. "You need me."

It was bold. But I was bound to this woman in ways I couldn't describe.

I turned, taking her with me and laying her on my bed, her hair fanning out like flames on my white bedspread. Rising up, I reached in my nightstand drawer for a condom.

"I'm on the pill."

I froze, a primal pulse wrecking my system. I met her gaze, firm and fierce.

"You sure?" I rasped.

"I don't want anything else between us."

I dropped the condom back in the drawer and moved back between her legs. I groaned, seeing how her pussy glistened and dripped onto my bed.

"Don't be gentle."

My eyes narrowed on hers.

Gripping her calf, I pushed it up and positioned the tip of my cock at her slit, moving slightly until I was soaked.

"This might hurt, baby," I said through tightly clenched teeth.

"Anything permanent usually does."

My eyes flared. *Permanent.*

Hell fucking yes, we were permanent. And with that thought, my hips shunted forward, driving completely inside her pussy.

Vaguely, I heard her cry mingle with mine, but I couldn't

focus on anything except the intense, exquisite pleasure of her tight cunt strangling my cock. Her muscles spread and seized around the massive invasion, unsure whether to try and push me out or pull me deeper, and I felt every deliciously bare and quivering inch.

I'd never fucked a woman without a condom before— never even considered it. But the second Keira offered, I knew this was the way I needed to have her—without anything left between us.

I pinned myself steady inside her for several long seconds, giving her a small reprieve to adjust to my size and length. Slowly, I began to roll my hips in and out with firm, deep movements.

"More." She gripped my shoulders, her nails digging into my skin.

"*Me.*" I pulled back and drove into her harder now, her hips rising to meet mine.

If taking her virginity hurt, Keira hid it well. She met each of my furious thrusts with uncivilized hunger. Our hips slapped together, her tight pussy sucking me deeper each time.

Breathing happened in rough gasps, my body realizing the in and out of oxygen was less essential than the gasping rhythm of my body joining with hers. I bent over her, taking her lips in a rough kiss. We bit and sucked, tongues sparring and stroking while our hips collided with frantic fervor.

She felt so fucking good. Better than I could've imagined. Better than anything I'd ever felt before. And for the first time since coming home, I felt myself healing.

I snaked my hand under her back and rolled us, putting her on top of me. Now I could see her body, marked from my mouth as it trembled with pleasure. I could watch her bare tits, red from the lash of my tongue, bounce with each thrust. I held one hand on her waist, dragging the other up to cup her breast and thumb her nipple.

"Archer," she moaned, splaying her palms on my chest, her nails finding new traction in my pecs as she rode me.

"That's it, baby," I bit out, feeling my balls tighten as her pussy squeezed and squeezed me. "Take what you want."

She gasped loudly, her eyes opening. "You," she whimpered, moving faster along my cock as the deeper angle let me hit her G-spot each time. "I want you."

For a split second, I was able to watch her climax overtake her. Her lips parted. Her eyes widened, the look in them was pleasure sharpened with fear of what was about to happen to her body—like she was unsure if she'd survive her orgasm. And it was the most erotic thing I'd ever seen.

And then she came, screaming as her back bowed and her cunt spasmed violently around me. Her body fractured against my hands, unable to do anything but be swept away.

Swearing, I gripped her hips and plunged through her clenching muscles one last time. I buried myself against her womb and spilled my release so forcefully, I groaned each time my cock pulsed, pleasure knifing through me, carving me limb from sated limb.

As soon as she started to sag, I pulled her down to my chest, pressing kisses to her hair and forehead while I gently trailed my fingertips along her back.

"That was…" She sighed adorably.

I smiled and held her a little tighter. "Everything," I finished, but she was already sleeping.

My eyes drifted shut, my body feeling like a loosely connected mesh of man. The woman in my arms had completely undone me.

My last pleasure-drenched thought before sleep took hold was that maybe this was how Orion ended up in the sky: he'd fucked a goddess and the indescribable pleasure split him into stars.

I didn't blame him for not surviving. If that was the only way to see her every night, I'd pin myself to the night sky, too.

CHAPTER FIFTEEN

KEIRA

Previous to this moment, I believed the most satisfying thing in life was sleeping in in the morning, in the softness of a good mattress, and buried under the warmth of covers.

Now, I knew better. I was *enlightened.*

There was nothing more satisfying than waking up in Archer's bed, the hardness of his shoulders underneath my knees, and his tongue buried in my sex.

And the things that tongue did to me, I decided, were definitely criminal.

It didn't abide by the laws of sense or progression of pleasure. It broke into my senses, vandalized all rational thought, and stole the richest pleasure from each one of my cells.

My hands curled into his hair, my thighs clenching around his head, I prayed I didn't strangle him before I came.

Selfish, I know. But that tongue…

I orgasmed with a strangled cry, my sore body arching against the sweet pull of his lips as his mouth devoured me.

When I had the strength to look down, Archer was smiling, the playfulness of his expression making him look so much younger than his normal responsible—*but still drop-dead-gorgeous*—self.

"We should get up," I murmured groggily though it wasn't the case.

"I was hoping you wouldn't say that," he said, his morning voice deliciously rough.

"I need breakfast." I pushed myself up and stared down at the man lying between my legs.

His hair was tousled. His lips red from their… endeavors. And his eyes… they were this icy green I hadn't seen before, the haze I normally saw completely wiped away.

"I already ate," he said huskily.

I tried to swallow. Several times. I knew I was sore. Used. My body stretched and bent and bruised in ways I never imagined. But still, I wanted more. Like a glutton brought to feast, I'd finally tasted the fullness of Archer Reynolds—I ate and ate but I couldn't get enough.

I pulled my lower lip between my teeth and winced at how sore it was. "I can just grab something on the way to the shop."

I turned to the side of the bed, instinct burning caution into my blood.

"You're not going anywhere without some food in you," Archer declared, his tone hardening into that *this-is-not-an-argument* tone.

Before I could stand, a thick arm slid around my waist and hauled me back against a hot chest. I took a deep breath, trying not to reveal how bad I was at this—at intimacy—even though I knew it wasn't my fault.

His fingers snuck under my chin and gently turned my head, his expression so tender it made my chest ache.

"You alright, baby?"

Air snagged in my chest, caught on all the tiny pins of promise the endearment planted inside me. He'd said it several times last night, and as I fell asleep, I told myself it was just in the heat of the moment.

I swallowed and managed a smile. "Just hungry."

He wanted to press, and he started to but then stopped himself.

"Alright, let's get some food in you." He grinned and kissed the tip of my nose. "Let me show you the bathroom and shower. I'll go use the guest bath."

"You don't have——" My protest cut off in a small squeak when he turned, giving me a full view of his naked front—*and his very large, very erect cock.*

"I do have to or you'll get something in you, but it won't be food."

Thank god he turned right back around and missed the immediate clench of my thighs.

I marveled at the heated tile on the bathroom floor and the numerous showerheads that sprayed my deliciously sore body from every angle. Once I'd pulled out a fresh pair of black leggings and a black tee from my bag—my standard tattooing attire—I walked into the kitchen to find Archer waiting for me, spatula in hand.

"Any requests for breakfast? My standard breakfast fare is bacon, eggs, and blueberry pancakes." He pointed the spatula at me and winked.

Jesus. Between the wink and hearing how he was going to cook, I almost came again.

"I can make breakfast," I offered, snatching the spatula from him with a small cheer.

"I'm making breakfast." Growly Archer was back. He moved toward me, and I took a step back, hiding the spatula behind my back.

"Are you sure? I cooked breakfast for Dad and me almost every morning——" I sucked in a breath when he cornered me against the island.

"And I cooked breakfast for my four siblings every morning my mom had to work," he returned.

We couldn't have grown up more different—his family brandishing the letter of the law and mine breaking it—but somehow, in so many ways, we'd ended up so similar. Responsible. Independent. *Islands that had somehow collided.*

We stared each other down, each trying to insist we were more capable than the other.

"I'll make the bacon and pancakes and you make the eggs?" He broke the silence with his truce.

"Deal."

We worked in sync for several minutes, moving to and from the stove, and sharing the workspace like we'd done it a million times before. Like something had finally aligned last night—our stars creating their own constellation.

I took the carton of eggs, realizing how crazy it was that I was here. In Archer's kitchen. Making breakfast with him after he'd spent the night making my body his.

I took a deep breath, my lungs filling with woodsy freedom… and bacon.

The sound of spitting grease filling the kitchen was as potent as the scent that came with it and my stomach started to grumble.

I began opening different drawers on the island searching for a bag for the eggs.

"What are you looking for?" he asked, glancing over his shoulder. "A fork?"

I shook my head. "Plastic bag."

His eyebrow lifted.

"Just trust me," I told him.

"Last drawer on the right."

I found the large Ziplocs and grabbed one, feeling his gaze track me back to the bowl of eggs, wondering what I was doing. Opening the bag wide, I set it on the counter and broke the eggs into it. Sealing the bag, I faced Archer with a small smile.

"Scrambled," I said and began to shake the bag.

Archer laughed and nodded, impressed, watching the yolks mix into the white. "Never seen it done that way before."

"I've got expert tricks," I quipped, and then stopped short, our conversation cut off when Archer's phone began to buzz on the counter.

He slung the towel he'd been wiping up the bacon grease with over his shoulder, the movement so smooth and sexy for a man who always tried to come off with hard corners and sharp, protective edges.

"Hey, Mom. How is he?" he answered the call.

And just like that, the single question popped the surreal bubble that had inflated around us.

Walt.

The man who was attacked... and the reason I was here in the first place.

My hands kept moving on their own, shaking the eggs while I stared at Archer, trying to read any slight alteration in his expression that would reveal more about the other end of the conversation.

"I see." His chin dipped several very long seconds later. *Not good.* "How long do they think?"

A small breath pierced my lungs.

Archer went back to the stove, grabbing tongs with one hand and pulling the bacon off the heat while holding his phone with the other.

"Okay. Yeah, keep me updated." He paused. "She's okay." Another pause. "She's here, Mom."

My cheeks burst on fire. I didn't know how relationships worked, but this wasn't the way I'd choose for his mom to learn about us—to learn about me. The girl who'd caused her son to leave his prestigious career because I couldn't tell him the truth.

"Keira." Archer placed his hands over mine. I blinked, everything coming back into focus. I didn't even realize he'd ended the call. "I think they're sufficiently scrambled."

I looked down, the eggs practically frothing in the bag.

"Yeah, you're right." I swallowed down the lump in my throat. "How's Walt?"

"Stable but not conscious." His hand tensed almost imperceptibly on mine. "They had to take him in for surgery last night to stop the internal bleeding. They're monitoring him for that, but also because of the head injuries."

"Oh no." The band around my chest tightened another notch. "So he didn't say who…"

"He's been unconscious the whole time," he replied, his mouth drawing into a firm line. "They took scans after they stopped the abdominal bleeding. He had some bleeding and swelling in his skull around his brain. They induced a coma to hopefully stop it from getting any worse or they'll have to operate again."

"That's… horrible."

I caught the way his fist flexed just before he reached over and turned the front burner of the stove on for me.

"It was intentional," he returned tightly. "Maximum damage."

"And your mom?"

"Worried. She was going back to sit with him. I guess reception is horrible inside the hospital, but she wanted to let us know he was stable."

"Who would've done this?" I asked without thinking. *Besides the mob,* I wanted to add.

Archer was silent for a second while I brought the eggs to the stove, pouring them into the heated pan.

"Not sure," he finally said. "He had a drinking problem. We all knew that. I don't know if he ran into other issues because of it, but it looks like that's going to be our next step until we can talk to him."

He didn't want to believe it, and I didn't blame him, but the probability that his excessive drinking got him into trouble with the wrong people was more likely than Boston's Irish mob realizing I wasn't dead and coming after Walt instead of me.

I mixed the eggs over the heat, allowing them to cook thoroughly.

"Can I ask you something, Keira?"

Immediately, my pulse picked up.

"Okay."

"How did the Kings find you so many times before in WITSEC?"

I turned the eggs while he flipped pancakes. It was almost comical to be talking about mobs and Witness Protection and faking death while making an All-American breakfast.

"I don't know," I immediately replied with, feeling my inner doors slam shut. Then I took a deep breath and slowly opened them back up. They creaked and protested, never having spread wide enough to let anyone else in before. "The first time, we thought that they just got lucky and we hadn't gone far enough. Then it happened again. And again. My dad argued with Lattimore—"

"Lattimore?" He put on an oven mitt and lifted the skillet with the cooked eggs.

"The FBI agent who coordinated everything with the US Marshals every time," I explained, scraping the eggs from the skillet onto our plates. "The third time, they set up a car bomb, but my dad realized in time. We made it behind the house before the car blew up."

"Jesus." He turned off the burners and we moved to the stools on the other side of the counter to eat.

"That time, when Lattimore brought us to a safe house until we could be relocated, I overheard them arguing. My dad thought I was watching TV in the bedroom, but I'd come out to get a glass of water and heard them talking." I picked up a forkful of eggs, blowing and watching the steam dissipate. "My dad insisted there had to be a leak in the Marshals."

'There's no fucking way this happens three times without a mole,' he swore. 'I'm not doing this again. I'm not doing this to her again.'

"That's a bold accusation."

"My dad was a bold man." I sighed when the first bite of eggs and bacon hit my tongue.

I realized my eyelids had shut when silence stretched on. My eyes popped open and I found Archer watching me intently.

"Like father like daughter."

I half-smiled and took a bite of his pancakes, complimenting him when I was finished. "These are delicious."

"So are your eggs," he returned. I didn't get a chance to thank him before he added, "We make a good team."

Instantly, my gaze dropped to my plate. *Team.* The fear in my chest fought to close those doors once more, but Archer wouldn't let up.

"What did Lattimore say?"

I took another bite of food.

'What other choice do you have, Pat? You knew the risks when you came to us—you told us the Kings wouldn't stop until you were dead for this betrayal. We have to keep going until we get him—'

'Then we'll make me dead.'

"I didn't hear him agree, but he didn't fight my dad on the accusation either. He tried to tell my dad to just hang on until we could get Jimmy Maloney to trial, and that was when my dad suggested that we die." I remembered thinking he was joking at first. My dad was always able to stay deathly serious while holding onto a joke. But it wasn't a joke. "That night, they hashed everything out. We moved again, but I knew it was just as temporary of a placement as the previous ones had been."

I scraped up the last bits of egg on my fork and licked it clean.

"Who else knew?"

"No one." I set my fork on my plate and tucked my hands underneath my thighs. "My dad trusted Lattimore and no one else. Five people knew about our deaths. Lattimore. The man who shot us. The two agents in the ambulance with us that day. And the head of the FBI."

Archer picked up my plate along with his and walked to the other side of the island to wash them, glancing up at me as he asked, "Is it possible that Lattimore—"

"No." I shook my head. "My dad trusted Lattimore, but not even enough to tell him where we'd go. It was the final precaution. We were given some cash, but my dad refused every other assistance of WITSEC. No new job. No new house. No new life. At least, not from them. The plan was that we'd leave Boston and not even the Marshals would know where we were headed."

He turned the sink off and dried the plates.

"That's why I know this can't be because of me," I said with a tone of desperation that made me worry I was thinking emotionally rather than rationally. "No one knew where we were headed."

I was unwilling to believe that after all this time I could be in danger again. No. I was afraid. I was afraid that the second I'd finally started to notch out a teeny-tiny corner of the world for my life, my past came along to rip it back up again.

"But you kept moving…"

A sad smile filtered over my lips. "Even after the dangerous life my dad had lived, nothing scared him as much as almost losing me in that car bomb." Tears welled like hot wax in the corners of my eyes. "I think he knew he'd never be able to shake that fear, and that's why we never came here."

His head tipped. "What do you mean?"

"We pulled out of Boston that day and he asked where I wanted to go, and I looked in the rearview, feeling the hole in my chest growing bigger with every mile, and told him Wyoming."

The tears melted hot streaks down my cheeks, and I quickly brought the back of my hand up to wipe them away. "I think he could see how badly I wanted to live here, and he didn't trust himself to bring me here without being sure he'd never have to make me leave. So, we kept moving until he got sick. Then he had no choice but to stay in Salt Lake City."

Archer hummed low as he walked slowly around the counter to me.

"And nothing happened there?"

I shook my head. "Even if one of the few people who knew our deaths were fake confessed to Sean—the Kings—" I cleared my throat, trying hard to hide the small unsteady slip. I could try to talk about a lot of things with Archer, but Sean Maloney wasn't one of them. Not yet. "Even if all the stars aligned and someone figured out it was really Patrick McKenna who passed away in Utah, I left nothing to tie me to here."

"Except your tattoo business."

I tensed. It was so unlikely—beyond unlikely. Everything about my business was anonymous. I never posted photos of my face or revealed my name, introducing myself as Kay to all my clients. I'd had a mobile setup in Utah, renting out different spaces on different days to work from. It didn't make cash flow consistent, but I still took the precaution.

"A business they would've targeted if they knew I was here. Not Walt. Not the post office," I returned.

His shoulders slumped with a loud exhale, his fear for my safety fighting with facts he couldn't deny.

"Speaking of... I need to head over to my shop." I slid off

the stool and was a half step away from him when a very broad chest blocked my path.

My gaze snaked up the solid wall of male, lingering on the bronze skin at his throat, those lips that drove me crazy, and then finally reaching that potent jade stare.

"I want you to stay with me," he declared.

I jerked back and stammered, "What?"

It was only one night. This wasn't—he wasn't… asking me to move in. No. I already had a place—a place I hadn't even fully unpacked into. And we… we were just starting—

As if reading my thoughts, Archer cleared his throat and said, "Mom said Walt's going to be in the induced coma for at least a week to make sure the brain swelling goes down. I want you to stay with me until I can talk to him."

"Oh." This was about danger not desire.

When it came to Archer Reynolds, all the lines seemed to blur.

"I just need to make sure, Keira," he rasped.

I wanted to insist that it wasn't necessary, but the words died well before they reached my throat. Part of me wanted to run, conditioned to flee from everything I could care for and ultimately lose. But the other part of me—the part that ultimately responded—desperately snatched at the opportunity to be with him and held on for its dear little life.

I swallowed and my lips slowly peeled apart.

"Okay."

Almost all the taut lines on his face disappeared, his relief palpable.

"Thank you," he rasped and bent down to press a kiss to my forehead. "I just need to call Hunt and then I'll take you."

I nodded, feeling my heart thump steady and firm against the front of my chest, watching him grab his phone and walk toward the bedroom to make the call. My walls were disappearing. My safeguards stripped down by his tender though slightly imposing care and fierce desire.

I was in danger here. Not my life, but definitely my heart.

CHAPTER SIXTEEN

ARCHER

"WELL, LOOK WHO IT IS." GUNNER'S VOICE CARRIED THROUGH the small seating area inside Brilliant Brews.

Brilliant Brews was Tara's baby. It used to be an old video store that went out of business after Netflix came around. She'd completely redecorated the spot to turn it into—as she described—a retro library feel. The walls were decorated with classic Wild West novels, some pinned open, some kept shut. The furniture was bold and funky—like the pink velvet armchair I was sitting on; it used to belong to Mom, living in her basement never to see the light of day until Ranger moved down there and Tara asked if she could have it.

There were little pieces of everyone's story stitched into the fabric of Wisdom, and with each day that passed, I realized that Keira was becoming stitched into mine.

We stopped in for coffee just like we'd done every morning for the past four days, settling into a kind of routine I hadn't known I'd crave. We'd stop for coffee, then head over to the tattoo shop where she'd meet with clients while I sat in the back room, not-so-inconspicuously assessing every client that came through her door while working remotely to organize, assign, and pull background information for RPG's current and upcoming cases.

Technically, I'd called Hunter the morning I asked her to give me a week and put him in charge of the office—something I'd done a few times in the past when I was away for a case. But this case was different. It wasn't a case; it was just her.

Keira liked to tease me because I wouldn't even let her go to the bathroom in the grocery store without having to stand outside the door and make sure no one suspect went in after. But if she had any serious complaints, I couldn't hear them over the way I made her scream every night.

On the kitchen counter. In front of the fire. In the shower. Yesterday, we hadn't even made it inside the house before I pulled her over the console in my truck and fucked her from the seat; the damn horn had honked with every deep drive of my dick.

Thank god it was several miles in every direction until I had a neighbor.

"Shouldn't you be working?" I grunted and shifted my seat, in a perpetual state of discomfort throughout the day when I had to keep my hands to myself no matter how many times my mind wandered.

It felt like my damn dick held its breath every second until it was buried inside her hot cunt. And I held my breath every moment until we were alone, and I could pull her into my arms and convince myself I'd kept her safe for another day.

"Shouldn't you?" he countered.

I glanced at the door, my focus momentarily captured by the bell announcing a new patron. *Darryl Nelson.* I nodded to the senior rancher for the Nelson Ranch and he tipped his hat. I wish it was this easy to identify everyone in town. The locals, sure. But with Jackson and the resort so close and the end of ski season coming up, there were more visitors passing through town than I was currently comfortable with.

"Don't make me fire you," I turned back to Gunner and warned. "I'm on a case."

"So, we offer body guarding from our own beds now?" He smirked. "Good to know."

Jesus, this kid.

My chest rumbled with a growl. It wasn't a secret that Keira was staying with me or that I'd taken this 'case' to a level of protection that was well beyond all professional boundaries.

She wasn't my girlfriend. I asked her to stay with me for her own safety not for a relationship. We didn't go on dates even though I'd spent every minute of the last week with her. Watching her. Talking to her. Getting to know her. I'd spent every night learning every dip and curve of her body better than I knew the back of my hand, only sleeping once she was curled against my chest.

Fuck.

I could growl all I wanted, but Gunner's cheeky insinuation was right. I needed to draw new boundaries because I didn't want to be her bodyguard. I wanted to be her boyfriend. I wanted more of the everything I'd warned her about… but I didn't want to scare her away.

"Here you go, Gunner!" Tara exclaimed, batting her eyelashes as my brother laughed and walked up to the counter with his classic bachelor swagger, taking the two travel cups from her with a wink.

"Thanks, doll." He returned to where I was sitting. "Where's Keira?"

"Bathroom." I nodded to the corner. The coffee shop was small enough that I could monitor the door from my chair. It was a local spot which was why I favored it over the Cosmic Cup which was next door to the Worth Hotel; Cosmic served Starbucks coffee and drew all the tourists.

"Any more info on Walt?" I had Hunter working with

205

Chief Diehl on possible suspects who would've had motive to attack Walt.

"Hunt told you he found out that Walt took out a second mortgage on his house a few months ago?" he asked, and I nodded. "Diehl called this morning and said he found some junk mail from online gambling sites after doing a second sweep of Walt's place, so it's possible he gambled and lost to the wrong people and this was some sort of warning."

I hummed. Definitely possible. More possible than any other explanation, but it still didn't sit quite right.

"I'll call him later and get a full update," I told him and took a sip of my black coffee. "Everything else at the office okay?"

"Yeah. Did you tell Hunter that his girl took the job?"

"Hunter's girl?"

"Zoey." I shot him a look. "Ran into her here yesterday and she told me you offered her the job."

One of the many tasks I'd accomplished this week was going through the rest of the applications we'd had for the assistant position and then, while Keira was safe at my house, I'd interviewed three candidates; of those, only Zoey made the cut.

She was perfect for the job. And perfect for my brother. I just had to hope that didn't cause a problem for either.

"I haven't told him yet. She said she won't be able to start until the situation with Walt calms down." I admired her sense of duty, unwilling to leave her job at the post office when there was no one to replace her.

He nodded and then lifted up the coffee cups. "Well, I'm looking forward to the day when having an assistant means I don't have to make coffee runs."

"Gunner…"

"I know, I know. I'm about to be fired."

"I wouldn't worry about me firing you. Hunter will have your head before I get the chance."

"Well, that would make the family dinner very awkward."

My brow furrowed. "What family dinner?"

My phone started to vibrate in my pocket, and Gunner's grin widened; it was Mom calling. "That one."

I glared at him as I answered, "Hey, Mom."

"Hi, honey."

"Everything okay? Any word on Walt?" I asked, watching my brother pull down his sunglasses and stroll out of the coffee shop.

"Nothing yet, but I'm heading over to the hospital this afternoon to talk to his doctors again. I was actually calling to talk to you about a birthday dinner."

"A what?" I wasn't sure I heard her right, my focus momentarily distracted as Keira came out of the bathroom but was waylaid by Tara.

"I was hoping you'd host a birthday dinner for me at your house since you couldn't make it to my party."

A subtle request.

"Mom…"

"And I'd like Keira to be there."

I clenched my teeth. It wasn't that I didn't want Keira to have dinner with my family. On the contrary, I wanted like hell for her to be a part of everything with my family. But I needed to figure out how to tell her that after only the last week, I knew this was it for me—*that she was it for me.* I needed to figure out how to ask her—hell, beg her if it came right down to it—to move all the things she'd just unpacked in her house over to mine.

I needed to figure out how to convince her that putting down roots with me didn't mean bulldozing over the tentative but independent ones that had already started to grow.

"I don't know that she and I are… I don't know that whatever we are… is there yet…"

"Oh honey, you might not, but only because you've been the most stubborn of all my children. It's just dinner. I think you can manage."

I gritted my teeth. "Let me talk to her about it, and I'll let you know. Love you." I hung up just as Keira stopped in front of me.

"Everything okay?" She took her coffee from my hand.

"Yeah. Just Mom." I bent and brushed my lips to her forehead.

Yeah, this was so far beyond fucking professional.

"News on Walt?" I swore her breath caught, but she took a sip of her coffee so fast I wondered if I'd imagined it.

"No, nothing since the scans yesterday." I held the door open for her as we walked outside.

They'd taken new scans on Walt and his doctors were optimistic by the reduction in swelling but said he would still need a few more days in the coma. That gave me some time to figure out what to say to Keira. *It gave us both time.*

I greeted a few acquaintances from town as we walked over to the tattoo shop, everyone giving Keira and me that look like we were together. I didn't correct them. Neither did she. I also noticed every large black SUV parked along Main. *How many fucking Tahoes could there be available for rent?*

I exhaled my frustration. Maybe I was making more out of this. Maybe that was easier than just admitting how much I cared about her, and how this was all because I was stubborn.

"What are you doing today?" I asked, the *Twilight Ink* sign on her little building now in sight.

"You don't already know?" Her hair caught on the breeze as she looked over her shoulder at me.

"Nope." The background checks I'd done on her initial list of clients was now a running joke, though it hadn't been funny at the time.

She entered the code to unlock the front door. Meanwhile, I scanned the exterior for the discreet security cameras to make sure they were all still in place; I'd run through the feeds and check for any suspicious activity once we were inside.

"Well, Jemma is coming in at one to start her back piece.

We're doing a full tableau of Monet's Water Lilies on her back, so I'm outlining today and then we'll see how far we can get with color." Her face brightened as she spoke about her work. *More roots. More permanence.* "Before she gets here, I've got a whole inbox of appointment requests that I'm going to go through and contact. I'm already booking a month out, but I don't want to keep them waiting for a response."

We went inside the shop, the door automatically locking behind us.

I reached for her wrist, stopping her before she walked too far. One tug had her back against my chest, and I notched my fingers under her chin. Her head tipped back without much provocation.

"I'm proud of you," I told her.

She flushed and swayed gently into me, my dick instantly thinking this was going somewhere it wasn't. *At least not right now.*

"Thank you."

I kissed her upturned mouth gently, her lips melting open. I groaned as my tongue tangled with hers, my hold on her tightening.

"You need to work," I stopped myself and rasped.

And I needed to get myself under control.

It was like every time I had her, it didn't sate me. Instead, it only made me hunger for her more.

"Yes, boss."

"I'll be in the back if you need me." I pressed my lips to her forehead and inhaled deep, needing her scent to hold me over until I could have her back in my arms.

I GLANCED up at the clock, shocked to see it was already well into the afternoon. There were no windows in the back and with the bright lights Keira worked under, there was no way I would've noticed the dimness of the setting sun.

I rubbed my eyes and let my head drift back. I'd been staring at a computer for too many hours this week. Usually paperwork and casework were broken up with other tasks during the day, but Hunter was holding down the office while I spent too much time sifting through video footage looking for anyone suspicious.

The most I'd found today was a black SUV that had parked outside the shop for about ten minutes yesterday. No one got out of it and the windows were too tinted for me to see who was inside, and I couldn't get a good angle on the license plate when they drove away. Basically, nothing. No reason that it would be suspicious except that I was looking for anything to be suspicious. Still, I sent the footage over to Hunter and asked him to take a look.

I peered into the front room and saw Keira talking to her client, Jemma. They were both standing, moving slowly toward the door. *She was almost done.*

I closed my computer and my phone started to ring.

"Hey, Mom," I answered with a sigh and leaned against the back of the chair. "I told you I'd let you know about dinner—"

"I'm not calling about dinner, Archer. Walt's awake."

I sat forward so quickly the chair went up on two wheels for a second. "What?"

Awake. Walt was awake.

"His scans today were so much better, so they pulled him out of the coma, not wanting it to start doing more harm than good."

"How is he? Have you talked to him?" I stood. "What did he say? Who did this to—"

"Archer," she broke in, forcing me to stop and take a

breath. My mind felt like it was running a million miles an hour. "I've talked to him, and he's still on a lot of meds, but honey, he doesn't remember anything."

The ground felt like it dropped out from under me. I flattened my hand on the desk and bent forward, my gut wrenching. "Nothing?"

"The doctor said that's to be expected given the injuries his skull and brain sustained. He may regain his memory of that night, but he may not. They said it's impossible to know."

I swallowed hard, my tongue moving around like a caged animal in my mouth, unsure of what to do.

He didn't remember.

That meant there was no proof either way whether or not Keira was in danger—nothing for my next decision to go off of except how I felt. And how I felt scared the shit out of me.

"I'm glad he's alright," I rasped, knowing that was most important.

"Are you okay, honey?" When I didn't reply, she continued, "I know it's hard for you to not have all the answers for the people you care about."

"I just want to be able to tell her she's safe." My voice was low, hardly recognizable.

"Sometimes, Archer, it's more important to know you have someone to face the unknown with, no matter what that is, than to have all the answers." Her voice turned thick with emotion. Strength and tenderness. That was Mom. That was how she lived. How she raised us. How she took care of this community. "Because you never know what life brings. She could be safe from the mob today but in a car accident tomorrow, you just never know. The only thing certain in life is the person or people you choose to live it with, and I think you and Keira know that better than most."

She was right.

Of course, she was, she was my mom.

Over the past week, I'd learned more and more about

Keira's life over the last four years. The places she'd lived. The things she and her dad had done. I realized now, in spite of every tumultuous turn life had thrown her, she hadn't looked to her dad for answers; answers hadn't mattered. Him being there with her did.

"The only answer she needs from you, honey, is that you are going to be there for her whether she's in danger or not."

"Thanks, Mom," I murmured.

"Anytime. And don't forget to let me know about dinner," she said, and we hung up.

Mom was right. I thought I could prove myself to Keira by being her protector. She didn't need a protector, though. She needed a partner.

"Hey, I'll be ready to go home in five…" My head snapped up, and I saw Keira standing in the doorway, regarding me with worry.

She'd taken off her sweatshirt and though she had a bra on under her black tank top today, the massive hickey I'd left on her neck last night was left completely exposed.

"Archer… what is it? What happened?" She walked up to me and asked.

I sent the message to Roman and placed my phone on the desk. I was just as unprepared for this conversation as I had been this morning, but I had no choice now. She needed to know the truth. About Walt.

About how I felt.

"It's Walt. They pulled him out of the coma."

CHAPTER SEVENTEEN

KEIRA

"HE'S AWAKE?" I GASPED. MY HEART PULLED TO A STOP IN MY chest. "Does he remember who attacked him?"

Archer's head dropped, his fingers strumming on my desk for a split second before he replied, "No. He doesn't remember anything."

There the conversation stopped like it was suspended on the edge of a cliff. As the last couple of days ticked by, I found myself losing my will to be right. Of course, I didn't want to be in danger. I didn't want the mob to be after me again. But if they weren't, where did that leave Archer and me? Our proximity—our relationship—had always revolved around my peril. If that was gone, I was afraid to hope that what was left would be enough to hold us together.

"Keira, I have no proof that you're in danger," he rasped, but I stopped him before he could continue.

I didn't want to hear it. I didn't want to hear the man I ached for—the man whose presence, passion, and protectiveness I'd gorged on for the last week—tell me that we needed to take a step back for whatever dutiful reason.

I thought I could handle it, but I couldn't.

"Well, that's a good thing, right?" I asked, a slight quiver in my flippant voice. "I guess this means you don't have to waste your time following me around all day. I can go home, and you can have your house back to yourself—"

"No." The word fired through the space.

"W-What?" My heart hummed with hope in my chest.

"Dammit, Keira." He dragged a hand through his hair. "I don't want you to leave my house." His Adam's apple bobbed. "Or me."

Heat spilled through me, and I stepped closer to him. "What are you saying?"

"I'm saying that I'm here to protect you—I will always be here to protect you. But it's not why I'm with you, and it's not why I want you to stay with me... I'm not sure it ever was." He reached up and tucked a strand of hair back behind my ear, tenderly trailing his finger along my cheek. "But if that's not what you want—if it's too soon, I—"

I crushed my lips to his, snaking my arms around his neck and plastering myself to his front.

His growl echoed against the thrashing of our tongues and when he wrapped his big arms around me and lifted me off the floor, I wrapped my legs around his waist, feeling the hardness my body ached for wedged right against my core.

I loved so many things about being with Archer, but the way he was so big compared to me, the way he could manhandle me into any position and then dominate my body, made me shiver every time I thought about it.

My back hit the wall and his hips began to grind into mine, rocking his cock against my swollen clit.

"Please, Archer," I panted, letting my head fall to the side so his teeth could have at my neck.

I loved it when he marked me.

"Tell me what you want, baby."

And baby. God, I loved when he called me baby.

I gasped, a bolt of pleasure searing me with a thought. "I want you to tattoo me."

His mouth peeled slow from where he'd been biting the corner between my neck and shoulder, steadily sucking a new bruise of blood to the surface of my skin. *My very own vampire.*

"What?"

Permanence.

"Take me to my table," I ordered, meeting his stare.

We both knew what this meant to me—to us.

Carrying me, he walked us into the front room. I'd already cleaned up everything and had my machine set up for my next client; I just hadn't known my next client would be me.

My butt landed on the table, and I pointed to my wireless tattoo gun. He picked it up and hit the power button, remembering how it worked from the time I used it on him.

"You sure you want me to tattoo you?" he asked low, coming to stand between my thighs. His other hand reached up and palmed my breast through my shirt, fireworks of pleasure shooting out from the firm touch.

"You know how to mark me," I said breathlessly. "I want you to mark me."

His lips tipped to my ear. "My cum against your womb isn't enough?"

I shuddered and moaned, my eyes hazy as they slid to his. "I want this, too."

His face screwed. He was trying to figure out what the hell to tattoo on me.

I reached between us and palmed my hand over his crotch, reveling in his low hiss. He took my wrist and pulled my seeking fingers away.

"Careful or you won't get the tattoo," he warned and then stepped back. "Take your bottoms off."

My feet touched the floor and then I wriggled out of my pants. Positioning myself back on the edge of the table, I rested my hands on my thighs and then spread them wide. Heat flushed up into my cheeks, the move bold.

He made a strangled noise but it was the rough way he

had to undo the front of his pants to release the pressure on his cock that really turned me on.

My pulse thrummed when he stepped back between my legs.

"Hold my shoulders," he instructed against my ear. "The things you do to me, baby…" he trailed off as his teeth found their previous notch in my neck.

I moaned, and my eyes grew hooded when his hand found my waist and then slid over my quivering stomach to my slick sex.

He groaned loudly when his fingers slipped into my wet heat.

"So pink and puffy and wet." He pushed two fingers inside me, curling into my G-spot.

"Archer!" I gasped. My nails dug into his shoulders. "Tattoo me."

His teeth pressed deeper for a second before he drew back. I opened my eyes just enough to see the tattoo machine come for my neck. I didn't even register its low hum over the buzzing of my blood, but I did feel the burn of the needle as it bit into my skin—*right where his teeth had been.*

"Are you…" I couldn't finish; he'd finished the first mark and at that moment stroked his fingers against my G-spot again, making me buck.

"Stay still or you'll mess up your bite marks."

Yup, he was. He was tattooing his teeth marks to the corner of my neck.

Just like the constellation, the string of smaller lines probably wouldn't look like much of anything from a distance. It was only up close with a view of both the front of the slope of my shoulder and the back that someone would be able to tell it was the tattoo of a bite mark.

I hissed when the needle etched the next line into my skin and then cried out when the pain was followed by a burst of exquisite pleasure from his fingers inside my pussy.

Pain and pleasure. Good and bad. Right and wrong. We'd been defined by both and broke the line between them.

My body spiraled high—the alternating pain and pleasure wreaking havoc on my nerves. My fingers dug into his thick muscles for support, and I gasped for air.

The press of his fingers along my inner wall became constant even as his other hand continued the small design of the tattoo. No more alternating. He bombarded my body with pain and pleasure at the same time, and the result was breathtaking.

"Archer, please," I moaned, sucking in air though it felt like I lost it all before it reached my lungs. "What are you doing?" I thrashed my head to the side, letting my hips buck freely against his expert touch for an instant when the needle retreated from my neck.

"The same thing you're doing to me," he ground out.

I dropped my gaze down, seeing the thickness of his cock jutting out from the waist of his boxer briefs, moisture beading at the small slit in the red bulbous tip. My muscles clenched, anticipating the feel of him inside me. The stretch. The soreness. The fullness. The heat that would fill me when he came. My core squeezed again, and he swore roughly, his cock stretching higher out of the fabric.

I bit my lip at the return of the needle. He worked faster now. Both on my sex and on my skin. The stroke of his fingers was accompanied by the press of his thumb on my clit, all the while he traced the outline of the edges of his top teeth on the back of my shoulder.

My eyes squeezed shut. My head tipped forward until it rested on his shoulder. I couldn't take any more. I didn't even know how much more there was to take, but I felt the hot coil inside me cinching tight, ready to snap.

"God, you're so fucking wet and ready for me," he mumbled, trying hard to focus on his task and hang onto his restraint.

His name tumbled from my lips in a mindless chant.

"Done." The pain disappeared. The machine landed on the rolling stand beside me, and the sound made my eyes fly open just as Archer pulled his fingers from me.

I felt the blunt rim of him against my entrance but only for a second before he drove inside me, my clenching muscles protesting wildly at the massive intrusion.

But then he began to move, and I swore my heart stopped just so that I wouldn't have to feel anything except the way he claimed my body.

I held his shoulders, and he gripped my waist, driving into me with such force that the table inched back with each thrust. My legs lifted so my heels could dig into his waist, holding him tighter.

"God, yes," I panted, the slap of our hips resonating around the room.

He fucked me hard and honest, the truth as bare as his cock was inside me. *He wanted to be with me.* And I lost it. My orgasm ripped through me like a tidal wave, crashing over me with wave after forceful wave. My body gripped and squeezed his hard length, pulling him deeper and deeper until I no longer knew where I ended and he began.

I forced my eyes open, wanting to watch him come. The cords of his neck tensed. The muscle in his jaw was locked hard. But this time, his eyelids weren't drawn tight, instead, he was staring at my new tattoo like he was possessed.

Possessed with possessing me.

I wanted to send him over the edge. I wanted to make this big, beautiful man break. So, I tipped my head slightly to the side and murmured, "I'm yours."

He shouted, his hips pistoning to new depths before the warm rush of his release erupted inside me.

He held me to his chest, and I inhaled him, that same scent from Boston. The rich, earthy one that started as freedom and then grew into hope, then home, and now... My eyes traveled up to his and by the time they met his piercing green gaze, I knew that scent—*him*—it meant something more.

"So, how did I do?" he said, carefully pulling from my body and tucking himself back into his jeans.

My eyes went wide. "You mean the sex?" I blurted out.

He threw back his head and laughed. "The tattoo." *Oh. That.* "I'm happy to hear about the sex though."

He pulled a couple tissues from the box on the rolling tray and began to clean me. Meanwhile, I tried to look at my shoulder, but the angle was too steep.

"I think I need a mirror for the tattoo," I told him. "As for the sex…" I drew out the pause purposely. "It was beyond compare."

He grinned boyishly and cupped my cheek, bringing my mouth to his. "Only because you have no one to compare to."

"Are you complaining?"

"Hell fucking no." He kissed me hard, making my toes curl.

We righted our clothes, cleaned up my table—and put it back in its rightful spot. I took a peek at my tattoo in the handheld mirror and nodded my approval. Discreetly possessive. *And so damn hot.*

I threw on my sweatshirt and declared, "I'm ready."

He stood by the door, arms folded, assessing me. "Are you?"

Not ready to go. Ready to stay. With him.

I walked right up to him until we stood toe to toe and then propped my chin high. "This is the only move I've ever wanted to make."

Before, moving was a necessity. Even this last relocation to Wisdom wasn't so much a want, it was a last desperate attempt at a life. But moving in with Archer? That was something the very beat in my chest ached for.

"Is there anything you need from your rental?" He

wouldn't even call it my house anymore. "Anything you want to bring over now?"

"Nope." I shook my head, just wanting to go home. "Actually…" The wrapped stack of frames on the wall in the back caught my attention. I walked over to them and lifted up the top one. "Can we take these?"

He took the largest one from my hands and then reached for the others.

"I was going to hang them at the house, but it just never felt right. So, I brought them here, thinking it would feel right, but it didn't. Maybe it just doesn't feel right to hang them yet; it's only been—" I broke off, a sudden swell of emotion choking me.

Four months. Only four months since my dad had died. Part of me was even afraid how I'd react once I unwrapped the paintings again.

"Hey." Archer set the artwork carefully on my desk and pulled me into his arms. "They'll stay safe at home until you decide where they belong."

"Thank you." I drew back and wiped my cheeks on the ends of my sleeves.

"Don't thank me." His lips found my forehead. "I'd do anything for you, baby. Any goddamn thing."

I pressed my sleeve-covered fist to my mouth as Archer picked up my precious paintings and carried them out to his truck. *Anything for me.* I'd only ever had one person to promise me that and make good on it; safety necessitated solitude. But not anymore. Not with Archer.

I STARED at the crackling fire.

We'd been curled on the couch watching a show on Netflix

until Archer got up to shower. I stayed on the couch until he was done and called out and asked if I was coming to bed; I told him yes, but I wasn't sure how long ago that was now.

The problem was that I was stuck—stuck on something I didn't know how to talk about because I hadn't talked about it for a decade.

I looked over at the wrapped paintings propped against the wall. Asking to bring them here, hearing his promise... it tied my insides in a knot that grew tighter as the evening went on. The last person to promise to protect *and* love me had given up his entire life and the only family he ever knew to make good on that promise.

What if one day, Archer was forced to do the same?

"Keira." Archer's hoarse voice cut through my thoughts. He walked out of the bedroom shirtless, his gray sweats clinging low to his hips. "I thought you were coming to bed?"

"I am."

"What is it?" He sat down on the couch next to me, placing his palm on my leg as if to say we weren't going anywhere until we talked. "Is it us? Is it this?" he probed. "If it's too fast, we don't—"

"Stop." I turned and captured his face between my hands and then pressed my mouth on his.

I felt him sigh in relief, and then he carefully pulled me onto his lap, letting his arms circle around me.

"Then what is it?"

"Nothing. We can go to bed."

His hands slid to my shoulders, starting to massage them and then work down my spine in slow, firm circles.

"Don't run from me, Keira. Please." He took my wrist and pulled my palm to his mouth. "Just tell me what's on your mind."

I wasn't running. I was hiding—hiding the truth because I felt guilty, and I shouldn't.

"Tell me." He kissed my palm again. "I can handle it."

"You shouldn't have to. You already handle a lot." My head ducked.

He held my hand in both of his, his long fingers working their massage magic over the swell of my palm and along my own fingers. We sat there for a few minutes with only the sound of the fire and our breaths.

"It's not about should, Keira. People tell me all the time I shouldn't have had to do the things I did for my mom and siblings at such a young age, but I learned a long time ago that when it comes to people you l—care about, there is no should. Only what I would do to help them—to ease their pain. And what I would do is anything. Everything."

My throat tightened.

That was Archer. That was the man who'd brought famous Boston food to my motel room, so I wasn't stuck eating the same greasy diner dinners for three weeks. That was the man who'd brought his TV to the room, so I could watch a baseball game. That was the man who'd snuck me out to walk the Freedom Trail because he knew the solitude and anxiety was tearing me up inside no matter how hard I tried to hide it.

I found his gaze and something released inside my chest. One more lock I'd kept on my past, but it had to give if I was going to stay with Archer. That was the trade-off. Greater intimacy required greater vulnerability.

"You asked me once why my dad turned on the Kings." I inhaled and my chest burned.

"You told me it was because of you—because he didn't want you around that life any longer."

"It was because of me, but not because of the life." I tried to swallow, but it felt like acid dripping down my throat. I'd only spoken these words once—the day I'd told my dad what happened. Never again until now. "He turned on the Kings because Jimmy's son, Sean, tried to rape me when I was sixteen."

Like my head grew snakes, Archer's body turned to stone underneath me.

"What?" The word was deadly soft.

I picked a blank spot on the wall behind his head and mentally stepped through the door I thought I'd shut forever that day.

"My dad took me with him to Jimmy's house one day. They had to meet about something, I don't even know what. When we got there, my dad told Sean to take me into the living room and put on some TV; he didn't want me hearing anything that they talked about." I shuddered, and Archer gripped my upper arms. "At first, Sean didn't want to do it; he wanted to stay and be a part of their conversation like he was old enough for that. Jimmy smacked him for not obeying my dad."

"What happened?"

"Sean was mad. We went into the living room, and he started to hand me the remote only to throw it into the couch." I gulped, my body feeling numb. "He started yelling at me. *'Who did my dad think he was talking to the future head of the Kings like that?'* I tried to run but he grabbed my hair and threw me onto the couch." Ice coated my veins. "He climbed on top of me. Put his hands on my chest. Reached under my skirt. Said I was going to learn who was in charge."

My eyes fluttered shut, too heavy to hold under the weight of the nightmare.

"Keira," Archer growled and gently shook me. "What happened?"

"Before I could even think about screaming, their housekeeper—Elise—came in. She was so nice. I'd babysat her toddler a few times." I gulped. "She came back in because she'd forgotten the grocery list and when she saw me struggling against him, she pulled him off of me and smacked him."

I couldn't tell which one of us was trembling or maybe it was both of us.

"So, you told your dad?"

Hot tears branded my cheeks like scarlet letters. "No." A sob escaped, but when he tried to console me, I shook my head and flattened my palm to his chest to keep him at a distance. If he held me now, I'd never finish telling him the truth.

"I was afraid. Afraid of what Sean would say to his dad. Afraid what his dad could do to my dad. But the housekeeper... I'll never forget Elise's face when she realized she'd smacked Jimmy Maloney's son. She was petrified, Archer." And petrified was an understatement. "She looked at me and said one word—please."

My tongue felt impossibly thick and heavy, but I forced the words out anyway.

"Please what?" he asked, his jaw knotting tight.

"I-I don't know. I thought she meant please don't say anything—that if anyone said anything she would get in trouble. But now..." I dropped my head back and wiped my cheeks clean in frustration, the familiar stone of guilt jostling around in my stomach.

"Now what?"

"A week after it happened, my dad stormed home one night. I was sitting on the couch and he came right up and kneeled in front of me. He looked me in the eye and said this was the only time he was ever going to talk to me about his work." I exhaled slowly. "He told me he'd just helped Jimmy get rid of his housekeeper's dead body. My dad hadn't killed her; he promised she was dead when he got there. He knew better than to ask questions, but he believed either Jimmy or Sean did it."

"Jesus." Archer's jaw looked like it might crack. "Why did he tell you?"

I didn't bother to wipe away the tears this time. "Because Sean made a comment when he was leaving—that my dad should tell me this mess was my fault."

To this day, I wasn't sure if it was pure arrogance or pure stupidity—maybe the unfortunate marriage of both—that made him say something.

"In that moment, I knew I'd made a mistake. Elise had said 'please' because she needed my help. She needed me to tell someone what had happened to me and get her out of there," I choked out the last. "Instead, I stayed silent, and he killed her because she'd hit him—he killed her because she wouldn't ignore that he was trying to rape me."

"Keira, it wasn't your fault—*Christ*—" Archer pulled me against his chest. Only there, against his steady hardness, did I realize how badly I was shaking. "It's not your fault, baby. You were just a kid, and she… she knew she was doing the right thing."

"But it cost her—"

"Yes, it cost her." He held me tighter. "Doing the right thing doesn't mean there aren't any consequences."

I took several breaths, just absorbing what he'd said and the way it stilled my soul.

"How do you always know the right things to say?"

"I don't. But after raising four siblings, I usually can get pretty close." That loosened a small laugh from the bind in my chest. "What happened after you told your dad?"

"After I told him the truth, he was furious. That was the first time I'd ever looked at him and saw a man capable of killing." Until that moment, who he was and what he did had always been very distinct in my mind—like the sun and the moon, two sides of him that never met until they eclipsed that night. "He went and confronted Jimmy."

"I take it Jimmy didn't respond like he'd hoped?"

Not a far leap, considering he knew this led my dad to turn on the Irish Kings.

"Jimmy told him that it was all in good fun—a boy being a boy and a little too handsy."

"*Fucker.*"

I took a trembling breath, curling myself tighter against his heat. "Dad said that was the moment he knew that deep down, Sean Maloney was growing up to be bad news and his father, Jimmy, wouldn't be the one to stop it."

"So, he went to the feds." Archer's hand on my back slid up and began to gently massage the back of my scalp.

"Mhmm. Said that would be the worst way to hurt them." I sagged against him, my eyes fluttering shut as his fingers worked magic—not just on my head but on my hurting heart.

"I'm sorry, Keira. I'm so fucking sorry," he rasped. "He should've killed him—I would've killed him."

My eyes snapped open. To hear Archer Reynolds, the man who had always shone as bright as his badge and used every letter of the law to define himself, say that he would've killed Sean Maloney for what he did was something that shook me to my core.

I pushed off his chest and wiped my cheeks clean. "Archer, you don't have to—"

He reached up and flattened his hands on top of mine, framing them against my cheeks and holding them there to make sure my gaze never left his.

"I would kill anyone who tries to hurt you, Keira," he swore to me.

Not just to me—to the little girl who'd been scarred from that moment, scarred into believing that protecting me came with a risk and that maybe it was safer for everyone if I was alone.

My lip quivered. "Dad would like you."

"I hope so." He grunted and flashed a small smile. Then

he pulled my hands to his mouth, kissing the slope of each thumb. "What can I do?"

I watched how the fire caught at the threads of gold buried in his mossy eyes. I'd never told anyone the truth about what happened—one more secret that needed to stay behind locked doors. But just like every other door, all Archer had to do was ask, and I couldn't stop myself from inviting him into my life. Into my past. Into my secrets. And into my heart.

"Take me to bed."

He lifted me and carried me into his room, tucking us both into the massive bed.

For a decade, the ideas of vulnerability and safety were mutually exclusive for me. And then Archer happened.

Now, I was completely vulnerable to the strong man determined to take care of me. *And I'd never felt safer.*

CHAPTER EIGHTEEN

ARCHER

"You know, I didn't notice the first time around how hot Charlie is."

My head whipped up from the steaks I was seasoning.

"Excuse me?"

Keira hid a smile, pretending to be focused on sweet potatoes she was cutting. "Charlie." Her eyes detoured to the TV in the living room where we'd put on Twilight for old times' sake. "I just never realized how good-looking he was the first time around."

Do not get jealous over an actor.

"Maybe I should turn this off," I grunted. *Or... get jealous.*

"You wouldn't," she gasped, hiding her smile.

I set the steaks by the stove and walked behind her, fitting my chest against her back and snaking a hand possessively around her stomach. "I would," I murmured in her ear.

Her head turned, and she chuckled. I followed her eyes to my workspace on the counter.

"What?"

"You're a messy cook."

I pulled back, insulted. "And you're just realizing this?"

We'd been effectively living together for almost three

weeks now. Even though Walt couldn't remember anything about the attack, Keira and I decided it was best if she was still cautious at her shop. So, she continued to see clients by appointment only. I did background checks on them and then either worked from the back of the shop or, in the few instances when I'd had to take meetings at the office to go over security protocols with clients, I'd sent one of my brothers to sit outside while Ranger monitored the security system.

As the days passed with no incident, I wondered more and more if I was just paranoid. But then, each night I pulled her into my arms after losing myself in her body and decided I'd rather be paranoid than risk anything that could take her from me again.

And if Keira thought my idea of protecting her was overkill, she didn't show it. It wasn't the normal progression of a relationship—not with danger looming like a shadow over our heads—but neither of us cared that we were locked away together for days on end. It was almost like being back in Boston, except better scenery, better food, and lots of sex. And if I was being honest, danger or not, I wouldn't mind living like this with her for the rest of our lives. *Though it would be nice to confirm that her life wasn't in peril.*

"No." She giggled. "It's just funny because everything else about you is so clean. Your house. Your office. Your truck."

I arched my eyebrow. "Everything?" I pressed my teeth into the corner of her neck. "Pretty sure my mouth is dirty, too."

She hummed and pressed back against me. "Well, that's true."

My lips slid up her soft skin in search of her delicious lips. Her head tipped onto my shoulder, letting my tongue delve deep into her mouth. My hand on her stomach slid up to cup her breast, kneading it through her shirt and bra. I'd just hooked my fingers under the edge when the door from the garage opened.

"Knock, knock," Gunner's voice called through the living room. "You better be fully clothed, Archie."

I pulled my mouth from Keira's, lifting my hand and quickly wiping her lips dry with my thumb.

"Come in!" I called, returning to my workspace on the counter and wiping it clean of the excess spices.

Gunner and Hunter came into the kitchen, each greeting Keira with a warm hug.

"Brought something for dinner." Gunner smirked and dropped a bag of chips and jar of salsa on the counter.

I shook my head. "You actually make this, Gun?" I teased, popping open the jar of homemade salsa.

As soon as I set it on the counter, Keira pulled out a bowl from the cabinet and dumped the chips into it. It was always like that between us. A natural push and pull wherever we went—whatever we did. Like two gears working in sync.

"Of course not. Hunter did. I prefer to save my hand skills for other areas," Gunner returned cockily. I growled at him when he winked at Keira. "Calm down, Archie," he teased and nodded in Keira's direction. "I want her to stick around. She's good for you." I watched him meander over to the couch and grab the remote.

He had no idea.

While I made sure she was safe, Keira had invaded all the corners of my life—the little pleasures I'd ignored because of the responsibilities I'd had to shoulder. Most nights, she insisted on cooking for me. She made sure to push my laptop screen shut when it was getting late and pull my brain away from work mode. She was the reason I'd used the bathtub in the master bathroom for the first time since the house was built.

Life had always been synonymous with duty and responsibility until she'd entered mine. Now, I craved more. More smiles and laughter. More life.

More love.

"It's Hazard's secret salsa recipe," Hunter said as he briefly embraced Keira.

She looked at me for explanation.

"Hazard Foster. He's the owner of Armorous Tactical Security and Training, a well-known security firm outside of San Francisco that specializes in high-profile cases as well as advanced tactical training," I explained, handing her a chip and pushing the jar in front of her. "Even though Hunt, Gun, and I all went through the academy, I made all four of us take Harm's four-month training course before we opened RPG."

"Ahh." She dunked the chip in the tomato salsa and fed the entire thing to her mouth.

Hunt and I exchanged glances, waiting for her reaction.

"Holy shit," she said, still chewing. "That is delicious."

That was everyone's response.

"Yup," Hunt agreed, taking a chip for himself.

"What's in it?"

I chuckled as Hunter shook his head. "Unfortunately, I'm sworn to secrecy," he told her and then chomped on the chip. "I'm sure you can wrangle it from Arch though. Mom and Ranger should be here any minute." He slapped me on the back just as the door opened and our two missing dinner guests appeared and then joined Gunner on the couch.

Mom immediately went for Keira, her face lighting with a look I'd seen a lot recently—like her son was the one who'd come back to life and she couldn't be happier.

"Is this for me?" She nodded to the wine sitting on the counter.

"Of course." I kissed her cheek. "Happy belated Birthday."

"Thank you, sweetheart." She hugged me tight. "What are you making?"

"Steaks." I faced the stove and cranked on the burner, the gas flame bursting to life. "And Keira is whipping up some mashed potatoes."

"I brought pasta salad." Ranger offered up the bowl in his hands, setting it on the island. "Hi, Keira." He adjusted his sweater vest and then pushed his hands into his pants pockets.

"Ranger," Keira greeted and embraced him, the shocked look on his face comical as he didn't know what to do. "So, do you know how to make this secret salsa?" She probed him, dipping another chip and popping it between her lips.

The griddle started spitting, drawing my attention, but I chuckled when I heard my brother's response.

"No, I don't have the secret recipe. However, salsa typically contains the same base ingredients of tomatoes, onions, and chilis. Even though it wasn't officially discovered until after the Spaniards conquered Mexico in the fifteen-hundreds, the origins of the dish can be traced back to similar variations made by the Mayans and Aztecs of Central America."

"Range, try not to fill her up on information before dinner!" Gunner called from the living room, listening to their conversation while flipping through the channels. If that wasn't classic Gunner, I didn't know what was.

"So, if you went to this training course, too, how come you didn't get the recipe?" Keira probed.

"Because I didn't complete the taser portion of the course," Ranger replied matter-of-factly. "Archer wouldn't let me."

"There was no reason for you to get tased," I said.

At the time, I wasn't sure how much fieldwork I was going to have Ranger do given his personality. However, I wanted him to be able to adequately defend himself, and I didn't want him to think he was less capable than the rest of us, so I signed him up for the course, but I told Harm that I didn't want him tased. Physically, he wasn't built like the rest of us, and he was the baby.

"I agree with your brother," Mom said. "Though I don't think there was reason for any of you."

I chuckled, watching her take a chip and dunk it in the salsa. She let out a sigh of enjoyment.

"Okay, maybe reason for at least one of you to get tased for this recipe," she then admitted with a quick wink at Keira.

"And which one would that be?" Hunter appeared, wondering cheekily which of her sons she was okay with torturing for some salsa.

Mom wagged her finger at him and opened up a bottle of wine, pouring glasses for her, Keira, and Ranger; Ranger didn't like hard alcohol or beer.

"Obviously, I love you all, so it would be among the four of you to decide," she declared.

"I vote Archie," Gunner said immediately, joining the conversation as he strolled over to the fridge and pulled out beers for the rest of us, using his palm to pop the caps.

"Of course, you do," I muttered.

Laughing, Keira picked up the cutting board of chopped potatoes and brought it over to the stove where the large pot of boiling water waited.

"Only because you'd volunteer yourself before picking any of us to take the shock," he retorted and my lips pulled tight. "You know I'm right. If self-sacrifice was an Olympic sport, you'd take home every medal, Archie."

"Happily for those I love," I grumbled and caught Keira looking at me as she strained the potatoes into the mixer. Her expression was soft with longing. She was thinking about our conversation the other night where I'd held her and sworn to do anything for her.

Love wasn't mentioned, but it was there. *It was felt.*

"Well, I'd pick you, Gun," Hunt chimed in, clinking their beer bottles together.

"Dick." They both drank, and then Gunner turned to Ranger. "How about you, Range? You going to make it a tie so that Mom has to pick?"

All eyes went to Ranger who blinked and then crossed his arms.

"No, I would pick Archer, too," he replied clearly.

Gunner laughed and clapped his hands. Hunt and I stared at our youngest brother, surprised he picked at all.

"Really?"

"Well, research has shown that taser effectiveness does decrease with increasing body mass. So, since Archer is the largest out of all of us"—he paused here when Gunner made an affronted sound—"he would be the least hurt by the voltage."

"Least?" I chuckled, taking a plate and placing a grilled sirloin on it before handing it to Keira so she could add on the mashed potatoes. "That shit hurt like a bitch, Ranger. There was no least about it."

Dinner became an assembly line. I added the steak, Keira scooped on the potatoes, and then Mom topped it off with the pasta salad before passing the finished plate to one of my brothers.

"Well, of course it still hurt. The electrical impulses are still sending fifty-thousand volts through your system to electrically incapacitate your nerves and send your muscles into shock," he went on, completely focused on the facts as he took a plate from Mom.

"We better sit now because if we wait for him to finish, dinner will be cold," Hunt broke in, taking his plate and directing everyone over to the table.

The next forty-five minutes was spent alternating between facts, feast, and laughter. Once it was officially concluded that, regardless of the vote, I would take the tase for the greater snacking good of my family, the conversation then moved onto other stories from our time training at Armorous, and then back even farther to our childhood.

"I wish there were embarrassing stories of Archie to tell,

but he's always so far above the law, I'm surprised he doesn't suffer from vertigo," Gunner remarked.

"What about that one time he passed out in my bushes in front of the house?" Mom asked, her eyes twinkling as she drained the last of her wine.

"In the bushes?" Keira's head whipped to me, her eyes wide and dancing.

"That doesn't even sound like me, Mom," I returned with a laugh. "That was Gunner."

Gunner set his beer on the table with a loud clink, claiming the attention. "True." He held up a finger. "But in my defense, that was all your fault."

"Me?" My eyebrows lifted and I shook my head. "How is it my fault you couldn't hold your liquor?"

Keira looked between us, and Hunt stepped in with the story.

"We all went out for Gunner's twenty-first birthday. Of course, Gunner was Gunner and overdid it within the first hour," Hunt explained and Gunner smirked and shrugged. "So, Arch and I brought him back to Mom's and dropped him off, thinking he could at least make it inside."

"I made it to the bushes and passed out," Gunner finished. "And would you believe it, Keira? These two assholes left me there."

I looked at my woman—the way she murmured in mock outrage, '*The horror*' and then covered her mouth and laughed. She fit in with my family. Granted, it was hard not to when they made a point of welcoming everyone, but she fit without effort. She fit like she was meant to be there.

"You looked pretty comfortable to us," I replied and reached for Keira's hand, giving it a squeeze.

He flipped us the finger, and then eagerly continued to share embarrassing stories about himself because that was who Gunner was—the life of the party. Carefree, a little cheeky, but always kind.

"Well, all I know is that Gunner walked into the kitchen the next morning with branches and leaves coming from everywhere." Mom stood and swayed.

Hunter quickly reached over and grabbed her empty plate that she was about to bring to the kitchen. "Looks like you've thoroughly enjoyed your glass of wine for tonight, Mom." He looked at Ranger who immediately rose and walked Mom into the kitchen, securing her to a counter stool before she toppled over.

"So, are you two official now?" Gun asked casually as we collected in the kitchen for clean up. "Or is Archie still pretending like it's normal for him to protect his clients from the comfort of his own bed."

"Gunner!" Mom gasped and then swatted him on the back of the head as he walked by.

I glared at my smirking younger brother, but before I could say anything, Keira's hand found its way to my arm, staying my anger.

"What? I think we all need to know so that you can stop asking us," Gunner countered, putting Mom in the hot seat.

I turned to Keira while they bickered and murmured, "Sorry. My brothers are annoying."

"Don't apologize." Her eyes twinkled. "I've waited a lifetime to feel safe enough to be able to feel annoyed."

My jaw tightened along with my chest.

My family was nosy—no, *invasive*. But they were loving and loyal as hell, and I wanted nothing more than for her to have that part of them, too. I wanted to give her everything she never had. That desire started four years ago with Boston's favorite eats and a tour of the Freedom Trail. It then grew to giving her the kind of safety and freedom she couldn't question. And now...

I slid my hand around her nape and brought my lips down to hers, kissing her in front of my mom and brothers.

Now, I wanted to give her family and a future here with me.

And love. God, I wanted to give her so much love.

"Guess that answers my question."

When I pulled back, I saw Gunner had his phone out.

"Seriously?" I lunged for him, but he easily sidestepped and put the island between us.

"Just sending it to Gwen. Calm down, Archie. Sis needs to know that big brother finally let his guard down," he teased, putting his phone away and taking the dirty plate from my hand. "Now, let me wash up. Your work here is done."

I eyed him for a second but finally caved.

"And I think it's time for me to head home," Mom said.

She and Ranger made their way around the island, saying goodbye to everyone and thanking us for dinner. When she pulled me in for a hug and kiss, she said, "She's perfect, sweetheart. And you both deserve this happiness."

Before I could reply, her embrace moved to Keira where she not so quietly whispered that she needed to set up an appointment for her tattoo. I stared at Keira, waiting for an explanation which I finally got once Mom and Ranger left.

"I'm not going to tell her no," she said.

Gunner chuckled. "And you know Mom won't listen if you tell her no."

I grunted.

The four of us cleared the rest of the table and made quick work of the dishes. There was a brief discussion about Gunner's case that he was leaving tomorrow for—personal security detail for the CEO of a national healthcare system at their annual retreat in Jackson—before my brothers who, no matter how much shit they gave me, knew when it was time to go because my growly demeanor made it clear I was done with sharing my woman for the day.

The alarm system beeped as it secured the house.

I went up behind Keira as she dried her hands in front of

the sink and turned her to me, lifting her in my arms. "Time for bed, baby."

She sighed audibly.

Sometimes, I wondered if she knew about the sound she made every time I called her baby, but I shied away from asking because I never wanted her to stop making it.

"Thank you," she murmured as I carried her down the hall and into the master bedroom.

I didn't bother with the lights, the moon and stars broke up the blanket of night and shone brightly through the large windows.

"For subjecting you to Gunner's jokes, Ranger's facts, and my mom's tipsy requests?" I chuckled, peeling her shirt up her body.

"For sharing your family with me."

"They're all yours," I told her. I'd meant it facetiously, but as soon as the words were out and she stilled in my arms, I realized I was completely serious. Tipping her head back, I tucked her hair behind her ears. "You didn't have anything like this when you were younger?"

She shook her head. "My dad did with the Kings, but I didn't. As much as he wanted to keep me away from that world, he also couldn't bring himself to leave it."

Until they'd forced him to choose between his loyalty to them or loyalty to his daughter.

"And what about you and him?" I sat her on the bed and kneeled in front of her, peeling off her slippers and then her socks and then gently massaging her feet one by one.

She gave me a sad smile, sighing when my fingers rubbed deeper into the balls of her feet. "We were partners. Him and me against the world—or at least the criminal one. But we didn't have nights like this." She swallowed hard. "I think once he betrayed the Kings, it stranded him. He was no longer a part of the world he knew, but he didn't know how to be a part of the real world either."

I hummed low, continuing to rub and encourage her to open up. "And you?"

"I was stuck trying to bridge the two." She rested back on her palms. "Don't get me wrong, I loved my dad. We were close, and he loved me more than anything. But there were parts of him—of his life and criminal past—that were always off-limits to me. His first priority was always to keep me safe, but keeping his secrets came in a close second." She sighed. "Like the sacrifice he made to keep me safe would never make up for the failures of his lawlessness and the danger they'd put me in."

I took a slow breath, the image of my mom in Roman's arms burned its way to the forefront of my mind, her throat mangled and bloody from where she'd almost been strangled to death. He'd arrived just in time to save her, while if it had been up to only me, I would've been too late.

"It's hard when those failures almost cost you someone you love," I rasped and then hissed low when her hand reached out and cupped my cheek, tipping my face up.

"Failure doesn't imply fault, Archer."

"She told you." It wasn't like it was a secret in town—that Mom had almost been killed by a famous serial killer who was still at large no matter how much time Roman dedicated to finding the bastard.

Keira nodded.

"I know." I sighed. "But I can appreciate how hard it was for your dad to accept that."

"Your family love and admire you."

I turned so I could kiss her palm and then said, "Well, they've certainly claimed you."

They didn't need to tell me how they felt about Keira, it was obvious. Not just tonight, but from the moment I'd told them about her, they'd gone above and beyond to ease the unsteady path it took us to finally find our way to each other.

Her breath hitched. "And what about you?"

My chest rumbled possessively. "I claimed you a long time ago," I said ruefully, watching her hand as it left my cheek and touched the discreet tattoos of my teeth marks on her shoulder. "Before that," I added, heat spiraling through my blood with the feral instinct to mark her body once more.

"Before?"

"From the moment you allowed me to enter your room in Boston," I confessed, sliding my hands up her legs to the waist of her jeans.

Her tongue slid out along her bottom lip. "I didn't realize…"

I gave her a half-tipped smile and confessed honestly, "Neither did I."

I hadn't realized that single question had changed my entire life. *May I come in?* Into her room. Into her life. Into her secrets and her past and her pain. Into her dreams and her goals and her future. *Into her heart.*

Leaning forward, I took her mouth, her tongue instantly tangling with mine.

We kissed deep as I stripped off the rest of our clothes until we were nothing but bared skin and souls. Laying her back on the bed, I skated my mouth down her torso, pausing at the delicious peaks of her tits for a quick taste before I settled between her thighs. And there I devoured her sweet honey until my tongue chased three orgasms from her body, leaving her limp and shuddering and begging for me.

Only then did I rise over her and with a firm flex of my hips, bury my cock completely inside her welcoming heat.

"So damn perfect, baby," I rasped against her mouth, anchoring my body to hers with strong but languid strokes.

Everything about tonight was perfect—was how it should be. Her. In my home. With my family. In my bed.

Keira purred under me, the ache for one more orgasm making her hips buck eagerly against mine. My cock swelled, strangled by the tightness of her small body.

I felt the words on the tip of my tongue. *I love you.* I wasn't a man who shied away from the truth, but with her—a woman who'd been starved of a relationship with depth and vulnerability—I had to tread carefully. So, instead, I confessed without words. I latched my teeth to their home on the side of her neck and sucked hard against her skin, drawing blood and pleasure from her body.

She came again with a breathless cry, her pussy gripping my swollen length and milking my own release. I growled against my hold on her neck as I climaxed, shunting my dick all the way against her womb and exploding hot cum against it.

Our bodies rose and fell in sync, coming down from one more high into each other's arms. Like every other night, she curled against my chest, and I pressed my lips to her forehead.

She wasn't the one who'd been claimed in that doorway, I realized. *I was.* Utterly and completely claimed by her.

I wanted to tell her I loved her, but not tonight. Not until I could say it knowing she felt safe and free enough to say it back. So, until that day came, I would continue to show her— to give her the words without having to say them.

CHAPTER NINETEEN

KEIRA

I CHECKED THE CLOCK ON THE TV AND THEN AGAIN ON MY phone, wondering what was taking Archer so long.

Maybe that I'd sent him back to my half moved-in house to bring over a bunch of my things.

At breakfast this morning, I'd mentioned that I wanted to stop back at the rental to grab some more clothes and underwear because I only had a few pairs to cycle through that I'd grabbed the night of his mom's party.

"Sounds like a you problem," he'd replied with that playful grin that made my lower parts tingle.

"I can start going commando to my appointments if you'd prefer," I'd managed to counter.

A small moan escaped when I thought about what happened next.

His stool had skidded on the floor as he stood and stalked next to me, trapping me in my own seat with a hand firmly planted on the counter on either side of me.

"If I go back over there, Keira, I'm bringing the rest of your stuff."

My heart skipped a beat. It was one thing to agree to stay when Walt couldn't remember anything about the attack, but this? Moving all of my meager possessions from the rental to

Archer's house was a bold declaration. Bolder than kissing me in front of his family. Bolder than tattooing me with his mark.

And after all the time spent with him and then with his family, I finally gave into the want.

"Okay," I'd said with a huge sigh of relief like the final weights I'd used to hold myself back were gone.

I wanted Archer. All of him. His protectiveness. His duty. His caring. His possessiveness. His home. His family. His heart.

The feeling welled inside me once more, and I reached for the edge of the couch to steady myself against its strength. I'd never allowed myself to want something so badly before. *I'd never allowed myself to think I could actually have something I wanted this badly before.*

Everything okay? I texted Archer.

His response wasn't immediate. From the dots, it looked like he tapped a reply, deleted, and then started again.

Be there in five.

I didn't know why, but I shivered.

I hadn't been back to the rental since that night, but I didn't remember it being that much of a mess that it would take him this long to bring my things. I didn't have a ton of clothes. The appliances and furniture had come with the place as part of the agreement. And my only other possessions were currently wrapped and stacked against Archer's living room wall. *My dad's paintings.*

I looked at the light gray wall and suddenly saw the one painting—the ship on stormy seas—in the bare spot. I blinked and the wall was empty again, but the urge to hang the painting lingered. I pressed my hand to the smooth paint, feeling for the first time that I might've found the right place for the only things I had left of my dad.

At the sound of the alarm disabling, I dropped my hand to my side and faced the door just as Archer walked through it.

And when he did, the smile I held onto knowing the roots

I was forming with him were about to grow deeper, died with the look on his face.

"Archer…"

He was in front of me in a second, hauling me into his arms and carrying me over to the couch.

"What is it? What's going on?" I asked as he sat, holding me tight in his lap.

Was it Walt? His mom? One of his brothers? Had I done something —my spilling thoughts were cut off by the hard edge of his voice.

"Someone broke into the house, Keira," he rasped, his arms tightening their hold.

And just like that, I regretted the tiny, hesitant steps I'd taken without wearing the weight of caution as a parachute. I wasn't protected. I wasn't safe. And as the ground felt like it opened up beneath me, I gasped for air as I free-fell into fear.

The freedom I'd inched and clawed for was ripped away from me in a second, and suddenly, I was back in my former life, existing like a ghost in the land of the living, unable to leave any marks, form any tangible relationships, *exist* because it left a trail.

"What?" My instincts kicked in, and I pushed against his chest, standing—stumbling to the side as I tried not to panic.

"Keira—"

"Just tell me what happened," I pleaded, trying to collect where I felt myself crumbling at every seam.

His expression was pained, wanting to reach for me but also wanting to respect my request.

"I went to the house to get your things, and the door was busted open. Inside everything was a mess. Furniture turned over. Every cabinet and drawer looked like it was searched through." His hands locked in front of him, turning white at the knuckles. "I called Diehl right away. He's still there cataloging the scene, but I needed to get back to you."

"I don't understand." The words spilled out brokenly from

my chest. "First Walt, now this." My head turned in slow measures through the fog of confusion and disbelief. "This isn't what they do when they come after people—when they come after me," I told him. "Even if they wanted to go after someone else to get to me, they wouldn't go after a drunken postman; they'd pick someone I care about. And they wouldn't terrorize my house, there's no point if I'm the only thing they're after."

"I don't disagree," he said with a low tone. "I already talked to Hunter on my way back here, and you're right. It doesn't make sense what is happening if it's you that they're after."

If.

"But it is me that they're after. My shop. My house." I drew a trembling breath. "They've found me, Archer. The Kings have found me."

How? I had no idea. But I guess that didn't matter—it didn't change reality.

The vulnerabilities I tried to bury bubbled up and erupted before I could stop them and my chest caved in with such a painful sob I thought my ribs might crack in the vacuum.

"What am I doing? I'm never going to be safe. This is never going to end." Tears spilled over my cheeks.

He stood and pulled me back in his arms, and in spite of everything that told me I shouldn't, I clung to him like he was the only thing keeping me above water.

"Don't say that, Keira. We don't know—"

"But we do," I protested. "You know you do. You know I'm the target here—you've always known, I was just too stubborn to believe it. I thought I was finally free, but that's never going to happen. They're always going to find me."

Pain lanced my chest like the sharpest lesson: I would never be safe from the Irish Kings. My dad was right to keep running—to keep moving. It was the only way to stay alive, even if it wasn't really living.

"I can't stay here. I'm a danger. They already hurt Walt, who knows who—"

"Keira." Strong, warm hands framed my face. "You're not going anywhere."

"How can I stay?" I cried quietly. "I can't stay. I should be alone—"

"Dammit, Keira, you're not alone," he growled low and stamped his mouth to mine. His kiss was hard and furious, warning my fears away from his woman. "You have me. You will always have me."

"I can't ask you to protect me again, Archer," I murmured against his mouth.

"Baby, you never have to ask a man to protect the woman he loves, it's just what we do," he declared.

I sucked in a breath. *The woman he loves.*

He lifted me when my knees started to buckle, returning us to our spot on the couch where we'd started.

"Archer…" I didn't know what to say. Part of me wanted to warn him away—to tell him that he couldn't love me because it was too risky and uncertain. But the words were like oxygen and once they infused my cells, I couldn't figure out how to deny them.

"I love you," he repeated, his big fingers brushing my hair from where it stuck to my face. "I love you no matter what."

There was a ripple of silence so profound I swore it shifted the mountains in the distance with its force.

A hot tear burned down my cheek. "I love you, too."

His arms snaked tighter, pressing me flush to his chest.

"Promise me you won't make me lose you again." I flinched, but he grabbed my chin before I could look away. "Last time, I lost you because you ran—because you thought you had no other option. I'm asking you to trust me this time. To stay here. With me. And fight this—whatever or whoever it is."

I tried to swallow but couldn't. Everything seemed

unsteady. The earth. The air. The present. The future. Everything except for him.

"Do you remember what you told me that day at the site of the Boston Massacre?" His question grounded me instantly in that memory and the sharp feelings it evoked. "You asked me how the colonists must've felt."

"I remember." I could picture the cobblestones at my feet.

"I said angry and you corrected me."

"I said they felt trapped." I shuddered, even just the word evoking the former cage where I'd had to live my life.

"Exactly," he said, his eyes searching mine. "Trapped by their past. Trapped by rules and dictates they couldn't escape. Trapped in a cycle that continuously took away their freedom."

My breath caught. I'd likened my former life to those of the colonists before—trapped by the very people who were supposed to protect them. But I could tell from Archer's voice that this was something more.

"So, what did they do?" he pressed.

"Rebelled?" My voice cracked on the word.

"They fought, Keira, when they just as easily could've run. They could've accepted that there was nothing they could do to change what was happening to them. They could've been governed by fear and retreated into whatever kind of life would be left for them, but they didn't," he said vehemently. "They stayed and fought—fought against men with uniforms and weapons, fought against the King and Crown and the only government they'd ever known. They fought against all the odds. Farmers and tradesmen against trained soldiers. Colonies against an empire."

My heartbeat revolted in my chest, hammering like a war drum eager for battle.

"Are you saying that this is my revolution?"

"I'm saying that there will always be something to run from in life, baby," he rasped softly. "But I want to be the thing that makes you stay and fight. I want to be the hope that makes you stand against the odds."

It was different tears that cleansed my cheeks this time. And though it seemed impossible, I felt in that moment the difference between safety and security. I wasn't safe—not from the Kings. But I was secure.

"Stay with me," he begged. "Let me fight with you."

With me.

Not for me. Not because of me. Not instead of me.

With. Me.

Like Orion had hunted with Artemis.

"Okay."

His breath exhaled in a warm rush against my lips just before he kissed me. It was a different kind of kiss than any before it—it was more than a kiss, it was an oath.

Archer kissed me for a long time, slow and steady, until there was no question that he wasn't going anywhere.

"So, what do we do now?" I asked when we finally broke apart. "Should I call Agent Lattimore?"

That was the protocol if anything were to ever happen, I was supposed to call Lattimore. One time, I'd asked my dad where we would go if they found us again. He'd smiled and said the Bahamas. I'd smiled back and pretended like I didn't see the worry in his eyes, knowing that would be the end of all hope for us ever finding peace.

"Do you trust me?"

I rolled my lip between my teeth and nodded. He set me to the side of him and fished out his cell.

"I want to call Roman first," he said. "I want him to see if he can get me photos of all the Kings' current associates; I'd like to take them to the hospital to show Walt, maybe it will trigger his memory."

"I could ask Agent Lattimore for those things…"

His lips pulled tight for a second. "You could, but then he'd know you were here."

My brow creased. "You don't think he… all those years…" *No, he wouldn't have done that to my dad and me.*

"No," Archer assured me. "But I also want to be damn certain this has to do with your past and not anything else."

"But it has to be the Kings… who else could it be?"

He exhaled low. "I don't know, baby. What I do know is that there's something missing here. Like you said, if they are after you, then why aren't they coming after *you?*" He dragged his hand through his hair. "Let me put it like this. If it were any other person who owned that shop, who rented that house, I would say that whoever is doing this is looking for something not someone."

I folded my legs under me and pulled a pillow into my lap. "But because it's me, it's hard to ignore that bad people could be looking for me."

"Right," he grunted. "So, I want to see if I can pinpoint exactly who is here committing these crimes before you call Lattimore and break down that last shield protecting your life here."

"I see."

He splayed his hand over my knee. "You can call Lattimore as soon as we're sure it's them and it has to do with you, okay?"

I laid my hand over his. "I trust you, Archer."

His chin dipped and then he rose, dialing his friend's number.

"Hey, Roman, I need to call in that favor."

I stood from the couch and listened to Archer on the phone. He didn't hide anything from me, keeping his entire conversation within earshot.

"I know you quit the FBI, but you know as well as I do that your connections run decades deep," he went on with a slight laugh that faded as soon as he got down to business. "Can you get me photos of all known major players within Boston's Irish Kings?"

I wandered around the back of the couch again while Archer was silent though I felt his gaze on me.

"I'm sure Ranger could give you the statistic on what the chances are of having to deal with a serial killer and East Coast mobsters in such a small town, but I don't have those figures on hand," Archer joked.

I paused in front of the stack of my dad's paintings. I ran my fingers along the edge of the tallest frame, remembering the day my dad had let me pick out frames even though he'd never hung the artwork.

"We're not running anymore, Dad," I murmured so softly to the lifeless paintings like they could get the message to him. "I'm not running anymore."

I didn't hear their muttered goodbyes and only looked up because Archer's presence collided with my space.

"He'll have the photos to me by tomorrow, so I'll go to the hospital and talk to Walt," he told me. "I'll have Hunt take you to the shop and bring you home."

I nodded but didn't respond.

He reached out and untied the cloth covering the painting, letting it slide down the canvas.

"Should we hang them?"

My head snapped to his, finding his gaze waiting. *How did he know the urge I'd felt earlier?*

"Here?" I squeaked. "Now?"

He chuckled, his hand finding mine, and pulled it to his lips. "I want every part of you here, baby. Now until forever."

I smiled. In the midst of everything going on, I smiled because I realized I finally had something that I couldn't lose; *him.*

"I love you, Archer."

He grinned at me. "I love you, too."

"I think these walls are where this art belongs."

CHAPTER TWENTY

KEIRA

Still at the hospital waiting to talk to Walt. Hunter's waiting to take you home. Call you when I leave and have service.

I SIGHED AND CLOSED ARCHER'S TEXT MESSAGE. WHEN I looked out the window, I saw Hunter's Jeep sitting in the parking lot.

It won't be like this forever, Keira. Just for now. Trust me.

And I did. I trusted him. *I loved him.* But it was still hard not to let a decade of old skepticism rear its ugly head.

I packed up the last of my things for the day. My client, Lisha, had left almost thirty minutes ago. It wasn't a bad thing that my shop was by appointment only for the time being, but I also hoped there would come a day when I wouldn't have to be afraid of who might open the door and walk in if I left it unlocked.

I pinched the bridge of my nose, feeling a small headache come on. I'd been working on an intricate Henna-design tattoo down Lisha's side for four hours and the detail work under the lights, combined with the constant concern that someone was after me was proving to be too much.

I just wanted to go home and curl into Archer's arms where I knew I was safe and loved by the man who fought to keep me free, but I'd told Zoey earlier I would stop over after work today. Even though I was exhausted, the distraction might be good if Archer was still going to be a while.

A shuffling sound caught my attention, and I turned just in time to see a flyer slide under the door.

Strange. My mail should still be going to my PO box.

Maybe it was something local.

I finished lacing my sneakers and went over to pick it up, my stomach falling to the floor when I bent over and saw the message scrawled on the flyer.

We will get what belongs to us.

It was handwritten in Sharpie over a Netflix advertisement. I reached for it and the paper slipped from my fingers the first attempt I made to pick it up. Clutching it tighter the second time, I rose.

Keep breathing, Keira.

I read the words again.

We will get what belongs to us.

My first thought was that it didn't make sense. I would've expected it to say *We will get you* or *We're coming for you.* Instead, it was cryptic. Too cryptic for a criminal organization that very simply wanted me dead for my father's treasonous actions.

Shaking my head, I flipped the flyer over, not really expecting more of the note or an explanation on the back, but just out of some instinct.

Nope, nothing on the back—

My gaze just landed on the note once more before I whipped the paper back over to the advertisement on the back. It was for a show on Netflix—*This Is A Robbery.*

I'd never seen it—never heard of it. Had no idea what it was about and wouldn't have even assumed it was anything but fiction except that there was something I recognized on the image.

My father's paintings.

The one with the ship. The one of the concert. The one of the couple in black. The one of the man's face that I'd sold to buy this building.

Why were his paintings part of a Netflix show?

Stones didn't just sink in my stomach, they skipped. Bouncing around from fact to fact. From past to present. From truth to lie.

I needed to go home. *I needed to look up this show.*

Pulling out my phone, I texted Zoey that I had a headache and that I would call her later. Then I grabbed my things, folding up the flyer and shoving it as far down in my bag as possible.

I didn't want Hunter to see—I didn't want anyone to see. Not until I knew what the hell was going on.

"Hey, Keira. Arch got held up at the hospital—"

"Yeah, he already texted me," I replied too quickly as I climbed into the passenger seat.

Hunter looked at me with a stare that was vaguely familiar. "Everything okay?"

I gulped and nodded. "Yeah, just a little bit of a headache from the day."

He grunted. "Need me to stop for anything? Advil?"

"There's some at the house, but thank you." I forced a smile.

He nodded and put his SUV in reverse.

I turned in the seat and faced the window. I should've feigned rest, but I couldn't stop myself from reaching for my phone and searching the show advertised on the flyer.

This Is A Robbery.

I should've waited to look because what I found made my stomach turn over.

253

"Everything alright?"

I nodded vigorously and squeaked, "Yeah. Just trying to pick out a new show to start watching."

"Ahh. Well, if you haven't started the Witcher, you guys really should," he suggested, and I tried to pay attention but his voice sounded like it was coming from the other end of a tunnel. "It's good. And Henry Cavill is in it. You know, he kind of grumbles a lot like Archer does."

I laughed weakly. "I'll look it up."

Clearly a fan of the show, Hunter started going on about the storyline and premise. And while in a different moment I would've been really interested to hear about a monster-killing Cavill in a land of mages and elves, right now I couldn't think about anything except the most famous art heist in history.

And the stolen paintings that were hanging in Archer's living room.

By the time I reached for the remote, I couldn't even remember if I'd said goodbye to Hunter. *Crap.* Hopefully whatever abrupt thing I did say, he chalked up to my headache and need to lie down.

My fingers were as cold as a corpse on the remote. I had to press and swipe several extra times before it registered that a living human was trying to operate it. My heart beat like a drum in my throat as I searched for the show on the flyer, pulling up the first episode though I wasn't sure why.

Maybe I needed to see it. To know that someone hadn't faked the stupid paper. *And doctored the internet.*

It only took four and a half minutes before the remote slipped from my hand, pausing the show poignantly on the image of Rembrandt's *Storm on the Sea of Galilee.* I turned my head slowly to the wall behind me, that very painting hanging proud on Archer's light gray wall.

Stolen.

My father had stolen all the paintings.

Even in my emotional state, I could piece together a timeline. The theft occurred in nineteen-ninety. Mob wars abounded in Boston and my dad had been instrumental in helping bring Jimmy Maloney and the Irish Kings to power. Maybe they'd stolen the paintings for money. But now that I thought about how my dad always talked about them—*"those paintings are the keys to freedom."* I'd thought he was speaking metaphorically—as in art was a freedom of speech, of expression.

No, he'd been cryptically literal, planting the seed that they were a Hail Mary in case of an emergency.

Oh god.

No wonder the small painting had sold so quickly.

Like a magnet held up to ferrous facts, everything that happened since I moved to Wisdom suddenly clicked into place.

Why the post office was ransacked. Why my shop and home were broken into though nothing was taken. Why Walt was attacked. The note.

It was all because of these paintings. They were like a ticking time bomb just waiting to explode.

And I just happened to have them in my hands when I'd pulled the pin.

I SANK ONTO THE COUCH, unable to stand upright without swaying.

Oh, dad. What did you do? Why couldn't you just tell me?

I was in possession of stolen art. Did this make me a criminal? *Did this make Archer a criminal?* Bolting from the couch, I tripped on its corner in my haste to reach the wall, removing the precious works from their hooks.

For no reason, I breathed a little easier once the weight of my crimes—*my father's crimes*—weren't hanging on Archer's walls anymore.

But now what?

Instinctively, I reached for my phone and went to call Archer, but at the last moment, a single word stopped me.

Please.

I gasped like a knife had been slipped right between my shoulder blades.

The paintings were here.

The paintings that they'd torn apart the post office to find. That they'd broken into my business and home to find. *That they'd almost killed Walt to find.* This house was the only place left for them to be.

Air bled from my lips.

I'd unknowingly put a target on Archer's back.

I took a deep breath. *Be safe. Be smart.*

I grabbed my phone and dialed Archer's number; it went straight to voice mail. I tried again with the same result.

Breathe.

The third time, I paced until his voice mail request ended and beeped for me to leave a message.

"It was the paintings, Archer. This whole time, it was the paintings, not me," I blurted out, barely breathing. "I know why all these things are happening, and I know how to stop them. I have to get in touch with Agent Lattimore and get him the paintings; it's the only way."

Just because Archer promised to protect me didn't mean I waived all responsibility of protecting myself—*or of protecting him.* If our situations were reversed, he would do what he had to in order to keep me safe and I shouldered no less of the same responsibility.

I wasn't going to do something stupid. I wasn't going to try to make a deal with the Kings or pawn off the art in exchange for my freedom. Dad's intentions had been good, but his execution was wrong. These paintings weren't a ticket to freedom, they were just one more tether that kept the Kings on his trail.

Well, I needed to cut that tie once and for all. I needed to get the art out of Archer's house—out of Wisdom—and into FBI hands. Because until I did, everyone here was in danger. Zoey, Hunter, Gunner, Ranger, Lydia, Tara, Jamie, Walt... everyone who I'd come to know and care about, everyone who'd stood kind and strong, allowing my hesitant roots to grow around them and drink from their warmth... everyone was at risk while I and these paintings were here.

I tapped away from the quick contacts in my phone to the number pad. Most kids were taught to memorize their parents' phone numbers and 911 in case of emergencies—the only number I was given to memorize was that of an FBI agent. *No one else would know what to do with me—a ghost with paintings stolen over three decades ago.*

I typed in Lattimore's number and hit call, praying this was still his cell and that he could still help me. As it rang, I replayed Archer's assurance that calling Agent Lattimore was the next step as soon as we had any concrete information.

"Hello?"

"Agent Lattimore?" I asked even though I thought I recognized his voice.

"Speaking. Who's this?"

I gulped. I'd never spoken to him on the phone—hardly spoken to him in person. There was a split second where I questioned myself—where I questioned everything.

Stay and fight.

This time, I would fight not just to protect the man I love, his family, and his hometown, but to protect my place with them.

Be brave.

"Agent Lattimore, this is Keira Mur—" I broke off and swallowed. "Keira McKenna."

I could hear the big thud of him sitting into whatever chair was nearby.

"Keira? Are you in danger? Is your dad—"

"I don't have a lot of time," I interrupted him. This phone call wasn't the time to regale the events of the last four years, nor go into details about what I'd found. "I need to meet with you. I have… information… about a crime."

"Okay. Alright. Are you somewhere safe? Do you want me to come to you?"

"No." I shook my head like he could see me. "I'm in Wyoming, but I'm not going to be safe here for long. I need to meet you somewhere else."

"Well, looks like we're in luck. I'm in Salt Lake City at the FBI field office here teaching a seminar. We have a safe house just outside of La Barge I can meet you at. It's a dark green house on Birch Creek Drive behind the Wyoming Inn; you can't miss it."

The name was familiar, and when I searched it on my phone, I saw it was a dot-on-the-map town about two hours south of here; I must've passed it on my move up from Salt Lake.

"Okay. I'll be there in just under two hours." I grabbed my keys from the small table by the door.

"Keira." His voice stopped me. "Is this about the Kings? Did Sean find you?"

My lips parted.

"No," I replied hesitantly. "Not exactly."

"Oh."

"It's about the Gardner Museum theft." I left him with

that bomb and hoped it meant he would get to the safe house just as fast as I would.

As I went to leave the house, my feet came to a stop at the door and turned. I took a deep inhale, letting the scent of him —the man who'd captured my heart—suffuse into my lungs and steady me.

My entire life, I'd been protected. This time, it was my turn to protect those I loved. And I hoped Archer would understand.

CHAPTER TWENTY-ONE

ARCHER

"Sorry for keeping you, Archer." Walt sighed and reclined his hospital bed. "This old body isn't what it used to be."

He looked much better than he had the last time I'd seen him, but I kept that to myself. His bruises were in the greenish-yellow stage and the swelling in his face was almost gone.

Though I'd arrived at the hospital early this afternoon, I'd had to wait while they ran some tests to make sure Walt would be cleared to head home in a few days. Turned out, there were a few other medical conditions to be addressed because of the drinking that kept him admitted longer than the blunt force injuries he'd sustained two weeks ago.

"Yeah?" I walked to the side of the bed and folded my arms. "Well, maybe once you bust out of this joint, you give that old body a fighting chance and lay off the alcohol."

A mixture of sadness, shame, and acceptance swept across the creases of his face.

"I know," he admitted, his voice hoarse. "I didn't realize how bad it was. Like a slope I didn't know how far down I'd slid until I was lookin' back up." He paused and cleared the emotion from his voice. "If it wasn't for the drink, maybe I'd remember what this is all about. If it's because of me... or if someone else is in danger."

His stare lifted, meeting mine with a knowing but unsettled look.

"Mom told you."

His nod confirmed my assertion. "Lydia said you're worried it's because of Keira."

I tensed waiting for him to ask why—to ask questions I couldn't give him answers to. But he didn't. Instead, his shoulders slumped like there was even more weight on them than before.

"I'm sorry if I let you down, Archer. Especially now." His eyes dropped to his lap. "Especially if I'm putting her in danger because I can't remember."

My chest seized. I reached out and placed my hand over his forearm, feeling the thin muscle tone and the bone underneath.

"Remember the first time you walked us home from school?" He looked at me, and his head tipped. I could tell he didn't remember that either, but it was a long time ago, so I continued before that bothered him, too. "I was ten. Gun and Ranger were what—six and seven, and they were arguing because you didn't have a map as you led us through the streets. Ranger insisted you had everything memorized."

He chuckled, the day coming back to him. "Gunner said no one could memorize that much information."

I laughed. *Some things hadn't changed.*

"They finally worked up the courage to ask you if you ever got lost," I went on. "Do you remember your answer?"

His lips pulled tight and he cleared his throat again before answering hoarsely, "That's the thing about this town, somebody will always help you find your way back." He placed his hand over top of mine and patted it like he was thanking me for the memory.

I nodded. "You just got a little lost, Walt, but we're all here to help you find your way back."

His eyes glistened, and he said nothing for several seconds before he trusted himself to speak calmly. "How can I help?"

He coughed, so I grabbed his water cup from the side table and handed it to him. He took several long sips through the straw while I pulled out the folder of paper from underneath my arm.

"I know you don't remember much from that night, but I wanted you to take a look at some photos. Just to see if anything jogs your memory."

I flipped open the folder and pulled out the two sheets of photographs that Roman had sent over of Sean Maloney's associates.

"Jesus," he swore not even a second later and jammed his finger down on the third photo in the top row on the second sheet. "Him. I opened my door the other night to him."

"Connor Walsh." He was one of the few older guys in the photos—probably one of the few remaining original Kings' men who hadn't been jailed because of Keira's dad's testimony or their own subsequent crimes.

I needed to tell Keira. And tell Diehl to get a BOLO out. And call Roman. And then Agent Lattimore.

"That's all I needed, Walt. Thank you." I put the photos back but a surprisingly strong hand on my arm stopped me from walking away.

"They wanted to know about the tattoo shop. If it was a front. If any large packages were sent there," he said, his tone hollow as though the memory was coming back in snapshots. "Packages to the tattoo shop's PO box. That's when they started hitting me."

"It's okay, Walt, don't hurt—" I tried to stop him. I knew enough of what I needed to take the next steps to make sure Keira was safe.

"No." He shook his head wildly, grabbing for me. "No,

Archer. Oh, god." His hand shook as he laid it over his mouth in horror. "I think I said her name. I just... I thought if they knew it belonged to Keira, they'd realize they were making a mistake."

My blood turned to ice. I couldn't blame him. He had no idea.

"I remember... that one looked at the other like her name was familiar, too." A tear slid down his cheek. "They asked about a Patrick. Patrick Mc... Mc..."

"McKenna."

Dread scored his face as his heavy eyelids widened.

His voice trembled. "B-But I didn't know a Patrick, and I told them that." And I was sure they beat him more for that, too. "They wanted her address—real address, Archer. And I think... I think I gave it to them."

He let out a choked sob, and I reached for his shoulder, gripping it to try and comfort him even though I didn't feel like I had much of that in me.

It didn't make sense. If they'd come to Wisdom weeks ago for Keira, why would they just be learning about Keira now? Something was wrong. There was a very big piece of this puzzle missing—bigger than Walt's possibly faulty memory.

But whatever it was, I had to get back to Keira.

"I'm sorry, Archer. I'm so sorry."

"You did what you had to do, Walt," I told him firmly. "But most importantly, you helped me."

Within two minutes, I was out of the hospital, my phone dinging just as I threw my truck in drive and floored it out of the parking lot. I checked the screen and saw three missed calls and a voice mail from Keira. *Fuck.*

I tapped to play the message.

"It was the paintings, Archer. This whole time, it was the paintings, not me. I know why all these things are happening, and I know how to stop them. I have to get in touch with Agent Lattimore and get him the paintings; it's the only way."

The paintings?

What the hell was she talking about?

"Fuck." My palm came down hard on the steering wheel when I tried to call her back but it just rang through to her mailbox. I tapped on Hunter's name next.

"Hell—"

I didn't give him a chance to finish. "Are you with Keira?"

"What? No. She wanted to go home, so I took her back to your place. Why?"

"Walt just positively ID'd one of Sean Maloney's known associates, Connor Walsh, as one of the men who attacked him at his house that night, and I just got a voice mail from her rambling about paintings and getting them out of town—"

"I'm at Mom's, but I'm heading back over now."

That wouldn't be fast enough. "Is Gunner at the office?"

"No, but Ranger should be."

"Update Diehl and get a BOLO out in Jackson for Walsh, and then meet me at my place." I barked out the order and then hung up, immediately dialing Ranger's cell.

"Hello?"

"Ranger, I need you to go to my house," I told him, trying to keep a measure of stability to my voice when it felt like every cell was fracturing apart.

"Your house? Is everything alright?"

"Keira's not answering, the Irish mob is in town, and I think she's going to leave the house because of some artwork. I need you to go over there and stop her."

"Of course. I'll go right now."

"Stay on the line with me," I instructed, the sound of him grabbing his keys and zippering his coat echoing through the cab of my truck.

My foot pressed harder on the gas, the mountains whipping by as I easily broke one more limit to make sure she was safe. Unfortunately, the faster I drove didn't get my brother to my house any faster.

"Pulling down your drive now," he updated me not even a minute later.

I didn't say anything, my teeth were clenched too tight trying to stop air from exiting my lungs unsure when I'd be able to take my next inhale.

The beeps of the electronic keypad lock filtered through the line as Ranger opened my door.

"Keira?" He called. "It's Ranger."

"Anything?" I asked almost instantly.

"No," he replied to me and then called her name again. "Keira!"

"Fuck." I saw red.

"She's not here, Archer."

Fuck.

A wave of guilt and panic swelled through me. Once more, she was in danger, and I hadn't been there to protect her.

"Any sign of a struggle? Or anything out of place?" I rasped, trying to think through this as though it were any other case.

"No. No sign of forced entry or a struggle," he answered matter-of-factly. "Everything seems like it's order..."

"What about the paintings?" I demanded roughly.

"What paintings?"

I shook my head. "Keira's dad's paintings. We hung them after everyone was over for dinner."

"Hung them where?"

I tensed. "In the living room." There was a beat of silence. "Ranger?"

"There are no paintings in here, Archer."

It felt like my chest caved in. "Was there a car in the drive when you pulled up?" The question ate at my tongue like acid.

"No."

No sign of forced entry or a struggle. Her car, gone. Her most prized possessions, gone.

"The TV was left on," my brother rattled off observations. "It looks like she was a few minutes into watching a show. Let me see—"

"Thanks, Ranger. It's okay. Hunter will be there—"

"What were the paintings of?" He interrupted me—startled me; Ranger never interrupted anyone.

"What?"

"The paintings? What were they of?" he demanded firmly.

I stammered for a second, needing to find a path out of the tornado of emotion whipping my brain to shreds to find the answer he wanted.

"The biggest was of a ship on the sea during a storm. Another was a woman playing a piano with some couple watching. This old-time portrait of a couple, but we didn't put that one up because it was weird—"

"No, Archer. It was stolen," Ranger broke in. "They were all stolen from Boston in 1990—"

"Wait, what?" I shook my head. "What are you talking about?"

I heard Ranger inhale, the way he always did before he vomited an encyclopedia's worth of information.

"In 1990, the Isabella Stewart Gardner Museum in Boston was robbed on St. Patrick's Day. Thirteen pieces of famous artwork were stolen by two men posing as police including, *The Storm on the Sea of Galilee* by Rembrandt, *The Concert* by Vermeer, and *A Lady and Gentleman in Black* by Rembrandt," he rattled off information. "It was the largest art heist in history, Archer, and those paintings have been missing for three decades."

My phone buzzed three times, and I tapped on Ranger's messages to find photos of the artwork that had been hanging in my home only five hours ago.

"What the…" My vision swam for a second, facts coming together and colliding like meteors into an unbelievable puzzle. "Jesus Christ."

The paintings. This was what she was talking about.

All of a sudden, the answer knocked me over like a damn wrecking ball. This whole time, she'd been right; the things happening in town weren't because of her past, they were because of the paintings. But in the same breath, I'd also been right; she had been in danger because she was the one with the paintings.

"The FBI has always suspected that the theft was orchestrated by organized crime, but they never had enough evidence to prove it and no one has been able to find the paintings," he went on. "Until now."

"*Ranger!*" I heard Hunter in the background.

"I'm on the phone with Archer now," Ranger said.

"Did you find Keira?" Hunt asked.

"No—"

"But we did find the art stolen from the Gardner Museum," Ranger chimed in.

"What? Stolen art? Wait, the art from the Netflix show?"

"Well, I guess technically we didn't find it since it's not here anymore, but Archer said the stolen paintings were hanging in here earlier today—"

My mind scrambled and unscrambled while they talked— a Rubik's cube that was twisting and turning until all sides of this case connected. Keira. The art. The mob. *Her father.*

"Archer, is Keira an art thief?"

"Well, it couldn't have been her since she wasn't born when the paintings were stolen—"

"But her father was," I broke in as I turned onto the drive that led to our office and my house. "She said the paintings belonged to her dad, that they were his most prized possessions."

267

"Not just his. The FBI estimates the stolen works are worth over five-hundred-million dollars."

I gritted my teeth. "Her dad stole the paintings for Maloney." I had no proof, but deep in my gut, I saw the full picture of what happened. "Patty McKenna stole the paintings for the Kings who held onto them as rainy-day insurance."

"What do you mean?"

"The return of stolen art or valuables is a common trading piece for criminals to use to reduce or completely eliminate any criminal charges. The longer they held the paintings, the more valuable they would become and the greater the crime someone could get away with knowing they had a get-out-of-jail free card in their back pocket," Ranger explained for me.

I pulled up to my house, my chest burning to see for myself that Keira's car was gone.

"One sec," I told them and hung up the call.

I was inside in just a couple of steps, seeing for myself the white walls where the paintings had been.

"Arch…"

"When McKenna knew he was going to testify against Maloney, he took the artwork because he knew it would be the only thing that would get Maloney out scot-free." I looked at my brothers. "That's why they kept going after them. They didn't just want revenge, they wanted their damn insurance back."

"And Keira didn't know?" It was hard for Hunter to ask the question, knowing how I felt about her. But I couldn't blame him for doing his job.

"No." I shook my head. "Her dad tried to protect her from that part of his life at every step. She had no idea what the paintings were or how valuable they are. She would've told me."

"Does she know now? Or is she on the run just because the Kings have found her—"

"She knows." Ranger pointed the remote at the TV, drawing our attention to the screen. It turned on to the first episode of *This is a Robbery* paused a few minutes in.

"So, wait. How the hell did they find her?" Hunter folded his arms. "If they didn't know about Keira until Walt told them, what the hell brought them to Wisdom? The paintings? If that was the case, why didn't they find them in Salt Lake City? Or before that? We're missing—"

My throat went dry. *Fuck.* Her words hit me like a punch in the gut.

"It was the smallest of them, and part of me felt guilty, but the other part of me knew that Dad would want me to have the freedom it bought me."

"She sold one," I rasped, recalling our conversation where she confessed to pawning one of her dad's heirlooms in order to buy Todd's place; her savings depleted from hospital bills.

"What?" Ranger's eyes bugged wide.

"She had no idea what the paintings were," I asserted again, gripping the back of the couch to steady myself. "When McKenna died, she needed capital to buy Todd's building so she wouldn't have to get a mortgage. With most of her money going toward her dad's medical expenses…"

"She sold one of the paintings to pay for it," my brother finished for me.

I nodded. "I don't know which one. She said it was small."

"Maybe *Chez Tortoni* by Manet," Ranger surmised.

"As soon as that thing touched the market, the Kings would know—they would be looking for the rest. They tracked down the seller, probably interrogated him like they did Walt." Hunter's gaze pinned me as I began to pace.

"The seller pointed them to Keira's PO box and Wisdom where they came looking for the paintings. They probably have been working discreetly this whole time because they don't want to draw attention to what's here, especially after the Netflix show."

"And the reward the museum promised," Ranger added.

My head tipped back and I exhaled a low curse, my blood sizzling like a live wire. "And then Walt gave them Keira."

"Why would Mr. McKenna have kept them all these years?" Ranger asked, his tone a mixture of innocence and curiosity. "He went to the FBI because he claimed to have had a change of heart. If he had turned a corner, why wouldn't he have given the FBI the stolen paintings? They're priceless. It doesn't—"

"He was trying to protect her," I bit out, truth bleeding from the gaping wound in my chest. "McKenna didn't go to the FBI because he was a good man or a bad man; he went to the feds because he was a father. He wanted to take them down to protect her, and he kept the paintings for the same reason—in case anything ever happened with the Kings or the feds, those paintings could guarantee her safety."

Hunter's lips pursed. "So, where is she now? On the run with the paintings?" His eyes darted around the house like Keira was about to leap out of a closet somewhere and surprise us all.

I shook my head. "She ended up watching that show and realizing what she'd been sitting on this entire time," I began, working through the timeline of what happened here. "She left me a voice mail saying that she was going to call Agent Lattimore, the FBI agent who helped them before in order to stop all this." I groaned. "She doesn't know that Walt told them about her—that the Kings know she's alive."

"She's trying to protect all of us," Ranger murmured.

I gritted my teeth and nodded. The bullet of truth ricocheted around inside my chest, tearing up everything in its path.

"If the feds get the paintings, she thinks the Kings will leave Wisdom." I reached for my cell.

"Because she doesn't know they're after her, too." Hunter drove his hand through his hair.

My phone was already at my ear, ringing once before Roman picked up.

"Hello?"

"Roman, we have a situation."

The tone of my voice didn't allow for any questions except one. "How can I help?"

"Where is the nearest FBI safehouse to Wisdom?"

He sucked in an audible breath. "Jesus, Archer, I'm not a Rolodex of FBI safe houses—"

"But somebody is," I broke in roughly. "Somebody you know can tell you where—"

"Yes, they could, but the whole damn point of a safe house is that no one fucking knows where it is—" Roman started to argue.

"Tell them if they give you the safe house location, I will guarantee the return of the stolen artwork from the Gardner Museum heist." My voice bordered on a yell.

Both my brothers' eyebrows raised. *Fucking bold was what I just did—bargaining with a chip I didn't technically possess.* But I didn't have a choice. My body thrummed, knowing my heart was beating outside of my chest right now—beating its way straight into danger with a bunch of priceless stolen art.

"The Gardn—Jesus, fuck, Archer. Are you serious?" I might not have recognized the infamous artwork from the robbery, but Roman knew exactly what I was talking about. "Does this have to do with the Kings and why you called me the other day? The Gardner... *fuck.* What the hell is going on?"

He was reeling, but I didn't have time for that. I didn't care that I'd just promised him priceless masterpieces that seemed to have disappeared off the face of the planet for over three decades, I needed the information only he could get me.

"What's going on is that we all underestimated the lengths

a father would go for his daughter, and now my woman is in danger," I ground out. "So please get me that location."

He paused for a beat. "Last I was in Wyoming, there was a safe house down past Big Piney in La Barge. They'd keep one somewhere between Salt Lake City and Jackson, so head in that direction. Give me ten minutes, and I'll text you the address."

"Thank you," I said roughly. "And Roman, the Irish Kings are in Wyoming; the FBI might want to send back-up."

I hung up the call and went for my gun safe in the console below the TV.

"La Barge is two hours," Hunter said as I pulled out stocks of ammo.

We were closer than Salt Lake City which was the nearest FBI building. Knowing the situation and Keira's high-profile death, I had to assume that Lattimore wasn't bringing much back-up to keep her identity protected, and that meant we were her only defense.

I looked at Ranger and instructed, "Make sure Diehl puts someone back at the hospital with Walt in case they try to finish the job, and then stay ready at the office. I'm going to have you pull up the address of the safe house once Roman gets it to me, so you can let me know what we're walking into."

Ranger nodded and pulled out his cell phone to call the police chief. Meanwhile, I nodded to Hunter, and we headed for the garage.

"When did you drop her off here?" I asked, grabbing a second handgun that I kept in my toolbox on the way out.

"A little over an hour ago." He climbed into the passenger seat.

My chin clipped down, and I roared my truck's engine to life. "Then we're an hour behind her."

And I hoped to god it wasn't an hour too late.

CHAPTER TWENTY-TWO

KEIRA

THE POUNDING OF MY PULSE MADE IT PRACTICALLY IMPOSSIBLE to hear anything else as I drove. The mountains seemed to crumble in my rear view the farther away I got from Wisdom, amplifying the solitude I felt in the front seat.

It was all in my head, but it felt like the fragile foundation of a family and a future I'd built over the last couple of months was quaking underneath me.

Lattimore was right, I couldn't miss the safe house.

I turned onto Birch Creek right by the Inn and as soon as I drove past that building, the small green single-story home came into view, a large black SUV parked outside. I pulled my car next to it and shut off the engine, trying to swallow through the tightening of my throat.

This is how you end this, Keira. Once and for all.

I grabbed my purse and got out of the car. Shutting the door, I looked at the trunk, but decided to leave the paintings in there for now. I wasn't sure about anything at the moment. I trusted the man who'd helped Dad and me four years ago, but I didn't know if he was still the same man or how he'd respond knowing Dad had these stolen paintings the whole time.

I walked up to the brown door and tested the knob. The brass was cold against my hand and didn't budge, so I knocked. The door opened almost immediately.

"Keira."

Agent Lattimore looked like he'd aged a decade in just four years. His belly was bigger than I remembered and his clothes were wrinkled. The lines on his forehead had deepened, his eyes more sunken in. While we'd walked away from the Kings and the world of organized crime, it was obvious that Lattimore hadn't; and it had taken its toll on the older man.

"Agent Lattimore," I murmured as he stepped to the side.

He scanned the exterior once before closing the door behind me and ushering me into the small living room at the front of the house.

Like every other safe house I'd been in over the years, the furniture was dull and sparse. Only a single couch and a chair were placed in the living room facing a small TV on the wall. There was a doorway into what looked like the kitchen and presumably dining room where whichever agent was on duty would sit with his laptop and try to figure out how the hell we were in danger again.

"Can't say I ever expected to see you again. Especially on these terms." He walked over behind the one couch and rested his hands on the back.

"That makes two of us," I murmured wryly.

"Where's your dad?"

My chin dipped. "He passed from cancer four months ago."

"Damn." He shook his head. "Sorry to hear that, Keira."

"Thank you." I locked my fingers tight in my lap, feeling how slick they were. "I'm sorry to call you after all this time, but I have new information on the Isabella Stewart—"

"Gardner Museum heist," he finished for me, shaking his head and continuing with that authoritative tone he always had that didn't leave room for me to interject. "I was on the original task force the FBI sent to find the thieves. We looked into the Kings, Keira, and your dad never had any information on the theft—"

"Because he had the paintings," I finally broke in, blurting out the truth. "Not the sketches or the finial but the paintings."

"No, you're mistaken." His big frame recoiled and blanched.

"I'm not, Agent Lattimore." I couldn't believe he was arguing with me. "I've lived with those paintings for almost a decade, and I only just realized what they were because of a TV show, but I know it's them. I have them with me—I can show you."

He groaned, almost as though he were in pain. "Shit…" He trailed off, staring at me with a strange expression I couldn't read. "You really do have them, don't you?"

I nodded slowly, peeling my fingers apart and pushing myself up to stand.

"Dammit." Lattimore shook his head. "I swore Patty was telling me the truth when he said he had no idea what happened to the art, but of course he did."

"I'm sorry." It wasn't my fault that my dad had lied, but I couldn't stop myself from apologizing. "Let me show you."

He nodded, turning his double chin into a triple. "Bring them all inside."

I made it to the door when he called to me, "Keira." I looked over my shoulder. "I'm sorry, too."

I wasn't quite sure what he had to be sorry for, but looking at the dismayed expression on his face, I sensed it was for this entire situation—for everything I'd already gone through and everything still in front of me.

I didn't respond.

I opened the door and jogged to my trunk. I was only going to bring in the Rembrandt seascape, figuring that was enough, but Lattimore said all of them, so I awkwardly gathered all the canvases and walked quickly back to the house.

As I struggled to open the door again, the thought struck me that Lattimore hadn't come outside the house at all. To greet me. To help with the paintings. Even to open the door for me now.

But before I could follow the breadcrumbs left by that thought, a familiar voice bled into the air.

"Hello, Keira."

Sean.

THE CANVASES of priceless art clattered to the floor at my feet as I stood tall.

Sean Maloney stood behind Lattimore who was now sitting on the couch, a gun held to the back of his head. Even if I didn't recognize the leering eyes or malicious curve of the younger man's smile, the stench of his violent arrogance was unmistakable.

I lifted my chin. "Sean."

He grinned. *Grinned.* "I thought Fattimore here looked surprised to see me earlier, but your face right now—" He broke off and used the end of his gun to blow a chef's kiss into the air. "Perfection."

"Keira—" Lattimore started to speak. Instantly, the gun leveled with the back of the older man's head, jerking twice as two bullets fired through the silencer into Lattimore's skull, killing him in an instant.

I tried to stifle my cry, but the tiniest noise slipped out, making Sean smile.

My dad had taught me early on that whenever I had to be

around anyone from the Kings, I should never give away my emotions no matter what they were.

"That fat fuck finally paid off," Sean mused, wiping the blood from the end of his gun on the back of Lattimore's own shirt, causing the lifeless body to slump forward. "You look incredible, Keira. Especially for a dead girl."

I had to get out of here.

My heart slammed against the front of my chest as I shuddered. I no longer held the paintings, but I was close to the door, somewhat close to my car where my gun was in the glove box.

I hazarded a glance over my shoulder. *Maybe I could make a run—*

"Ahh!" I cried out, toppling forward as a burning pain in my thigh took me to the ground. Agony ripped through me like a hot knife through butter. I shook violently, not even hearing the shot he'd fired before it pierced my leg.

"You're not going anywhere," Sean informed me casually like he forgot to mention that before shooting me.

Distantly, I heard the click of his footsteps on the wooden floor, but my focus was on my leg. Blood oozed from the bullet wound in my outer right thigh, creating a red halo in the denim around the wound.

My fingers trembled as I reached for my leg, knowing I needed to put pressure on it to stop the bleeding.

His shadow cascaded over me.

"You won't get away with this," I said though my teeth were locked tight.

"I already have."

I yelled, more pain blinding me as he grabbed me by my hair and dragged me into the living room.

Blood smeared on the floor behind me, and I knew I was in pain, but adrenaline was pumping high enough that it wasn't crippling me. Once we were in the living room, he released my hair. Miraculously, I managed to catch my head before it smacked against the hardwood.

Keep pressure, I instructed myself. *You're not alone.*

And I had to believe that. I had to believe that Archer got my message—that he would find me.

Sean towered over me, his gun casually held by his side.

"I knew that fat fuck would lead me to you," he went on blithely, showing himself to be exactly the kind of man I knew he'd grow up to be. Arrogant. Narcissistic. Violent. "I have to admit though, playing dead was a clever choice. Worked for quite some time, too—even longer if you hadn't traded a piece of your past for a chance at a future."

Chez Tortoni. My stomach rolled. It was only because of the painting that my safety had been compromised.

"Fuck you," I spat.

He crouched next to me, taking the barrel of the gun and dragging the metal along the curve of my jaw. I wanted to turn away. The feel of that metal seemed to hurt worse than the bullet in my leg, but I forced myself to stay still. I wouldn't show weakness. *I was my father's daughter.*

"You had that chance. Instead, you cried to daddy and got Elise killed." I flinched at his words, and I saw the way my pain fueled him. "We'll make up for that though, don't you worry." The gun dragged lower, down my neck to my sternum and then over to my breast.

I wanted to vomit as he dragged it lazily around my nipple.

"Must kill you a little to know it's dear old daddy's fault that you're here," he went on, staring at my breast the entire time. "We had no fuckin' clue you both were alive. Hailed Banksy as a hero for shooting you both. I should've known something wasn't right when we went for those paintings, promising to barter something real special to the feds to get Dad out earlier only to come up empty handed."

I cried out when he jammed the gun painfully into my breast for a second.

"But nope. Dad never suspected a thing," he sneered. "And then *Tortoni* came on the market."

I gritted my teeth, my hand soaked with my own blood as Sean used his free hand to cup my face, forcing me to look at him.

"Sent my men to find the seller in Salt Lake City who, after we relieved him of a few fingers, gave us a PO box in Wyoming of all fucking places." Sean shook his head and sighed. "Still, no fucking idea you were anything but a pretty little corpse."

"Sounds like you've been a pretty little dumbass this whole time," I goaded him.

He punched me in the stomach, and when I gasped for air, his fingers dug mercilessly into my face to keep my jaw open, bruising the skin underneath. I couldn't do anything to stop him as he bent over and drove his tongue into my mouth like a venomous snake.

"Mmm." He smiled as I gagged. "That's going to taste so good soon. Now"- -his gaze slid down my body—"where was I? Ahh yes, still alive." He wedged the gun between the buttons on my shirt and tugged, ripping it open. "Ransacked the post office to figure out who the PO box belonged to. How nice of them to let you buy the box and only give a business name," he remarked and then rattled off parts of this story that I already knew. "My guys checked your shop. No paintings. So, I told them to get the owner's home address from the drunk postman, and that is where things got interesting."

"Interesting? You almost killed him."

"Almost?" His eyebrows lifted. "I'll have to punish Walsh for not finishing the job." Bile rose in my throat as his gun traveled lower, pressing between my legs. "According to Mr. Postman, a Keira *Murphy* owned the business. Keira. *Murphy.* I might be Irish, but I don't believe in that kind of luck. So, I told Walsh to observe, meanwhile, I had a little talk with Banks." His head cocked. "Talk isn't the right word."

I winced as he pushed the gun into my groin. My hand gripped my leg tighter almost willing myself to feel that pain rather than anything else.

"He confessed quickly, the poor bastard. Thought it would make things easier for him," Sean rambled and then sighed. "The things I did to that man are too unspeakable to say in your presence, darling Keira. Needless to say, I was surprised and pleasantly infuriated to learn you were alive this entire time—*and had our fucking paintings.*"

"They aren't yours. They belong to the museum."

"Too bad daddy didn't tell you that four years ago, so you could've returned them and saved yourself from this moment."

"He's going to find you."

"Who? Your boyfriend?" He chuckled. "You don't think I've thought about that? How do you think I got you here when you've been living guarded and under lock and key for weeks? I knew you were alive the day after we tortured the postman. I just had to get you to come to me."

"I would never come to you." I tried to pull away from him and instantly the gun pressed into my injured leg, making me cry out as a black spot of pain flickered in my vision.

"Ahh, but you would, Keira. You would if you thought you were in danger." He looked at me like he thought he knew me, and I wanted to vomit. "Truthfully, I thought you'd call him sooner." He nodded to Lattimore. "Little Keira always needing someone to save her, but when you didn't, I had to help you along."

I gagged, realizing what had happened. "The break-in…"

"Staged. And the flyer," he eagerly admitted. "I knew you'd kept the paintings with you. Breaking into your house was just to send you to Lattimore—to send you somewhere I could get to you. But you didn't call him." His expression soured. "So, then I had to make it really obvious for your pretty little head; I had them leave the flyer so you'd realize exactly why you were in danger—an unwilling culprit in your father's final crime. I thought you'd realize sooner what you were holding on to." His sad smile was sickening. "Must kill you to know that daddy kept this from you. Ironically, to protect you even though this secret is going to get you killed."

"I hate you."

This time pain exploded on the side of my face where he punched me. For a second, I thought the cracking sound came from a gun but it wasn't; it was from his fist connecting with my cheekbone.

The pain in my face evaporated under the wave of agony from my leg. I must've let go of the pressure when Sean hit me. Darkness swarmed and my head went light from either the blood loss or the pain or both.

Be brave.

I gasped for air and clung to consciousness. I refused to give this man any weakness.

"From there, it was easy. I've been sitting on Lattimore for weeks. All I had to do was follow him and then wait for you to get here—wait for you to show up begging for someone to save you once more."

"Well, there are your paintings. You can take them and leave." I tried to twist away from him and for a second, I thought my last-ditch effort might've worked when he released his hold on me and stood.

"I will, but not before I get what I'm owed." He stepped between my legs, but when I tried to move back, he pressed his heel into my shin, pinning me in place as his free hand went to the waist of his pants where I could see he was hard. "I told you I would find you that day, Keira. And look at you now, found."

He slid his belt open.

"Touch me, and I will kill you," I warned him though I wasn't in any condition to make good on that threat.

"Touch you?" He laughed. "I'm going to fuck you, Keira. I'm going to fuck you with my gun in your mouth, and when I come, I'm going to pull the trigger and blow your pretty little brains out."

Oh god. Air vacuumed from the room, my lungs seizing in protest and my stomach going into full revolt.

Sean came back into focus as he got on his knees and shoved his pants below his waist.

"God, the look on your face knowing what's coming…" he groaned and touched himself. "It makes me so hard."

My head grew light. I wasn't sure if it was from the wound in my leg or the way he looked as he spoke, his fingers reaching for the waist of my pants. They were rough and clumsy and full of hate—nothing like the way Archer touched me.

And that was all I wanted to think about. *Archer.*

I hated the hot tears that slid from the corners of my eyes when he dragged my pants down, but I refused to let him think he won.

"He'll kill you for this."

Please find me, I wished like Archer was still my very own warrior constellation, one who would bring down the heavens with him to save me. *Please know I love you,* I wished even harder.

I gave into the darkness and pain, unable to fight it any longer.

"No, he won't because he's not here. It's only you and me, Keira. You're all alone—"

No.

I heard gunshots, and I tried to open my eyes but they were too heavy. Everything was too heavy. A massive weight landed on top of me like a sack of potatoes and I distantly thought this was the end—that Sean had gotten everything he wanted.

But then I heard his voice.

"Keira!"

I was afraid to believe it was Archer—afraid to believe he'd found me in time. But then the weight was lifted off me, and all I saw was him, my protector.

My love.

Archer pulled me into his arms, barking orders at Hunter who dealt with Sean's body.

"Are you okay?" He pulled up my jeans and underwear where Sean had shoved them down my thighs, cursing loudly when he realized the blood on my legs was my own. "Jesus, Hunt, call an ambulance. Keira's been shot."

"I'm fine," I insisted weakly, and even though I swore I was telling my arms and legs to move, nothing did.

My head lolled against his chest. Everything was swimming in darkness.

"You're safe," he promised me and my eyes drifted shut. At first, I thought it was my brain playing tricks on me, but Archer kept repeating the words over and over again. I felt my leg jostle and I forced my eyes open, seeing Hunter hand Archer a tourniquet. My eyes shut again as he tightened it around my leg.

I shivered. I felt so cold. Cold and pain, but not alone.

"I'm here, baby, I've got you." His words were in my ear now, my body lifted against his chest. I finally relaxed against him, my adrenaline disintegrating as the pain in my leg became excruciating.

Blackness ebbed and flowed along with my consciousness. I wanted to apologize. I wanted to tell him I was sorry for not waiting—sorry for being in danger. Again. *I'd just wanted to protect him.* But I felt myself losing the strength of my grip on consciousness.

"I love you."

"Stay with me, Keira. I've got you."

"Archer." My voice broke.

He held me tighter. "I love you, too, baby."

Whatever I wanted to say came out as a soft moan, and I finally gave into the gravity of him, knowing he would always protect me.

Four years ago, I'd entered an ambulance choosing to die so that I could have a life, choosing to pay the steep price of solitude for safety. This time, as Archer's heart beat against my cheek, I chose to fight so that I could live, trading vulnerability for the reward of love.

CHAPTER TWENTY-THREE

ARCHER

"Archer!"

I whipped around and saw my mother running down the hospital hallway, Ranger power-walking after her, trying to get her to slow down and not look like she was in an airport about to miss a flight.

"Mom," I said, my throat so hoarse I was surprised I could speak. Mom pulled me into her arms, and damn, if I didn't hug her back hard. "She's still in surgery."

Four hours. She'd been in surgery for four hours.

"Oh, sweetheart." She clutched me tight.

The lump in my throat had lodged when the ambulance arrived at the safe house and Keira went unconscious from her injuries, but when we'd traded the ambulance for the medevac, the lump began to swell. Larger when we reached the hospital in Jackson. Larger when they rushed her into surgery. Larger when it had been three hours since I last saw her, held her.

"She's going to be okay, Archer." She rubbed my arm. "Keira's a fighter."

I gritted my teeth, feeling the words like a punch to the gut.

Four years ago, I'd watched on TV as the girl I'd unexpectedly fallen for was shot by a member of the notorious Irish Kings. I wasn't with her. I hadn't been able to stop him. I hadn't been able to help her. Even though it was faked, in that moment, it had been real for me.

Today, I'd been there. I'd gotten there in time to kill the fucker who'd set her spinning like a top out of control. I'd burst through the door of the safe house to see Sean on his knees with his pants dropped, about to finish what he'd started almost a decade earlier. I saw the barrel of the gun in his hand. And I fucking fired. Two rapid shots to the back of his head.

I'd killed him like I'd promised her I would.

But still, we were here. I'd gotten to her this time. I'd been able to stop him this time. But now I was afraid it wouldn't be enough.

"What if she doesn't make it?" I rasped.

"The good news is that it couldn't have punctured her femoral artery, otherwise Keira would've bled out in five minutes, barring any other kind of vascular or boney damage. So, if she made it to the hospital, that's a good prognosis," Ranger offered, thinking that his facts would be helpful right now. "Was the shot higher up in the thigh or lower? Because if it didn't hit an artery, it still could've hit part of the venous system. The femoral vein. The subsartorial vein. The great saphenous vein. Or the popliteal vein if it was closer to the knee—"

"Ranger," Mom chided softly, giving him a small smile.

"Sorry." He ducked his head, his blond hair falling boyishly over his forehead.

"It's alright, Range." I managed to speak even though my throat was impossibly tight. "You're just trying to help."

And his version of help was to throw every fact in the book at a situation so that he didn't have to worry about feelings.

"We don't think about what ifs, Archer," she reminded me. "We focus on what *is*. And Keira is in the best hands, in a good hospital, with a strong spirit, and people who are praying for her."

I pulled my lips between my teeth and held them there, nodding quickly but not quite convinced. When I looked up, Hunter was striding over to us.

"I got you food and clothes." Hunter held up a bag in each hand. "And Gunner says to call if we need anything."

I nodded. There was nothing Gun could do right now—nothing any of us could do, so it didn't make sense to pull him from his assignment.

"Thanks."

"Why don't we sit—"

"Mr. Reynolds?"

I whipped around, following the voice to the nurse who approached us.

"Keira..." I rasped, feeling like the world around me fell away—like there was nothing until I knew that Keira was okay.

"She's out of surgery and in a recovery room."

I let go of the breath trapped in my lungs, the strength in my body deflating like a popped balloon for a second. Thankfully, Hunter's quick reflexes had him grab the two bags he'd just given me before they fell to the floor.

"Thank god," Mom murmured behind me.

"Can I..."

The nurse nodded with a hopeful smile. "My name's Maria. I can take you to see her, but she hasn't woken up yet. She lost a lot of blood," she explained, and then looking to my mom and brothers, added, "I'm sorry, I can only take one person—"

I didn't let her finish. No offense, but I didn't care that neither my mom nor brothers could come back to the room. I just needed to see her.

I started walking toward the sliding doors that led into the depths of the hospital and with a few hurried steps, the nurse caught up.

"The gunshot missed her femoral artery and the bones of her leg, but it did nick her superficial femoral artery. Even though there were no clinical signs, thankfully, the surgeon did an imaging series before we assumed no vascular damage. He saw the small arterial bleed there, and immediately changed the course of her surgery. If he hadn't, she would've ended up back in the hospital after several months with more serious complications."

My brain felt like those eggs in the plastic bag—shaken up until everything scrambled together.

"Is she okay?" That was all I needed to know.

"She will be. We got the bleed under control and repaired the damaged artery with a saphenous graft. She'll be here for a week, and then a few weeks of rest, and without any complications, she'll be good as new."

We reached Keira's room, and I don't even remember the seconds it took for me to go from the door to her bedside.

"Keira." I touched her cheek. Her hair. I brushed it back behind her ear, and then took her hand with my other one. "Why isn't she awake?"

I had a feeling she'd already told me why, but I couldn't remember.

"She just came out of surgery, Mr. Reynolds, and as I said, she lost a lot of blood. Just give her some time," Maria instructed and then quietly left the room.

I didn't want to give her time. I'd given her four years of time believing that she'd died. I needed to know she was alive now. More than the machines beeping and tracing her heartbeat by my side. More than the nurse—Maria—telling me that she'd wake up eventually. I needed to see it with my own eyes.

"Come on, baby. Wake up," I pleaded, dragging my

thumb back and forth over her hand before I brought it to my mouth, kissing each of her knuckles.

She looked even more pale than she normally did, the bruises from where Sean had hit her were more evident now. Her hair even redder like it had stolen some of the blood from her body. But it was the way her chest hardly moved that got me. She was breathing, which was good, but the movement was so slight, I swore I could be imagining it.

I'd never been more grateful for taking another life. I'd have to answer for it; I knew the police and the feds would have questions, especially with Agent Lattimore dead. But I had a feeling Hunter was holding them off for me for right now.

"You're not allowed to die on me this time," I told her, like rough instructions would make her body listen. "You found me, my home, my family because you belong in it—in all of it. You've fought for so long to be able to finally live your life on your own terms, you can't give up now."

I sucked in a breath, feeling her hand twitch against my lips.

"I'm here, baby," I murmured. "I'm not going anywhere."

A small sound came from her lips and my heart picked up its pace. Her eyelids lifted slowly, revealing those vibrant green eyes. *Thank god.*

"Archer…" Her voice was impossibly hoarse. "You didn't ask to come inside."

It took me a second because I was emotionally spent to get her small joke. I let out a watery laugh and bent forward, pressing my lips to her forehead.

"I thought I'd lost you again," I confessed, moving my face lower until our eyes were level.

"I found you," she returned, and I looked at her, confused. Maybe this was the drugs in her system talking because she didn't make sense. "Everything started to go black, and Sean was standing over me." She stopped and took several seconds to swallow and speak again. "I thought it was over, Archer. After all this time. Right when I finally found my life, I was going to lose it."

"You're okay, baby." I stroked her cheek and swiped away the tear that fell. "You're okay. Sean's dead. It's all going to be okay."

She slid her hand from my hold, letting the tips of her fingers land on the edge of my left collarbone. "But in the darkness, I found you. Eighteen impossibly small, impossibly bright dots. My Orion. You never left me."

"And I never will," I promised and brought my lips to hers.

CHAPTER TWENTY-FOUR

KEIRA

One week later...

"Ready to go home?" Archer looked at me, his expression filled with every ounce of love and care he'd shown me over the last week while I was in the hospital.

"Ready."

My surgery had gone well, but because of the precarious nature of my injury, they'd wanted to keep me for a week for observation to make sure nothing ruptured or that there weren't any complications. I was cleared this morning to go home, but with crutches and strict orders to rest and take it easy for the next three weeks while everything continued to heal.

Archer gathered my things and his; he'd insisted on working out of my hospital room every day no matter how many times I promised that it was fine if he needed to go to the office. He wouldn't go; he wouldn't leave me. And I was secretly—selfishly—glad that he didn't.

We walked—well, Archer walked, I hobbled—side-by-side out to his truck. When we got there, he put our things in the back, opened the passenger door and proceeded to lift me into the seat without even allowing me to attempt it.

"You're going to enjoy this, aren't you?" I pursed my lips.

I wasn't the kind of girl who liked feeling helpless, and I knew that was bound to get me into trouble if I wasn't careful. Thankfully, it was already crystal clear that Archer was going to do a heck of a job taking care of me.

"I enjoy anything that puts you in my arms," he said with a wink as he buckled me in.

He climbed in the driver's seat and as we pulled out of the hospital parking lot and started driving toward those familiar mountain ranges and open blue sky, I never looked back.

"What is it?" Archer asked, and I realized I must've made a small noise.

"This isn't like the first time."

"Well the first time, you didn't actually get shot," he grunted, a knot forming in his jaw.

Every time he talked about what happened, a wash of anger that he tried to hide came over him. Anger at Sean. Anger at himself. Even though Sean was dead, the scar of watching me die the first time had been ripped open in a bloody and brutal way, and it would take time for Archer to heal, too.

"I mean afterward," I told him. "Last time, when we drove out of Boston, I looked in the rearview until I couldn't see the city anymore."

I'd looked for him.

"And this time?"

"This time, I'm heading toward a future I chose with the only thing I want in the seat beside me," I told him, loving the way his hand reached over and took possession of mine, bringing it to his lips.

"I should warn you that we're heading home to a little bit of a welcoming committee," he drawled, making me laugh.

"Oh yeah?"

"I convinced my family that they had to wait until dinner to come see you, but that was the best I could do. Damn vultures."

I laughed harder.

Lydia had stopped by every day to see me with at least one, sometimes more, of her sons. Her visits were tied in frequency with Zoey's, my friend making sure to bring me a pastry every day along with enough romance novels to make the time pass quickly. I enjoyed all the stories, though at the end of the day, none of them compared to my own real-life hero.

"Mom's going to make her famous stuffed peppers. Ranger wants you to play chess with him. Hunter's probably going to probe you about Zoey starting work at RPG. And Gunner... well, Gunner's probably going to be Gunner."

"I wouldn't have it any other way." I laughed, my heart feeling impossibly full.

As we approached the house, I noticed Archer's expression turned serious.

"What is it?"

"The doctor said you have to take it easy for the next couple of weeks."

I know. I slipped deeper into the seat. "I've already pushed back my clients," I told him.

I knew that I had to do it, but that didn't mean I had to like it. We'd argued about it a few days ago. In my mind, tattooing someone wasn't what I could call strenuous, but I couldn't deny that it involved some up and down, and moving around the table.

"It's only for a few weeks."

I nodded, staring at the familiar line of trees that led up to the driveway to RPG and Archer's—our home.

"I guess I'll have plenty of time to binge watch the show about the artwork my dad stole," I joked.

While Archer had left the safe house in the medevac with

me, Hunter stayed behind until the feds got there. Apparently, when they heard the scene involved the recovery of the artwork from the Gardner heist, it was a pretty big turnout from several branches of the FBI, including some retired agents who'd flown out, waiting decades for this moment—for the art to be recovered.

"Speaking of that…"

My head snapped in his direction. "They're the real ones, right?" I was suddenly hit with the thought that maybe they were just forgeries.

"Oh, they're real. Hunter spoke to Agent Troisi with the FBI last night that they verified the authenticity of the works."

I sighed in relief.

"But they do want to know about the reward."

"Reward?" My brow furrowed.

"Keira…" He glanced at me and then quickly looked back to the road. "The museum had a ten-million-dollar reward posted for the return of the paintings."

Ten… million…

"You don't have to decide right this second, but they do want to know where to send the—"

"I don't want it," I broke in immediately, shaking my head.

"You didn't know what the paintings were or that they were stolen; they aren't holding you responsible—"

"I know, but I still don't want the money." It didn't feel right. Or real. My dad had stolen those paintings and then, in his own distorted sense of chivalry, kept them in order to protect me. I didn't want money for returning something that he never should've taken or hidden in the first place.

"Well, it's up to you, but I'm sure they'd be happy to keep it if you can't think of anyone else you might want to give it to."

Please. The word hit me like a battering ram.

"Her daughter." My lips parted, and I looked at Archer. "Elise's daughter." I inhaled deep. "I want the museum to

294

keep half the reward, and I want to give the other half to her daughter if we can find her."

"Keira—"

"I know it's been a long time"—*almost eight years*—"but she's probably a teenager now, maybe thinking about college. I want to make things easier for her, whatever she wants to do," I said thickly, watching the scenery fly by almost as quickly as the thoughts going through my mind. "I know I'm not responsible for Elise's death, but I have to do this."

When he didn't respond right away, I shifted in the seat and instantly caught his intense stare, the green of his eyes deepening in color.

"You're amazing," he rasped, the muscle in his jaw flexing with the strength of his emotions. He squeezed my hand. "I'll have Hunter talk to the FBI and see if they can locate her."

"Thank you," I murmured, feeling one more weight lifted from my chest.

We pulled into the garage, and Archer was out of the truck and by my side in moments.

"I have a surprise for you," he declared, setting me down carefully and handing me my crutches.

"What?" I balked. "More than the ten million dollars?" *Like receiving a fortune for stolen art wasn't enough of a surprise for one day?*

"No, definitely not that much," he teased playfully. "It's inside."

"Inside?" I squeaked. How could he have a surprise inside? He only came home to shower all week. "I don't know if I can handle any more surprises."

Surprise had never been a good situation for me, but like most things, I had a feeling Archer would flip that on its head, too.

"I almost lost you again." The pain in his stare was like a straight shot to my stomach, and I shuddered as he pressed a kiss to the side of my head.

"No, you saved me this time."

The thud of my pulse grew louder as he held the door open for me, and we walked inside in silence.

My first thought that there was some sort of surprise party waiting for me rapidly vanished when I confirmed that no one was in the house. My second thought was that it had something to do with my dad's paintings. *No, not my dad's*—one day, I would remember that they were stolen artwork on the first try. It didn't have to do with the paintings though because they were still gone—the walls that had been filled with color and life, if only for a few days, were blank.

I started to scan the rest of the space when I saw it—*all of it.*

"Archer," I choked up, the crutches announcing every step I took toward the massive easel set up in the middle of the room, a bright white canvas resting on top of it.

"How... Why..."

"Zoey might've helped a little," he confessed and then cleared his throat. "One time, you told me you got into tattoos because of their permanence... and because it was too hard for your art to move with you."

I recalled the conversation. The heat of his stare followed me as I touched the canvas on the easel, then the glass palette set up on the side with a box of paints displayed on the side, a cup of unused brushes standing like fine fireworks just waiting to explode with color.

"You're not moving anymore, Keira. This is your home. With me. In this house," he rasped, giving me a small smile. "I want you and your permanence marked into every piece of my life, baby—my skin, my bed, my family, my home... and right down to the damn walls."

I blinked back tears as I turned to him. "Archer... I love you."

Thank god he made it to me first before I dropped my crutches in order to get into his arms.

He kissed my head, my hair, and then framed my cheek with his hand.

"I love you, too, and I want to give you everything, Keira," he breathed, holding me close.

I tipped my chin up, drowning in the consuming warmth of his gaze—*of his love.*

"Well, right now, all I want is a kiss—a real one," I declared.

In the hospital, he'd been careful—cautious because of my injuries and because it seemed like we almost always had a crowd. But now, it was just the two of us, and the hunger in his eyes easily matched my own.

I dragged my tongue along my lower lip, replaying a similar request from four years ago.

"That's all?" He placed tiny toying kisses on the freckles on my cheeks.

A small grin lifted my lips. "Okay, maybe something else." For the first time, I felt alive and happy and free, and I knew this was only the start, and it was all because of him.

"Anything."

"Forever, Archer. I want forever."

With a low noise, his mouth came for mine the way I needed him to—the way we both needed. Fire ignited between our lips and we let the burn consume us, the kiss building into something long and deep and ravenous. When he finally broke away, we were both gasping, our lungs fighting for the small thread of air separating us.

"Forever starts now, baby," he promised.

I smiled as his lips found mine again. "Finally."

EPILOGUE

KEIRA

One year later...

"That's it. All done," I declared and straightened, grabbing the handheld mirror on my table and holding it for my client.

The young girl, Della, sat up, holding one arm over her bare breasts. As she scrutinized her new tattoo, I decided that she couldn't be that young, maybe a year or two younger than me.

Be Bold.

The inscription I'd placed in the skin just underneath and slightly to the side of her left breast was simple but poignant; it reminded me of Dad's advice: *be brave.* Even if she hadn't confessed to being an ink virgin, it was always easy to spot them. Hesitant. Over-thinking. Slightly flinchy. And she'd specifically wanted the second 'b' to be capitalized.

She definitely wasn't like my usual clients who paid for grand masterpieces sprawled over their skin, but there was something about her request that intrigued me. I was tempted to ask Archer to do some digging out of curiosity, not fear, but

I decided against it, afraid he would insist on being here today and ruining my surprise.

Della's bright blue eyes snapped to mine and she beamed. "I love it. Thank you so much."

I smiled. "Of course." I returned the mirror to my table and gave her my back so she could get dressed.

Once she was finished, I walked us to the front of my shop and reached for my credit card machine.

"Do you have any plans for the weekend?" I made small talk while she reached in her very expensive purse for her credit card.

"Well, it's my birthday tomorrow—twenty-three"—she flashed a wide white smile—"so I'm meeting some friends at Jackson Hole to go skiing."

I guessed right. She was around my age, just living a more normal life at twenty-three than being in hiding from the Irish mob.

"That sounds like a blast." I took her card, about to mention that my brother-in-law was doing the same thing this weekend when there was a forceful knock on my door.

I had the door set to lock automatically while I was with a client. Surprisingly, the worries about my past faded more quickly than I ever imagined they would. Maybe it was because I realized I finally wasn't alone—because Archer had proven to me every single day that he would always be there for me—loving and protecting me.

"Excuse me," I murmured, sticking her card in the machine so it could at least run while I answered the door. As I walked by Della, I swore I heard her mutter '*shit.*' But the knock sounded again, distracting me.

I unlocked and opened the door, eyes widening at the giant, suited man on the other side.

"Excuse me, I'm looking for—*Miss Bolden*—" he broke off, his expressionless eyes zeroing in on the blonde.

"I know, I know, Seth." She held up a hand. "I just… have to pay. I'll be right there."

I was startled by the exchange, but then the pieces of her name finally clicked.

Della Bolden.

As in the Boldens—the family that owned the Jackson Hole resort.

My gaze whipped to hers, and in it, I saw a painful feeling that I knew all too well—*an ache for a normal life outside a cage.* In her case, a gilded one.

"She'll just be a minute," I added, folding my arms and standing between the man who was obviously Della's bodyguard and her.

He gave me a once over and then, whether he was frightened off by my red hair or decided it wasn't worth the argument, he stepped back outside, and I closed the door.

I didn't say anything as I walked back over to the counter, pulling her receipt from the machine and handing it to her along with her credit card.

"If I could just have your signature."

I couldn't believe it. I'd just tattooed a Bolden—Wisdom royalty. I knew there was something unique about her.

She scribbled her name. "I'm sorry about that. Sometimes, it feels like I can't even breathe without permission," she confessed and then flushed, regretting saying so much. "If you could please not… mention… that I was here."

Famous in a small town… a fate worse than death. Well, almost.

"Your secret is safe with me," I promised.

She gathered her things, and I handed her a bag with ointment for her new tattoo along with instructions.

"Della," I called as she reached the door, and she looked over her shoulder. For some reason, Dad's advice bubbled to the tip of my tongue. "Be brave. And enjoy your birthday."

She stared for a second, like for the first time, someone had given her permission to enjoy her life. And then, with a small nod, she was out the door, shuffled into a large black Yukon that sped away.

Alone again, I made quick work of cleaning up my tools and space before pulling out the special kit that I ordered a week ago. *A natural henna dye kit.*

I was all about permanence, but the tattoo I was painting on myself for tonight could only be semi-permanent because in a little over eight months, it would go from a part of my body to a part of our lives.

Biting my lip, I pressed my hand to my currently flat stomach. I couldn't wait to tell Archer.

My Orion.

He'd made it all of three months after the shooting before proposing to me, and after that, only another four weeks before we'd had a small ceremony at the Worth Hotel. It was perfect. I didn't want anything big or glam—I didn't have enough family or friends for that to even be possible. But I had everything I needed with him by my side, surrounded by his family and our close friends.

I didn't have an ultrasound yet, so I pulled up an image online, and using the mirror, I spent the next hour painting the henna on my lower stomach where our baby was growing.

My heart picked up steam on the drive home. It was a miracle—*or a lifetime of trained secret-keeping*—that I hadn't blurted out the truth to him already, knowing that we'd stopped using birth control several months ago.

The garage door opened with painful slowness, and I pulled my new Jeep Cherokee into its spot. According to Archer, my Corolla wasn't safe enough for the four-point-seven-mile drive between the house and my tattoo parlor.

"I'm home," I called, walking inside. Instantly, I was hit with the most amazing smell… and a pretty amazing sight: my husband, shirtless, standing in front of the stove.

"Hey, baby," he greeted me with a half-tipped smile that

instantly dumped heat between my legs. "The roast is almost done."

"Mmm." I set my things down and walked through the living room, stopping before I reached the kitchen.

It took him a few seconds before he questioned where I was and why I hadn't immediately come over to him for a kiss.

"Everything okay?" He covered the pot and went to the sink to wash his hands. "How was your client?"

"Good. Interesting." I bit my lip. "I also gave myself a tattoo today."

His gaze snapped to mine. "Oh, yeah? Of what?" I heard the possessiveness in his voice. My husband liked to be the only thing that got to mark me.

Heat flooded my cheeks, and I couldn't hold back a smile.

"Come see." I flicked open the top button of my long T-shirt dress.

His low growl reached me a second before he did. "I thought only I got to mark you," he rasped low, his hands making quick work of the buttons down my front.

"You are," I promised him breathlessly, reaching up to the neckline of my dress and pulling it from my shoulders; he'd undone enough buttons for the material to slide freely down my body and pool at my feet.

His confused expression lingered for only a second before he stepped back to examine me, his stare instantly locking on the large brown design on my stomach.

His jaw muscle clenched. His hands balled and released at his sides. He stared for several long seconds before he finally lifted his head.

"Keira…"

The only other time I'd seen this man so overcome was the moment I'd opened my eyes in that hospital bed, and my heart swelled so big I thought it might burst.

"We're pregnant, Archer." I beamed, feeling hot tears slide free. "We're going to have a baby."

A baby.

Our baby.

With a loud shout, he hauled me into his arms and claimed my mouth in a possessive kiss. The roast could wait —*and it did.*

Eight months later, Fiona Reynolds entered the world with her mother's fire and her father's strength, and we both had her name tattooed over our hearts.

The End.

The Reynolds Protective series continues with HUNTER.

PS - FBI Agent Roman Knight's story is part of my Covington Security series. You can find his story, BROKEN, here.

HUNTER

Zoey Roberts is on the run—that's what happens when someone is stalking you.

Winding up in Wyoming was her latest move and last resort, but giving up everything was the only way to protect herself. New state. New apartment. New life. And for good measure, she takes a new job at the safest place in town—the local security agency, Reynolds Protective Group.

But safe isn't always smart. And working for the handsomest man she's ever met quickly turns perilous when she's faced with those washboard abs, broad shoulders, and charming smile on a daily basis.

Hunter Reynolds is nothing if not determined. From the moment he met Zoey, he was determined to win her heart. So, he pursues her. Patiently. Steadily. Until she finally lets her guard down.

Just when Zoey believes Hunter could be her chance at happiness, she's threatened once more. Hunter immediately goes from hot boss to protective bodyguard, and it's not long before their forced proximity sends their attraction to explosive heights. But when her deranged stalker grows bolder,

Zoey remembers why she moved to Wisdom in the first place —and why love will always be out of the question.

Order Hunter.

WHERE REALITY MEETS FICTION...

Dear reader,
I always jump at the opportunity to put a little bit of reality
into my books, especially when it's something I find unique or
fascinating.

So, after my husband and I watched the Netflix docu-series,
This is a Robbery, I knew I had to incorporate the Isabella
Stewart Gardner Museum theft of 1990 into this story given
the mob background I already had planned.

The facts mentioned about the robbery in this book are true.
Thirteen works of art were stolen on St. Patrick's Day in 1990.
No arrests were made. The thieves dressed as cops, entered
the museum, and spent an hour and a half cutting the prized
artworks from their frames. Many of the suspects the FBI has
investigated belong to the mob (Italian, not Irish as in this
book.)

As much as I wish the parts of this book about the recovery of
the works was true, sadly, none of the iconic and priceless
pieces of art have been found. The empty frames hang in the

museum as a reminder of the works that have been missing for over three decades.

The FBI estimates that the contents of the heist are worth about $500 million.

There is still a $10 million reward for their safe return.

OTHER WORKS BY DR. REBECCA SHARP

The Vigilantes

The Vendetta

The Verdict

The Villain

The Vigilant

The Vow

The Kinkades

The Woodsman

The Lightkeeper

The Candlemaker

The Innkeeper

Reynolds Protective

Archer

Hunter

Gunner

Ranger

Covington Security

Betrayed

Bribed

Beguiled

Burned

Branded

Broken

Believed

Bargained

Braved

Carmel Cove

Beholden

Bespoken

Besotted

Befallen

Beloved

Betrothed

The Odyssey Duet

The Fall of Troy

The Judgment of Paris

Country Love Collection

Tequila

Ready to Run

Fastest Girl in Town

Last Name

I'll Be Your Santa Tonight

Michigan for the Winter

Remember Arizona

Ex To See

A Cowboy for Christmas

Meant to Be

Accidentally on Purpose

The Winter Games

Up in the Air

On the Edge

Enjoy the Ride

In Too Deep

Over the Top

The Gentlemen's Guild

The Artist's Touch

The Sculptor's Seduction

The Painter's Passion

Passion & Perseverance Trilogy

(A Pride and Prejudice Retelling)

First Impressions

Second Chances

Third Time is the Charm

Standalones

Reputation

Redemption

Revolution

Hypothetically

Want to #staysharp with everything that's coming?

Join my newsletter!

ABOUT THE AUTHOR

Rebecca Sharp is a contemporary romance author of over thirty published novels and dentist living in PA with her amazing husband, affectionately referred to as Mr. GQ.

She writes a wide variety of contemporary romance. From new adult to extreme sports romance, forbidden romance to romantic comedies, her books will always give you strong heroines, hot alphas, unique love stories, and always a happily ever after. When she's not writing or seeing patients, she loves to travel with her husband, snowboard, and cook.

She loves to hear from readers. You can find her on Facebook, Instagram, and Goodreads. And, of course, you can email her directly at author@drrebeccasharp.com.

If you want to be emailed with exclusive cover reveals, upcoming book news, etc. you can sign up for her mailing list on her website: www.drrebeccasharp.com

Happy reading!

xx

Rebecca

54223111R00190